MATCHING MELISSA

A Downtown Divas Romance

Dianna Dann

Wayward Cat Publishing

While inspired by wonderful Historic Downtown Melbourne, on Florida's sunny Space Coast, this book is a work of fiction and all the characters within it are products of the author's crazy imagination. Any similarities between characters in this book and actual people, living or dead, are purely coincidental.

ISBN 978-1-938999-51-2
Library of Congress Control Number: 2023918244

Wayward Cat Publishing
Palm Bay, Florida
www.waywardcatpublishing.com

Cover art © 2023 Wayward Cat Publishing
Illustration of girl © Heather McGrath via istockphoto
Illustration of cat © OleksiiK via istockphoto
Illustrations of gifts © nessa2 via istockphoto

MATCHING MELISSA

Chapter One

So, I dumped a tray of dirty dishes all over the most gorgeous guy in town. What of it, if the remains of a strawberry smoothie oozed down his obviously expensive suit jacket? And who cares if he turned out to be my major crush back in high school? Who hasn't embarrassed herself in public like that? It's not as if the relationship was ever going anywhere in the first place. Except that, as I stood there, watching the smoothie, a dab of mustard, a glop of mayo, and bits of leftover sour-cream-and-onion chips soak into his striped tie, I remembered what Isabella had said... No. Nope. It couldn't possibly have been Ryan Duval she was talking about.

The whole day started out as a disaster. It was Sunday, a big brunch day in Downtown Strawbridge. The end of the first week in November, too, so the Central Florida heat was a touch less stifling, and the tinge of the holidays was in the air bringing more people to venture downtown than usual. I'd stayed out much too late the night before with Vanessa. No amount of Diet Coke could wake me up. And Café Flamingo was hopping.

She sits on the corner of Strawbridge Avenue and Woodplum Street with the best people-watching this end of Historic Downtown Strawbridge. You walk in and you're hit with visions of pink flamingos and tropical green leaves on the walls. Waiting, or lounging with a smoothie, on your left, counter farther back where you order your sandwiches, salads, soups, and drinks. Seven booths on the far right, along Woodplum, with enormous windows cleaned daily. Eight four-seaters and eleven doubles inside with two four-seaters and two doubles out front, along the busy main road through town. It all screams Florida casual. And it's not a bad place to spend your life.

But that day, as soon as I walked through the door, I learned that we had two waiters and a dishwasher out sick. So I ended up running around barking orders, waiting on tables, refilling tea canisters, bussing the dishes to the kitchen and praying we'd have enough to last until I could get them washed. Still, everything was going to be okay. Our customers were patient and understanding, and we weren't too far behind.

I took time off to calmly visit with the Divas—my downtown business friends—when they came for lunch. They brought me a birthday cake and I sat with them at an outside table and enjoyed a slice as if nothing was out of the ordinary. And they all wanted to talk about "the one." Last month, I'd dragged them to see Isabella, the new psychic in town, and she'd said that my soul mate was already hanging around, waiting for me to notice him.

It all started because I'd challenged the Divas to a series of ghostly encounters leading up to Halloween. I just thought that if they could be open-minded about it, maybe they'd be more likely to believe me about my ghost sighting. And as part of that challenge, I booked us a group appointment with Isabella's Insights. I remember the whole thing as if it were yesterday. We were in Isabella's new…what do you call a psychic's storefront? I think she called it her sanctuary, which, at the time, made me think of Batman. It was basically a dimly lit room with shelves filled with psychic stuff, like tarot cards and incense burners. We sat around a red-velvet covered table and I told her we wanted to know about romance. Because, that's what psychics are for, right? Isabella, a wild, muumuu wearing, hair-piled-atop-head, bright-lipsticked, happy sort, didn't exactly tell us what we wanted to hear.

She said Vanessa would be a model, but wouldn't tell her anything about a guy, which I found suspicious. She told Karen she'd marry an artist. She said that Kaya's true love would be a man with kids. There was something weird about Pari and something about Sophie getting married in the winter…I think. And to me, she said there was a man who was watching me…waiting. I admit, my first thought was of Ryan Duval. That thing he'd said all those years ago when we were still in school. But he was drunk when he said it. He didn't even remember it the next day. And by the time Pari was saying how creepy it was to have a guy basically stalking me, I'd forgotten all about him.

Naturally, though, the Divas wanted to launch the Pink Diva Man Hunter Plan—I'm the Pink Diva because everyone thinks I love pink. Anyway, that started me thinking again, as I had been doing since we left Isabella's. Who was this guy? Did I really want to find him? Why not? I tried to tell myself I didn't have to actually date him if I wasn't interested. Even though Isabella did claim he was my "ever after" guy. Honestly, at that point in my life, I wasn't looking for ever after. I might *never* want ever after. I just wanted to know who Isabella was talking about.

I politely excused myself from my Diva birthday party and went back inside to continue the pace, but found myself analyzing every guy I knew, regulars and friends. That guy who orders a smoothie with fresh mushrooms in it every other day or the one who sits at the same two-seater every fourth Friday reading a magazine called *Emu Today & Tomorrow* could be *the* guy. And it started to seem more and more like a true love situation. Like a Big M thing. And I don't want to be that kind of girl. I'm not the swooning Prince Charming hunter. Oh, I swoon, mind you. I enjoy having fun and hanging out. But long term stuff—I don't even like to think of the M-word—is just not on my menu. Is it? Why was I tingling all over just thinking about Isabella's prediction? Was I suddenly on the soul mate train? I did my best to shake out of it.

By two o'clock, the busy had a tinge of letup in it. I could feel the tension ease just a tiny bit and the light at the end of the lunch-rush tunnel beckoned. I started to feel hope again. And then this huge bright sunny moment appeared out of nowhere. Suddenly, looking out the side window, across Woodplum Street, to the little pottery shop that's my neighbor—a sign! At least I thought it was a sign. A distinct, definite, universe-is-telling-you-something sign.

In the huge side windows of Mabel's Pottery & Glass were banners exclaiming, "Going Out of Business Sale! Everything Must Go!"

It was finally happening. Forget my stalker/love interest. Forget the M-word. It was time to expand. I had an agreement with my landlord, Mr. Jenkins, who also owned several more buildings on this side of Strawbridge Avenue, that as soon as Mabel decided not to renew her lease, that little storefront would be mine. For my catering business. No more would I have to operate out of Café Flamingo's back room. I could put Flamingo Catering into the mainstream—go bigger and better! Forget Romance Melissa. Woman In Charge Melissa was back.

Elated, I hoisted a large round tray filled with dirty dishes and stacked cups—silverware and napkins piled on top—to my shoulder, leaning backward and sideways to bear the load. Picture me, petite to the extreme, and you won't wonder why sometimes customers gasp a little when I do that. Smiling like I'd just won Downtown Bake-Off, with a triumphant glance over at Mabel's window, I turned toward the kitchen…and dumped everything onto a suit.

A broad shouldered, expensive suit with a purple silk tie. Now covered in mustard and mayo, the remnants of a strawberry smoothie oozing toward the pants.

"Mel?" the suit said to me.

Looking up, aghast, the entire restaurant now shrouded in stunned silence—has Melissa, Woman In Charge, ever done such a horrible thing?—I recognized the man wearing said suit.

"Ryan," I mumbled and everything decompressed. Customers went back to their sandwiches and soups, a few employees scurried at my feet cleaning up my mess, bless them, and time slowly began to tick away again. With a nervous chuckle, I said, "Long time no see. How's the real estate business?"

Ryan Duval was not amused. "Damn!" He sloughed a leaf of lettuce off his lapel. "I'm late as it is."

"Let me comp your lunch. And you'll send me the dry cleaning bill."

But he was already headed to the door. "Forget it. You've done enough."

I watched him through my front window as he stomped along Strawbridge Avenue and turned left onto Woodplum, continuing along the side of the c afé. He had his phone out, holding it with one hand while the other continued to wipe down his now ruined suit. My heart raced, my cheeks burned, and there was a hollow pain in my chest.

"He was cute," Susanne, my manager, said. "Until you dumped trash all over him."

"Now he hates me," I mumbled.

Susanne was about ten years older than me with stylish streaks of grey in her dark hair. She stood almost a half-foot taller, too, and liked to use that to her advantage whenever she thought I was making a major life mistake, like when I told her I might get a tattoo of a flamingo on my ankle. "Let's consider what your mother would say," she'd said, looming over me.

"You know him?" she asked now, as I continued to stare out the side window, though Ryan was gone.

"I used to."

"Well, I don't think you reconnected very well."

"Susanne, as usual, you are a master of the under-statement."

Ryan Duval wasn't exactly the one that got away so much as the one I'd never had. Talk about longing from afar. But after a series of disastrous encounters, I'd finally given up on him.

"That was years ago," I told myself, and got back to work.

Chapter Two

Luckily, a couple of my part-timers showed up at two to help out, so things got almost back to normal. Café Flamingo is open Monday through Saturday from eleven to seven, and eleven to four on Sundays. As the last customers start finishing up, we can begin the cleanup routine and usually get out of the place within a couple of hours after closing. I was supposed to meet Vanessa at Burgers for dinner and my staff literally pushed me out the door as soon as the last guest had left.

"It's your birthday," Susanne said. "Get out of here."

"We got it under control," Petra called from the kitchen over the spray of water into a sudsy washbasin.

I live just two blocks north of Downtown Strawbridge in a quaint little neighborhood of old, creaky houses. Mine's an adorable mission revival built in 1937, with a detached garage and an alcove in front, with a set of wide steps leading up to it. A big arched front window, and a *terra cotta* tiled roof. My life is simple. Hardwood floors. No clutter. A sofa, a chair, a TV. There's a little table off the kitchen with four mismatched chairs. You'd think my kitchen would be top-notch with all the latest gadgets, but no. I don't cook at home. My fridge has some yogurt in it for emergencies, and plenty of Diet Coke, but I'm just not home that often. No plants. Nothing that needs me on a regular basis, unless you count the gray stray cat that shows up once or twice a week looking for a handout; and I do keep a plastic bin with a bit of kibble just inside the front door for him. Don't tell Sophie. She'll want me to bring him inside and make him my own. And that's not going to happen.

A quick shower and a change of clothes and I was at Burgers by six ready to unload on Vanessa and let her do some unloading as well. The casual dining hotspot was our usual joint which happens to be across the street and a door or so down from my café. I waved at Diego West as the hostess showed us to our table. He and I spend a lot of time in each other's restaurants. No one can really understand the demands of the food service business like those of us in it. So we do tend to gravitate to each other's places.

"I've never done anything like that before," I told Vanessa after describing my literal run-in with Ryan Duval.

"It's no big deal. Your customers love you."

"Not this guy." I'd said it with a pout and a hollow sort of echo in my voice and I hoped that Vanessa hadn't caught it. Ryan Duval didn't like me. He never did and you'd think I wouldn't care. It suddenly struck me that I might not know myself as well as I thought I did. But who has time for self-reflection when you're a badass working girl?

We'd gotten our favorite table for two, tucked into the back corner of the busy restaurant, where we each sat facing a wall. By the time I'd finished with the horrid tale, a bacon double-cheese sat, cut in half, between us with a plate of fries and a bowl of onion rings on the side. We loaded up our plates hungrily. It was dish Sunday. My favorite night of the week, when we could manage it. Just me and Vanessa readying ourselves for the week ahead.

"Then who cares? If he's not the forgiving type, who needs him?"

"I guess."

"Okay, I know that tone. What aren't you telling me?"

I sighed. "You know him. Ryan Duval. The beach

party guy."

She looked at me, confused.

"The guy at the ballpark. My windshield?"

"Wait. Beach party guy and ballpark guy were the same? And that's who you dumped trash all over? Well, he deserved it." She laughed and I reached across the table to pretend at a slap.

"Not funny."

"You must have made a big impression on him at the beach party."

"Why do you say that?"

"At the ballpark, he knew you right away."

"We went to high school together. I'm sure I told you about him."

"So there's history there."

"Ugh. Let's not talk about it anymore."

"Did you two go steady?" she said, teasing.

"No. We never dated. Well, okay, we went out once, sort of. But nothing came of it. End of story."

"You don't act like it's nothing. Why is it bothering you so much?"

"It's just…"

"Tell me."

"I'd rather not."

"Oh, come on."

"Not while we're eating."

"That bad?"

"You really don't want to know."

"Is he handsome?"

"Insufferably."

She made a cooing sound, the vocal equivalent of patting me on the head. "Maybe he's your mystery man."

"No way."

"Don't say no so quickly." She popped a French fry into her mouth. "He could be the one."

"Isabella said it was someone I know."

"You *do* know him."

"She said it was someone in my life now. The last time I even talked to him was when I bought my house. Anyway, I dumped trash all over him, so even if he was the guy, it's safe to say he's not anymore."

Diego West swept up to the table. "*Hola*, ladies! *¿Cómo estás esta noche?*"

"¡*Hambriento!*" Vanessa said.

"Wonderful." He turned to me. "Have you recovered from your encounter?"

"Were you there?" Vanessa asked him.

"*Sí*, yes. Very messy."

"I'd like to forget the whole thing, if you don't mind."

"Good luck with that. This is Downtown Strawbridge. The story's got to be all the way to Stogies by now. Well, enjoy your burger. I'll see you again soon." And with a wink, he was gone.

We sat in silence for a moment or two, chewing—me trying to pretend I didn't know what Vanessa was thinking, until she said, "What about Diego?"

"What about him?" I didn't want to let on that I'd already considered Diego…and every other guy that looked at me for longer than a split second that day.

"He owns Burgers. You own Café Flamingo. He winked at you. It's like the setup for a romantic movie."

"He flirts with all the customers; it's part of his job."

"He doesn't work for tips. And I don't see him at any other tables."

"We're both married to our restaurants," I said. "It'd never work out."

"You're going to find a reason to say no to everyone on your list, aren't you?"

"What list?"

"You promised us you'd make a list."

"I was only half serious." That was the highlight of my birthday lunch earlier in the day. What guy did I know, but hadn't realized was totally in love with me? Who was my shy admirer? They literally wanted me to make a list? I suppose it was my own fault. I did rather eagerly agree to the Pink Diva Man Hunter Plan. "But I promise I'll be open about it. So, Diego is a maybe."

"Back to our other possibility."

"Absolutely not."

"I don't think you're in a position to discount any

possibles."

"Oh, really? So I should just date anybody? How about Doug?"

"Your dish washer? Ew."

"He's really nice."

"He's an ex-con. And in his fifties."

"But you said—"

"I said possibles. The right age, single, and good looking. Preferably never killed anyone."

"Doug didn't kill anybody. And looks aren't everything."

"But he has to be good looking *to you*."

"Fair enough."

"So…is he on the list?"

"Doug? Absolutely."

She slapped at my arm playfully.

"I'll give you Diego," I said. "But not Ryan Duval."

"Have you even started the list?"

"Honestly, I haven't had time to think about it."

"Whenever you say 'honestly' I know you're lying. But we should do it with all of the Divas. It's a group project."

The Divas are all business women in Historic Downtown Strawbridge. There's me, of course, with my Café Flamingo. Vanessa owns Glam It Up!, the best hair and nails salon in town, and she looks the part. She and I hang out more than the others, probably because we like to go out all the time. Being louder than the rest of the group, we like to spend quality time together so we can get really, really rowdy and not have to worry about it.

Pari Logan is a psychologist. She wears business suits. With her dark hair and eyes, she's like the complete opposite of me—short, blonde, and usually in jeans. Pari's best friend is Karen Morgan whose family owns the huge office supply store midtown. Karen's the tallest of all of us and strawberry blonde. She's a bit shy and I often feel like she's judging me when I go a little nuts while out on the town. But she's too sweet to make it obvious.

There's Kaya Channing who owns a fabulous retro clothing shop a little ways down the street from my café. Not that I can wear anything in there. Did they not have short people in the Forties and Fifties? And what's with all those pointy-toed shoes? Anyway, Kaya's what I like to call our center. She's down to earth and normal. She doesn't flaunt her smarts, but she's probably got better brains than me. And she always knows how to get right to the heart of the matter. If you need advice, Kaya's your girl.

I think Kaya's been getting closer with Sophie Childers. She's the Diva who brought us all together this past summer. Very smart. And very quiet. She's bookish. In fact, we call her Bookish Diva. And aside from being bookish, she runs the bookstore called Bookish with her grandfather. I'm Pink Diva, because everybody thinks I love pink. Pari is Fashion Diva because she's always dressed to perfection. Though, she does seem to be loosening up lately. Karen is Bella Diva. Something to do with an umbrella, don't worry about it. Kaya is Vintage Diva, because not only does she have that store, she's a walking advertisement. And Vanessa is, of course, Glam Diva.

"Well, speak of the devil," I said.

Ryan Duval had just sat down at a nearby table with a date.

Chapter Three

Don't stare, Van." She was practically turned around in her seat, blatantly watching him.

If only Ryan Duval had been seated behind me. Instead, I was forced to see him out of the corner of my eye. He sat along the back wall—the one my chair was facing—a few tables behind Vanessa. His date had a pile of brown hair on top of her head and wore a very small, purple, strapless dress.

"So, the guy must like purple," I mumbled. "Stop turning around. He can see you."

She giggled and winked at me. "He's very handsome. And definitely going on the list."

She wasn't wrong. Ryan Duval had grown from a skinny, shy high school nerd into a GQ cover model. He was average height and his light brown hair was flecked with blond, like it couldn't make up its mind whether to go one way or the other. Ruggedly handsome, I suppose you'd call him. You could tell just by looking at him he was one of those high powered real estate moguls, raking in millions, running roughshod over the little guy.

"He's too symmetrical," I said.

"That's the best you can do?"

"Come on, Van. You know what too symmetrical means. Means he's sinister. Not to be trusted."

"I bet he's got a crooked smile."

"Crooked all right."

"Oh, my god!" Vanessa said.

"Shhh! What?"

"He's the one, Mel. It's got to be him."

"Quiet. He's looking at us."

"I just realized," she whispered loudly over the din of the restaurant. "You two had a meet cute."

"A what?"

"A meet cute. All the romantic comedies start with a meet cute."

"I think you mean cute meet. Adjective first."

"Not this time." She took a bite of her half of the burger and risked another look behind her. "Just think about it. Sophie fell on top of Reese in Bookish."

"That wasn't cute at all."

"Of course it was. And Pari met Sam when she caught him on his hands and knees in front of her office door."

"The intergluteal cleft moment."

"Exactly. Those were meet cutes."

"Are you sure it's not cute meets?"

"This is not a language problem, Mel. And you upended a tray full of dirty dishes all over this guy. He's your soul mate. Obviously."

"Oh, cut it out. He's not on the list."

Vanessa looked over my shoulder toward the front of the restaurant and smiled. When I turned, I saw Sophie winding through the tables to visit us. Reese, sitting at a table for two, waved with both hands like a dork. Naturally we did the same in return.

Vanessa shouted, "Helloooo Reese!"

"Have you heard from Madaline yet?" Sophie asked me as she grabbed a fry from my plate.

"No, why?"

"You missed the last BOMB meeting."

The Historic Downtown Strawbridge Business Owners Management Board, or HDS BOMB, doubled up on meetings in November and that was just too much for me. Not that I attended them regularly any other time.

"And Madaline is going to complain?" I said.

"Not at all. She wants you to be a judge for the Downtown Strawbridge Holiday Baking Contest."

I think my mouth fell open.

Vanessa gasped. "That sounds fantastic."

"It's going to be between some of the business owners or employees. And they want all the judges to be restaurant people. Please say you'll do it."

"Of course I'll do it." *Sure. Why not? It's only the holidays. I'll have plenty of time. Why can't I say no?* But none of that panic showed up on my face.

"Great," Sophie said and grabbed another fry. She turned just a bit and waved at Ryan.

Vanessa gasped and whispered way too loudly. "You know him?"

"Yeah. And he's Mr. Cornell's new landlord. Wanted to know if Gramps was interested in selling the building."

"He wants to buy Bookish?" Vanessa said.

"Just the building."

"I thought he was a real estate agent." I'm sure I said it a bit too loud.

"He still could be, but Mr. Cornell said he's bought a few buildings downtown."

"Why would he think your grandfather would want to sell his building?" Vanessa said.

"Could he kick you guys out?" I said.

"He wouldn't do that," Sophie said. "He was talking about how great Bookish is for the Downtown aesthetic. He's got this whole 'let's keep downtown quirky' thing going. Really into the kitch."

"Kitch?" Vanessa said.

"He just has this cute idea about downtown. Wants to preserve its uniqueness. And he thinks Bookish fits right in. We had a whole long conversation about it this afternoon with Gramps."

"Are you selling, then?" I said.

"No way."

"I think Melissa should put him on the list."

"Really?" Sophie said with a quick look to Ryan's table. "Not a bad choice, if he's single. Who else is in the running?"

"I told her we need all the Divas to get together and help put the list together."

"Great idea." She turned back to smile at Reese waiting patiently for her return. "I'll see you two later." And she was gone.

Vanessa let out a sigh.

"What is it?"

"Reese is so adorable. And now Pari has Sam."

"Maybe we should make you a list instead of me. It's not like I really have time for dating."

She shoved a whole onion ring into her mouth. "Noph. Ish yur tun."

Suddenly Ryan was standing over us. I saw Vanessa try to swallow as she covered her face with a napkin.

"Hi," he said.

"Ryan," I said, not exactly sweet-like. My face burned hot.

He held out his hand and I stared at it for a few seconds as he said, "I'm sorry about earlier. I was short with you."

I wiped the burger grease from my fingers and let my hand slip into his. It was shocking how his touch sent tingles up my arm to my heart. And odd that he made the gesture. I wanted to say, "don't you remember we used to be friends?" But that was so long ago. Instead, I mumbled, "I'm the one who dumped trash all over you," trying to reign in my trembling voice. "And I'm really sorry. You'll send me the dry cleaning bill, won't you?"

He looked at me oddly, as if he were weighing his words carefully. "It's really nothing."

"Nothing!" Vanessa said. "I heard there was strawberry smoothie running down your pants."

Ryan suppressed a smile and gave a quick nod. "It's forgotten. I came over to tell you that I understand you didn't receive a letter from Mr. Jenkins."

I shook my head. "Not recently. Am I expecting one?" And why would Ryan Duval have anything to do with it?

"Apparently he had a stroke."

16

"Oh," both Vanessa and I gasped. "I hope he's okay," I said. "Is he—"

"He's doing well."

"—in the hospital?"

"Yes. But it was a mild one."

"Are you related to him?" Vanessa asked. "And who is he?" She looked at me.

"He's my landlord." And as soon as I said it, a feeling of dread washed over me. "What do you have to do with it, if you don't mind my asking?"

Ryan smiled at me—but it was a tad sheepish, as if he knew he had news that was fabulous for him, but not so great for me. "He should have sent out a letter to all of his tenants downtown explaining. But, well, he was incapacitated. I've been talking to everyone myself."

"What for?" I nearly yelled at him. I knew what he was going to say and I didn't want to hear it.

"I recently purchased all of his properties."

"Oh," Vanessa piped up again. "So you're Melissa's new landlord. How interesting." She fluttered her eyelashes at him and practically cooed.

I tried to kick her under the table but missed. "You'll have to excuse her," I told Ryan. "Private joke, that's all."

"I'll be sending out new rental agreements for signatures A-SAP."

As he started to turn back to his table I said, "What about Mabel's Pottery?"

"What about it?"

"I had an agreement with Mr. Jenkins that I could lease the building when she moved out. I hope he told you about it."

He shook his head. "First I've heard of it. What would you like to put in the spot?"

"I want to run my catering business out of it."

And again, he had a far off look, as if considering very carefully what to say. Then he opened his mouth and let it stay there for a second or two before closing again with a grimace. "I don't think a catering business is what Downtown Strawbridge needs right now."

"What do you mean?"

"I'm looking for shops with style. Shops to bring more customers downtown. Something quirky and cool."

"Catering's cool."

Vanessa let out a "hah!" and I glared at her.

Ryan was shaking his head. "No. I don't think a catering storefront is what I'm looking for."

"But Mr. Jenkins promised me."

"Tough luck," he said.

"This is about earlier, isn't it? Because I trashed your suit."

"What are you implying?"

"I think I stated it quite clearly. I dumped a tray of dirty dishes all over you and now you won't let me rent one of your spaces."

"You already rent one of my spaces, Ms. Stathem."

"Whoah," Vanessa said. And who could blame her? Ryan had gone from distant politeness to seething civility in an instant.

"I'll get you that new lease right away." He gave me a curt nod and returned to his table where his date didn't seem to miss him at all.

"Damn," I said.

"Uh, Mel," Vanessa said, nudging me. "Who's staring now?"

I quickly shoved a big bite of burger into my mouth. "I cah blev thith."

"You can find another spot for the catering, can't you?"

"Why aren't you upset about this?" Clearly Friend Protocol called for her to be as livid as I was. "It was perfect. Right across the little side street from the restaurant. I could oversee both businesses with ease."

"You're right. I'm sorry." She patted my arm with one hand and shoved another onion ring in her mouth with the other. "But he's still pretty cute, isn't he?"

"How can you say that? He's clearly getting back at me for the tray thing."

"It was a pretty big thing."

"What difference does that make? There must be a law or something that he's breaking. Is there a law that says he has to rent to me?"

"That doesn't sound like a law. Either way, he's still cute. And there was chemistry there."

"That was anger, Van. Bordering on hatred."

"Oh, come on."

"You wouldn't dare make me go out with him after that, would you?"

"I suppose not." She sighed. "But the meet cute."

"There was no cute meeting or cute meet or… whatever. Just no."

"I wonder what Isabella would say about all of this."

"I don't care. I am never going out with that guy."

"You mean again."

"What?"

"Earth to Mel. You said you went out with him. Where is your head?"

Ryan let out a laugh and his date turned to glare at me. Had they been listening to us?

"I really don't like that guy," I said.

Vanessa smirked. "Another romantic comedy trope. You're a goner for sure."

Chapter Four

How to Ruin a Scrumptious Recipe

Attempt One: Add a Lot of Alcohol

The pertinent thing about me and Ryan Duval is that we'd known each other for years. I remember him vaguely from middle school. But we didn't really get to know one another until high school. To be blunt: I was a snotty, no-nonsense, studious girl who knew by tenth grade she was going to open a restaurant. And Ryan Duval was the hot track and cross-country star who was never without a date on the weekends. But somehow, we were good friends by senior year. We'd managed to find a group of kids who were like us. I mean to say, sure Ryan was popular, but he wasn't the varsity quarterback. And I was the smart girl, but I wasn't hard on the eyes, either. We were…the middles. And the kids we hung out with were the same.

Ryan and I had something of a love/hate thing going on, always playfully jabbing at each other. I'd tease him over whatever new girl he was going out with—"Can she spell vapid?"—and every Friday he'd ask me what book I was dating.

I can admit, all these years later, that I had a major crush. But there was that nagging something in my head warning me not to make a move on it. I'd had a plan since I was a sophomore. I was going to college, where I'd get a business management degree, and then I was going to open a restaurant, just like my mom and dad did—only mine was going to be casual dining. I stopped telling people about it when their response was, inevitably, "Shouldn't you go to cooking school?" I was tired of explaining that I didn't want to be a chef in a restaurant. I wanted to own a restaurant. So, by my senior year of high school, I was keeping my plans to myself. Same with my heart.

But during Spring break of that year, the cheerleaders were throwing a pool party in Summerset, the fancy neighborhood south of town with all the big houses on acres of land. And Ryan was invited. We, along with seven or eight of our friends, were hanging out behind the band room during lunch on Friday before the holiday started and we teased him when we found out he was going.

"Don't let 'em drag you into the cult," Karl said. He always thought of rich, popular kids as members of some religious coven or other.

"It's just a party," Ryan said. "Jessica was invited, too."

We all turned to Jess and she grinned at us sheepishly. "Who knew I was popular?"

The bell rang and we all dispersed, tossing our trash in the big can along the covered walkway back toward the main buildings.

Ryan walked beside me, quiet for a few seconds until he finally spoke. "So, I was thinking. Maybe you'd like to come with me."

"You're not serious."

"No, I am. I know everybody who's going to be there, sure. But you guys are my friends. It'd be good to have one of you to hang out with."

"Jessica's going to be there."

"She's taking Josh."

"Ugh," I said. She and Josh couldn't keep their hands off each other. I couldn't blame Ryan for not wanting to stick with them. "I don't know. I'm not really the party type."

"Come on; it'll be fun."

So I gave in. Ryan picked me up the next day at three, wearing his bathing suit, an unbuttoned collared shirt, and flip flops. I was wearing a dress and sandals. At least it was a sundress.

"You think there's going to be actual swimming?" I said.

"You don't?" He looked down at himself. "Oh, well."

While there wasn't actual swimming going on, in the technical sense, there were lots of people in the pool. Some efforts at water volleyball were made, but it was mostly a lot of splashing. There were hot dogs and hamburgers grilling out in the yard, plenty of snacks and drinks inside the huge house, and swarms of kids everywhere. It was as if the entire school was invited. Sound systems both inside and out. No parents to be seen, a full bar, and tubs filled with ice and beer. By five, I knew I was going to have to drive Ryan home. He played beer pong, and chugged a few cans from the bottom, and after we ate dinner, he started on the rum.

The sky was dark when we were standing by the pool talking. Lights from the porch and lawn cast strange shadows on our faces. That lovely chill Central Florida air gets in the evening rose up—admittedly, northerners wouldn't call it a chill so much as a lack of unbearable heat—and the kids in the pool were now huddled quietly together in small groups, drinking and whispering, or making out. The others were out of the pool playing with firecrackers and sparklers, performing awful drunken *karaoke*, dumping ice all over the lawn and rolling around in it.

"So," I said, "this is what a party looks like."

He smiled a drunken smile and swerved a bit. "Yep."

"You're drunk, Ryan."

"Yep."

"I didn't realize you drank."

"There's a lot of things you don't know about me."

His eyelids were puffed and his red eyes glassy. He

burped.

"Oh, yeah? Tell me what I don't know."

"I've always—" hiccup—"liked you, Mel. Even way…way back in high school."

"We're in high school, dork."

"Middle school, then. I've loved you…" He held out his arm to the sky with a flourish. "…from afar." Hiccup.

"Okay, alkie, are you ready to go home?"

He lifted his hand holding a red cup full of sloshing rum and Coke and poked me in the chest with a finger. "I'll follow you anywhere."

And then he leaned in, a weird eyes-half-closed goofy look on his face, and I thought he was going to kiss me. Ryan Duval was actually going to kiss me! Wait. *Drunken* Ryan Duval was going to kiss me? Before I could decide if I wanted to be kissed by this particular version of my crush, he said, "Oomph," and vomited down the front of my sundress.

But it was okay, because as he spewed food and alcohol all over me, I took a step back, tripped, and fell into the pool. So…no stains. I was hauled out by some football players. They told me the next week in school they thought I was drunk and might drown. They were at the party as, like, bouncers, or security or something. Anyway, they dragged me out and deposited me on the deck, drenched and still holding my purse now filled with water. Towels were wrapped around me and I was led to a lounge chair and given a hot chocolate. All in all, while I didn't know all of them that well, everyone was really nice.

Ryan came over and lay down beside the lawn chair on the textured, wet concrete, sprawled like he'd been shot. "Everything's spinning."

I nodded, even though he couldn't see me. "It sure is."

I had to stop twice for him to lean out the passenger side of the car to vomit while driving to his house. He apologized profusely to his dad who ended up taking me home. His dad was pretty cool about the whole thing. He laughed a few times as I rode silently. Ryan couldn't come along—I refused to let him.

"Well, my dear," Mr. Duval said as he pulled into my parents' driveway. "Thank you for a lovely evening."

I laughed.

"I hope Ryan didn't do anything…wrong."

"You don't smell the vomit?"

"Oh, I do. But everything else went okay?"

"Sure. He's my friend. Still."

Ryan called me the next day and apologized.

I told him it was no big deal. "I hope you'll still love me from afar," I said with a chuckle.

"Huh?"

"Nothing." I recovered quickly. "There was a song playing when you puked all over me. Bad joke."

"But we're still friends?" he said.

"Of course, dork. Always."

And that was that. The extent of our high school romance. He didn't ask me out again. And I didn't ask him out, either. He only invited me to the party as his friend, anyway—so he wouldn't be alone. Never mind the silly thing he said when he was drunk. I was determined not to give it another thought.

Chapter Five

I love Mondays. Everybody's so laid back, or hungover, or desperately trying to pretend Friday is just a few days away. The restaurant isn't as busy as usual and all the orders are high carb. Sandwiches and fries all day long. I get so much done on Mondays. But, as I sat in my little office in the back room at Café Flamingo listening to Mr. Jenkins phone ring in my ear, I fumed…just a little.

It wasn't surprising that Mabel wasn't renewing her lease. She had so many rules for anyone entering her shop, she ended up chasing most people away. No food or drink. No children. No pets. No large purses or packages. And of course, the old standby: You Break It, You Buy It. The store was filled with pottery and glass knickknacks in dazzling glass display cases with tiny spotlights casting shards of light all over the place. You never knew when you might get hit in the eye with a dash of white light and stumble into something expensive. It was too scary to shop there, in my opinion. Not that I would. I'm the opposite of the type of person who wants to buy a pottery bowl to put up on a shelf just to look at.

But I'd heard a rumor a few months ago that she was planning to retire and dared to go in. It's a narrow space, but roomy enough for my needs. I would have tables and chairs for customers to browse invitation books, layout plans, and photos of past catering events, table setting suggestions, and more. Two desks for my manager Lucy and me to conduct business. And I happened to know that the space was once a bakery so there was a kitchen in the back. No more sharing the Café Flamingo kitchen, although I imagine I would still need it for really big events. The space was perfect. And Mr. Jenkins promised me I could lease it when Mabel moved out.

"Hello?" Finally an answer. I knew you had to let the Jenkins' phone ring for a while as he and his wife were very slow. Bless them.

"Is this Mrs. Jenkins?"

"Yes." She sounded suspicious.

"It's Melissa Stathem. From Café Flamingo?"

"Oh, yes dear. You've heard then, have you? He's going to be just fine." She didn't sound convinced.

"Is he still in the hospital?"

"I'm afraid so. But he should be home later today. Our son Peter is bringing him. You've met Peter haven't you? He's a bowler, you know. You bowl, don't you?"

"Mrs. Jenkins, I'm sorry to interrupt. I was wondering when would be a good time for me to talk to Mr. Jenkins."

"Oh, I'm sure he'd love to hear from you. Everyone is so worried about him. It would be a lovely idea for you to send him your best. Rally his spirits and all. So sweet of you to think of it."

"Sure, sure." It's not that I didn't already know my intentions were...well, evil. "I was hoping to talk business with him. When do you suppose he'd be ready for that?"

"He's retired dear. Didn't you know?"

"Actually I didn't. But I did hear about it from—"

"So you do know. Yes. Yes, he's retired."

"Thank you, Mrs. Jenkins. I'll check in later."

"So sweet, my dear."

This avenue of attack wasn't going to work. Not only were Mr. and Mrs. Jenkins in their eighties or nineties, they were the sweetest souls I'd ever known. Even if Mr. Jenkins agreed that he'd promised me Mabel's storefront, he'd never have the audacity to make demands of Ryan Duval. I was going to have to convince him myself. I'd need reinforcements. Time for a Diva intervention.

The Divas gathered in the back corner booth at Café Flamingo at six o'clock that evening. I'd like to say I was the one who called the meeting, but before I had the chance, there was a Diva alert on my phone: "Emergency Diva Dinner at CF tonight!" And by Diva rule, whoever calls the meeting gets first dibs on the topic. And who do you suppose the alert was from? Vanessa, of course. You can imagine what she wanted to discuss.

While any female business owner in Historic Downtown Strawbridge was technically considered one of us, we Divas stuck with the original six most of the time. Me, the Pink Diva; Vanessa, Glam Diva; Vintage Diva Kaya; Fashion Diva Pari; Bella Diva Karen; and Bookish Diva Sophie.

Here's the Diva Data you need to know:

Vanessa Torres, my best friend, runs the hair salon at the other end of downtown with her grandmother. Silky brown hair to her waist, always done up in some spectacular way. Long, always painted nails. The label "Glam" doesn't do her justice. Think Sophia Vergara, but not quite as tall. Can you imagine petite me standing next to Sophia Vergara? Don't even try.

Kaya Channing owns the vintage clothing shop not too far from my café. Curly, shoulder-length brown hair. Girl next door beauty. Sensible and kind. Her major quirk is dressing in her wares. I've seen her around town dolled up like a sixties *Mod Squad* girl. Even had her hair straightened into a bob. Sometimes people don't even recognize her!

Pari Logan, the psychologist, has an office in the big building at the east end of downtown. She's got this thick, really long, almost black hair that's to die for. Well, except that it's so hot here I sometimes wonder how she can stand it. She keeps it up mostly, in tight buns. It works well with the skirts and jackets she tends to wear. She's always so well dressed and made up you'd think she would be in fashion. But no, she likes to analyze people instead. I hope she hasn't analyzed me too much.

Karen Morgan's family owns Morgan's Office Supply

midtown. She's a tall strawberry blonde with the tiniest bit of freckling across her nose and usually a pencil tucked behind one ear. She wears reading glasses on a pearly chain around her neck and cardigans with pale fabric skirts and sandals. You get the idea she doesn't realize how beautiful she is.

And then there's Sophie Childers who works at Bookish, the used bookstore across from my café, with her grandfather. Medium height. Dark hair in a pixie cut. Sharp features. Smart as a whip. But that's what you get from reading. Sophie's more like me when it comes to clothes. We're jeans and tees kind of girls. You'd think I'd have been friends with her before Kaya and Vanessa, but Sophie's…well, she's bookish. And a bit shy. So, she was the last of the original Divas to become my friend.

"We just had lunch yesterday," I said as I slid into the booth next to Sophie.

Whenever I had the choice, I sat beside Sophie. Next to tall Karen, I looked like a child. Next to Kaya, uncool. Next to Pari, I was disheveled no matter how much I may have put myself together. And next to Vanessa, I was just plain, most of the time.

"Vanessa said you were working on a list," Sophie said.

"A stalker list," Pari chimed in with a smirk. You think a psychologist is going to be above that sort of thing, but Pari could joke around with the best of us.

"Obviously, if he turns out to be a creepy stalker, I won't date him."

"Either way," Karen said. "We want input." She pulled a small, black, ring-bound notebook from her purse, flung it open, and clicked a pen that had magically appeared in her hand. Miss Office Supply was ready.

"Aren't I in the best position to know who's stalking me?" I said.

"Not necessarily," Vanessa said. "You could be overlooking the most obvious candidate."

I knew exactly who she was talking about. I said, "If he's so obvious, I wouldn't be able to overlook him."

"You might do it subconsciously," Pari said. "You'll

pretend not to notice anyone you don't want to go out with." Ah, real psychology there.

"Well, sure," I said. "I'm not going to go out with anybody I don't want to. Am I?"

"We don't expect you to date somebody horrible," Pari said. "But we also don't want you to pass over someone who might be a good fit for you just because you don't see it."

"So we thought," Karen said, "we'd all help you make the list."

"I already know this is Vanessa's idea. You don't have to cover for her."

"What ever happened with you and Jake?" Sophie said.

"Why?" I said. "Does he ask about me?" Jake was her boyfriend Reese's business partner. They owned and ran Summer Sun, a beachwear and outside-stuff store down by Trudy's Treasures antique shop.

She opened her mouth to answer me, but nothing came of it.

"It's okay." I chuckled. "I totally forgot about *him*, too."

"You were in love with him," Pari said.

"Oh, come on. It wasn't *love* love. Anyway, he was sort of a jerk. Not really my type."

"So, he's off the list," Sophie said.

"Even if I make a list, what am I supposed to do with it?"

"Ask them all out," Karen said.

"I guess." It's not like I'm old fashioned. It's that, to be honest, I don't date—not in the traditional sense of the word. I go out with Vanessa. I meet guys at the clubs. I've been out once or twice in the last few months, but only after I've snogged the guy at a bar. It's not the greatest way to meet a man, but I'm a busy woman. I don't really have time for…dating.

"No," Kaya said.

Everybody stopped chatting and looked at her. She was shaking her head and, if I dare say, looked a bit peeved.

"What do you mean, no?" Vanessa said.

"Just. No," she said. "It's not going down like that. I just spent the past two months traipsing through cemeteries in the dark, watching spirits be conjured into existence—I put on zombie makeup and marched through town. I went to a seance that scared the bejeezus out of me and spent a night in a haunted office building. All because this girl—" she pointed at me—"insisted."

"Well, I—"

"I'm not finished."

I think we were all a bit scared. We'd never been lectured by Kaya before. In fact, I'm not sure Kaya had ever said so many words at once when the whole group was together.

She went on. "So this is how it's going to happen. Each of us is going to pick a man. And we're going to set up a date for you with that man. And each date is going to be crazier and wilder than the one before it. And if you don't come out at the end of all of this in love, that's okay. But I will at least have the satisfaction of knowing that we put you through some of the same batshittery you put us through. Can I get an 'amen?'"

And, unfortunately, all the other Divas and several people in the booths nearby joined in with a hearty, "Amen!"

Well, this was just great. I suppose I had only myself to blame. "Can I have some say in who the guys are?"

"You can give us a list," Kaya said. "But we're making the choices."

"This is going to be so much fun," Vanessa said.

"You're supposed to have my back," I whined.

"Oh, don't worry," she cooed. "I'll make sure no harm comes to you…physically."

"What's that supposed to mean?"

"I'm just saying, a little humiliation now and then does a girl good."

They were all laughing, but I knew better. They wouldn't do anything too wild. If anybody had a wild streak it would be me. Bookish Sophie would plan a date for me at Poetry Night held monthly in the local cigar shop. Pari would probably send me on a romantic picnic in a park. Karen would host another movie night and pair me up with somebody cute. Vanessa would probably have me on some kind of spa date. It was Kaya I was going to have to watch out for. I had no idea my ghost challenge had freaked her out that much. She was out for revenge.

"So, let's have the list," Karen said.

I sighed. "Now that I have to actually choose guys, I feel silly. I just want to preface this by saying that I don't really think any guys are into me. I have no idea who Isabella was talking about."

"Just give us the list and we can go see Isabella again later."

"Okay." I'd hemmed and hawed all I could. "Diego West, I suppose."

"Meh," Karen said.

"He's not a 'meh,'" I said.

"I just mean I don't think he's the one."

"Quinn Norris?" I said.

"Possibly," Sophie said. "But can't you think of anyone who's not in the restaurant business?"

"How about Benjamin?" Karen suggested.

"That cute boy at Namaste?" I said.

"Isn't he, like, twenty?" Kaya said.

"Is there an age limit?"

"At least an age minimum."

"I've got seven years on him," I said. "Too young, right?"

"I thought he was gay." Sophie said.

"Oh, yeah," I said. "I think you're right."

"Should we ask him anyway?" Pari said.

"What about Bryan at ChocShop?" I said.

"He's still in braces," Vanessa said.

"So? He could be thirty and in braces."

"But he's not," Karen said. "He's seventeen at best."

"You do like 'em young," Kaya said.

"I'm just tossing out names here," I said. "How about Officer Palmer?"

"He belongs to Pat Willard and you know it."

"Still," Sophie said. "They seem to have hit a speed

bump. If we set him up with Melissa, it might get Pat to sit up and take notice."

"Hey," I said. "This is all about me. We can fix Pat's relationship another time."

"Well, who else have you got?"

"Eric Lawson," I said.

"Too tall," Karen said.

"And too into health food," Pari said.

"You can't go out with Pari's ex," Vanessa said.

"Sure she can," Pari said.

"He's certainly good looking," I said. "What about Hugh?"

"Hugh, who?" Karen said.

"My friend Hugh?" Sophie said.

I nodded.

"I'm not sure I want to do that to him."

"Thanks a lot," I said leaning into her with a chuckle. "Leland Booker, then."

"Oooh," Karen said. "You two can sample all of his cigars."

"That's got sexual innuendo all over it," Kaya said.

"Is Noah still dating your cousin?" I asked Sophie.

"Yep."

"So, he's out."

"I know an attorney you might like," Pari said.

"But it's supposed to be someone who knows me already. Someone who's worshiping me from afar."

"I'll ask him," she said. "You never know."

"This is really dumb," I said.

"Sure it is," Kaya said. And then wickedly, "But it's going to be a lot of fun."

"For you, maybe."

"Exactly."

"I know someone," Vanessa said. "She knows him. He knows her."

"No," I said. "I told you he was not on the list."

"Who are we talking about?" Kaya said.

"Nobody," I said. "Just forget it."

"I think she's talking about Ryan Duval," Karen said.

"How did you know?"

"Everybody knows."

"Oh, right," Kaya said. "The incident."

Downtown Strawbridge was like a little hamlet where everybody knew everyone else's business. We should all be speaking in British accents and sipping tea—don't tell the Trenthams at Across the Pond, the all-things British shop downtown, that I said that.

"She's already been out with him," Vanessa ratted me out. "A few years ago. So he could definitely be the one."

"It was in high school and it wasn't technically a date," I protested.

"Didn't you two go to a party senior year?" Kaya said with a smirk. "I seem to remember that being a date talked about all over school."

"Please, Kaya," I said.

"You have to tell us about that," Vanessa said.

"No thank you."

"Okay," Kaya said. "Leave her alone. I'm just joking."

"I'm not going out with Ryan Duval," I said.

"You are if we say you are," Kaya said.

"Seriously. No. Look, he's my new landlord, for one thing. It wouldn't be appropriate. But the worst part is, he won't let me rent out Mabel's space—" I pointed out the window to her shop across the street, "—for my catering company. I had a deal with Mr. Jenkins but Ryan won't honor it."

"That's not right," Karen said.

"Isn't there something you can do?" Sophie said.

"Was there a contract or something?" Pari said.

"Unfortunately not," I said. "It was a verbal agreement. So you see? You can't fix me up with him. He's off the list."

They all looked around the booth and nodded to each other. But Kaya was shaking her head.

"Maybe," she said. "But I don't think we should promise anything."

"If you fix me up with him, I won't go."

"You have to," Kaya said.

"It's only fair," Pari said. "I didn't want to do the ghost challenges, but I went along, happily."

"We can make them all double dates if it'll make you feel better," Sophie said. "So, even if one of us chooses Ryan, there'll be a buffer."

"Anyway," I mumbled. "I bet he wouldn't agree to go out with me."

"What did you do to him?" Vanessa said with a laugh.

"I didn't do anything. Just make your fix-ups and let's get this whole thing over with."

"That's not the right attitude," Karen said. "Let's see some enthusiasm." She lifted her glass of iced tea and shouted, "Here's to the Pink Diva Man Hunter Plan!"

"Ugh," I said.

Chapter Six

Technically, the HDS BOMB (Historic Downtown Strawbridge Business Owners Management Board) was the Board of Directors for the HDS BOA (the Historic Downtown Strawbridge Business Owners Association). But everybody liked saying HDS BOMB much more than HDS BOA, so all of the HDS BOA meetings were called HDS BOMB meetings, even though the actual HDS BOMB, of which I was a member, met separately.

As a board, the HDS BOMB planned and handled all of the downtown events. We settled disputes between business owners—sidewalk sales caused the most trouble with one store accusing the other of taking up too much space or one store claiming the other was encouraging customers to bypass their sale. We put out a newsletter letting everyone know what everyone else was up to. And we enjoyed lunches all over town—strictly business, of course.

But the HDS BOA was open to all downtown business owners, or their representatives, and that's the meeting I went to on Wednesday to talk about the holiday plans and to see if I could rally support for my leasing of Mabel's storefront. For these larger meetings, we almost always met for lunch in one of the back rooms at Tracks and Quinn Norris, the owner, donated some of the money his restaurant took in to the Association. You never knew who was going to show up at these meetings. Typically, people only showed up if they had something to complain about. But the holidays were upon us, so we had a nice crowd that Wednesday.

I sat with the other board members at the front of the room, so we looked like a wedding party, except for the folders and laptops beyond our lunches. Octavia, our Vice President sat next to Madaline Richards, real estate salesperson extraordinaire and our President nine years running. Quinn was next to me on Octavia's right and Eileen Simmons, our Secretary, sat at the other end of the table on Madaline's left with Trudy Spencer and Harry Trentham. Trudy, Harry, and I were just board members. No titles, no responsibilities. Just there to vote. It was a great gig.

There must have been twenty people in attendance, sitting at white-cloth-covered round tables, unobtrusive flowers in the middle. Sophie's granddad Mr. Childers, the owner of Bookish, was there, looking handsome as ever. Leland Booker, the dashing and disheveled owner of Stogies cigar shop was sitting with Mr. Swanson, owner of Venerable Trinkets—the only antique store downtown that wasn't involved in a war with the other two. And I waved at my bestie Vanessa who was sitting with Karen.

Isabella Bolton was at a table in the back with Carolina Davies. Now there was an unlikely friendship. Isabella: psychic, draped in silks and satins, hair a fluster, stars painted on her ridiculously long fingernails. And Carolina: Devout Christian, seller of religious knick knacks and thingamabobs, pure and wholesome, wears an apron everywhere she goes. And yet, there they were, huddled together with smiles on their faces, sharing what looked like a plate of fried clams.

"What's he doing here?" I found myself blurting out as my crab cakes were put before me. Ryan Duval was sitting at one of the front tables talking with Mr. Simmons of MacAuley Awley's Irish pub.

"Who?" Quinn asked.

Quinn Norris was ruggedly handsome and had just the tiniest bit of a Scottish lilt to his voice. He was the kind of guy who looked just like himself whether he was in ripped jeans and a dirty t-shirt or a three-piece suit. You know what I mean—you'd never turn around at an event, gasp and say, "I didn't recognize you in that!" Like you do when you see your eighth-grade math teacher on the dance floor at The Fort wearing a mini skirt and thigh high boots.

"That guy with Mr. Simmons." I told him.

"I don't know him."

"Well, he's not a business owner, or a manager. He shouldn't be here."

"Are you going to kick him out? We really need a Sergeant at Arms. You should volunteer."

"Very funny."

"It'd be hilarious."

"Octavia." I reached over Quinn's trout *Amandine* and grabbed at her sleeve.

She turned and smiled. "Crab cakes," she said. "I should have gotten the crab cakes."

"Why is Ryan Duval here?"

"Who's Ryan Duval?"

Quinn cleared his throat and explained, "He's the one talking to Simmons. I take it Melissa objects to his participation. Don't you think she should throw him out?"

Octavia laughed. "I'd pay to see that. I don't know who he is."

"He's my new landlord, apparently," I said.

"Oh," she sang.

"He shouldn't be here."

"I'll check it out." She scooted her chair back and, over my frantically whispered objections, sauntered over and introduced herself to Ryan. She ended up gabbing with the entire table for way too long and when she finally got back up front, Madaline was calling the meeting to order.

"First on the agenda, please take a calendar on your way out, but there it is on the screen. Quinn, why isn't the calendar on the screen?"

"Give me a minute." He took another bite of trout and pulled his laptop closer to his plate.

"Better," Madaline said.

Behind the Board's table there was a big screen on a rolling base, so all eyes were peering our way. I should have turned toward the calendar, but instead, I was staring at Ryan Duval. And of course, he caught me. He smirked.

Madaline went on about the calendar of events and when she finished, she said, "Which brings me to a sad announcement. As many of you know, Wilfred Jenkins had a mild stroke. But he's okay—" she put her hands up to quiet the worried gasps. "That being said, even before this happened, he'd decided to retire. And luckily for him, he's found a buyer for all of his Downtown properties. Mr. Ryan Duval, would you stand please and say hello."

This was too much. People were applauding the man.

"He's not a celebrity," I grumbled to no one.

"He looks like one," Quinn said, nudging me.

"Too symmetrical."

"Am I not symmetrical?"

We gazed at one another as Madaline continued. "We'd hoped to have Mr. Jenkins emcee the Holiday Baking Contest."

"You've got the good looks of asymmetry, Mr. Quinn," I said.

"Our judges for the competition will be Quinn Norris of Tracks—"

Quinn waved to the crowd.

"Melissa Stathem of Café Flamingo—"

"You're asymmetrical, too," Quinn said as I nodded to the BOMB gathering.

"Diego West of Burgers, and from Brunch, Melanie Carter."

"Witherspoon," Melanie called out from the back of the room.

"What about a spoon?" Madaline said.

"My last name is Witherspoon now."

"Since when?"

"Since my husband left me, Maddy. Is that okay with

you?"

"Witherspoon. Are you sure?"

"I think I know my own name."

"I went to school with a Melanie Witherspoon."

"Yeah, I know. That was me."

"Really?"

We were all looking at Melanie now and she made something of a 'duh' face.

"Okay," Madaline recovered her gaffe as best she could. "Anyway, Ryan Duval has graciously agreed to take Mr. Jenkins place and emcee our competition."

"Madaline," I said. "If I may...we offered the emcee spot to Mr. Jenkins as a means of honoring him for his years of service to Downtown Strawbridge. If he feels up to it, we should let him do it."

"He's already said he can't."

"Shouldn't we choose a replacement with the same intent, then? Someone we want to honor?"

"Who would you suggest?"

"Well, I don't know. But we should give it some thought."

"I've already approached everyone I could think of—"

"You're saying you can't find anyone other than Mr. Duval to emcee? Not one other person would do it?"

Madaline stood there, looking at me as if I were speaking a foreign language. She shook her head. "No one."

"Did you ask Mayor Hawn?"

"He's already got a job at the festival. You know that."

"He can't host the holiday pie eating contest *and* emcee the baking competition?"

"We're not following Robert's Rules of Order at all," Quinn shouted.

"And he's riding in the parade," Madaline said, clearly annoyed. "And judging the best decorated tree contest and the best decorated store front."

"Okay, okay," I said throwing my hands in the air. "What about the Senator?"

"Of course I've already asked him. He would rather

not. Look, Melissa, we don't have time to make these last minute changes. I've already told Mr. Duval that he could do it."

"Where's a gavel," Quinn said.

"I understand," Ryan said, standing. "If you'd like take nominations and have a vote, I don't mind."

"We can't nominate people without asking them if they want to do it," Mr. Simmons said.

"Let's just vote now," Madaline said.

"This is out of order," Quinn said.

"All those in favor of having Mr. Duval emcee the cooking competition, raise your hand."

I watched, frustrated, as it seemed everyone in the room but Quinn and I had arms in the air.

"Those opposed."

All eyes were on me. But I'm nothing if not determined. So I raised my hand. "I'm just making a point," I said. "It was supposed to be an honor."

"And I'm just supporting Mel," Quinn said.

"And the others?" Madaline looked over her nose at Vanessa and Karen who, bless them, had their hands up.

"Divas stick together," Vanessa said.

"Hmph," Madaline said. "Still, the ayes have it."

"It is an honor," Ryan said with a smirk and had the nerve to bow to the room before sitting down to applause.

"I'm assuming, of course," Quinn said, "that asymmetry is a good thing in faces."

"Symmetry is evil," I said.

His eyes widened as he gaped at me. "You really don't like the guy. What did he do to you?"

"Mr. Jenkins was going to let me lease Mabel's storefront, but now that Ryan owns the building, he says he doesn't want a catering business there."

"Why not?"

"Exactly! I'm right, aren't I? There's no reason I shouldn't have that space."

"No, I mean, what was his reason?"

"Oh, some nonsense about the Downtown atmosphere. He wants quirky shops."

"He has a point."

"That spot is perfect for me."

"But is it right for Downtown?"

I glared over at Ryan. He was so at ease, chatting with Mr. Simmons. So galling. "I don't see why not. I really need people on my side here," I said, turning back to Quinn.

"Readying for battle?"

"Well, yes. If it was your battle, I'd be on your side."

"I'll put in a good word for you, if that will help."

"It will. Thank you."

"Although, I did just vote against the man for emcee."

"Ugh. And symmetrically evil people always hold grudges."

Chapter Seven

The meeting broke up slowly, a half-completed, unaccomplished feeling of disarray floating through the crowd.

"What was that all about, anyway?" Isabella found me at the door.

I started to explain—about the tray of dishes and Mabel's storefront, but she stopped me.

"No, I mean the meeting. Why were we even here?"

I had no answer. But the minutes would reflect that we discussed and approved the holiday calendar. Funny how that happened.

"Do you remember what you said in September? When the Divas had a reading?"

Isabella peered at me with a smile. "Not at all, I'm afraid. A reading is stuck in time, you see. Whatever I said then was for then. Would you like another appointment?"

"Maybe. It's just that…you said there was a guy who liked me, but that he was shy or something. You said, he was around…watching me."

"That's hardly unusual."

"And Pari said, 'like a stalker.' Remember?"

"Ah, yes, Pari. She's a sharp one, isn't she. So glad she's found herself."

"Yes, but about me—"

"Why don't you just let love happen, Melissa?"

"The Divas won't let me."

She laughed and patted my cheek before turning to leave. Things like that happen when you're petite with a squeaky voice.

"That was fun," Quinn said. He handed me a white bag. "You didn't get to eat your crab cakes."

"Thanks."

He winked at me as he left to get back to work. It had to be Quinn. Of all the guys around me, he was the only one who seemed interested in me. And yet, he wasn't interested enough to ask me out. And I'd never thought about asking him out. I was trying to come up with other possibilities as I left Tracks and then smacked myself—in my imagination, anyway. Who cared, right? Why was I suddenly becoming obsessed with finding a steady guy? Sure, the Divas seemed to be pairing off. And the more involved they got with their love lives, the more Diva time was spent on the subject. But that was no reason to give in to it.

"Well, you're doing a great job." Ryan Duval was standing next to my little red Jetta, leaning against a shiny black Audi.

"What?" I pushed past him and stuck a key into my car door, only to find it was the wrong one.

"It's all over town, apparently. I've had three people suggest I let you rent out Mabel's space."

"Is that so?" Flustered, I dropped my keys. Then, naturally, I stomped my foot and said, "Urrrgggh." Why was I so rattled? I had a good case against this guy. Bias in renting, or something. There had to be a real estate rule about it. When I bent down to grab the keys, we bonked heads. "What the hell," I said and gave him a little shove.

"I was just trying to help." He practically threw my keys at me.

"Well, stop."

"It's not personal, okay? It's not about the tray of dishes."

"I thought you sold houses. When did you become a real estate mogul, anyway? And why Downtown Strawbridge? Why my Downtown?"

"Your Downtown?"

"Café Flamingo has been here since…well, since before you were here."

"I grew up here."

"Oh, forget it." Trying to find the right key when you're having a meaningless argument is nearly impossible.

"Stop sending your friends to talk to me."

"I didn't send anybody." Forget the keys; this was war.

"Then why would they care who I rent to? What would possess them?"

"We stick together here. You're an outsider."

"Again—" He looked at me as if I were stupid. "I grew up here. And now I own six properties in Downtown Strawbridge. I'm an insider."

"You ran into me."

He startled. "What?"

"In the restaurant. You ran into me. It was your fault. I didn't want to say before, because…well, customer is always right and all that."

"You're nuts."

"Don't call me nuts."

"You weren't looking where you were going and you know it. You should have been begging my forgiveness."

"Why? Because you're some highfalutin real estate guy? And I said I was sorry. I offered to pay for your dry cleaning. But you couldn't be bothered. You stormed out."

"I had somewhere to be."

"Exactly!" I stuck a key into his chest and he stepped back, alarmed. "You were in a hurry and you ran into me. And now you're holding it against me like a petty, grumpy business tycoon."

He rolled his eyes. "Tycoon? Give me a break."

"I'll break something," I mumbled, finally finding the right key.

"Was that a threat?" He was on the other side of the Audi then, opening the door. "Who says highfalutin anyway?"

As angry as I was, I couldn't help but smile as I slid into my car. I had said that, hadn't I? It was his fault. There was something about Ryan Duval that really ticked me off and made me act stupid. I tried to think back to the last time we'd met up. Had things really gone that badly?

Chapter Eight

Numbers are calming. It's words that get me. This is probably why Vanessa and I are closer to each other than we are to the other Divas. If we were all word games, Van and I would be sudoku and the others would be crossword puzzles. Give us a ledger filled with numbers, even on the computer, and we're happy. Balancing the day's money that Wednesday evening was just what I needed to get Ryan Duval out of my head. I was checking the till for startup the next morning when Vanessa knocked on the glass door of the Flamingo.

"I was just at Kaya's and thought I might catch you before you left," she said breezing into the café with a bag from ChocShop. She waved to Lydia who was mopping the floor, the chairs upturned on the tables. In the kitchen, the sounds of cleanup echoed out to us over the heavy metal screeching from the radio. "Doug's closing tonight, I hear. So, why are you wrist deep in cash?"

"I work here, remember?"

"But you have people."

She followed me back to the register behind the counter and I continued counting ones.

"What do you have in mind?" I mumbled. "Twenty-two..."

Vanessa was dressed for a night out, which, for her,

isn't much different from being dressed for work. But there was a distinct extra pouf to her updo, and a waft of grape-scented hair spray hung around her.

"Something new. I just heard about it today. *Improv.*"

"What's that, like…stand-up comedy? Forty…"

"No, it's like that show, *Who's Line is it, Anyway?*"

I looked around the café. "Who's line? What are we, in a play? Am I on hidden camera?"

"What?"

"You're the one talking gibberish."

"I said, '*Who's Line is it, Anyway?*'"

"I heard you the first time. Why are you asking me? Fifty-two. Fifty-three."

"Stop counting. You can't listen and count at the same time."

"Oh, can't I? Sixty—" I looked at her with my 'I can do whatever I want' face as I counted out the singles. "Sixty-one."

"Improv. They're doing improv. Like that show."

"What are you talking about?"

"The show *Who's Line is it, Anyway?*"

"Wait. Stop." I put the ones into the till and turned to her. "Slow down. Is the word 'anyway' part of the name of the show?"

She rolled her eyes and shook her head. "I know you have a TV. It's not standup, but it's a lot of fun. At least it is on that show."

"I might recall seeing the name on the guide, but I've never watched it. Are we talking SNL stuff?"

"Improv! As in, they improvise."

"Where's it at?"

"The Fort, but it starts at eight. We gotta go now."

"I can't." I'd finished checking the till and was carrying it to the back room where the safe was. "I've got to drop off the bank bag and get home to—"

"There's no time. You look fine."

"I'll meet you there," I called to her. "I promise."

"I'm coming with you." She'd followed me into my office. "You'll never get there if I don't hurry you. Seriously, you don't need to change."

"It's not that."

"What then?"

"Can't I meet you there?"

"Okay, what's going on?"

Here's the deal: Vanessa didn't know about the cat—the stray that I'd been feeding a few times a week for the last month or so. I don't know why I hadn't told anyone. I suppose that's not exactly true. If I told someone I was feeding a cat, the mere fact of mentioning it would make me a cat owner. And I didn't want to be a cat owner.

"Fine," I said. "Come with me."

Once the bank bag was successfully dropped into the night deposit drawer outside the bank, I drove Vanessa to my little house on Coral Street. As I pulled up onto the driveway, I saw that the cat wasn't waiting for me on the porch.

"What's wrong, Mel," Vanessa said as we climbed the steps to the alcove where the front door faced the driveway.

"Oh, all right; I'll tell you." I unlocked the door and we both sighed with joy at the air conditioned living room.

"How can it still be so hot in November?" she said.

"Technically, it's much cooler."

"But not cold. I haven't forgotten—what's bothering you?"

She followed me into the bedroom and as I changed into something that said "I'm with Vanessa" instead of "I just hold Vanessa's purse while she's dancing," I told her about the cat.

"What's his name?"

"I can't name it. If I name it, it's mine. Anyway, I haven't seen him or her—"

"It?"

"Exactly. It. I haven't seen it for about a week now."

"And you're worried."

"A little."

"Sounds like you own a cat."

"He's not my cat. But still."

"Someone else is feeding him, that's all. It's a good

thing."

"I suppose. How's this?" I twirled. A cute knee-length dress with three-quarter sleeves in a leafy fall print.

"It'll do."

I could tell she was thinking about the cat. That was the last thing I needed.

We parked in the lot behind The Fort, as usual, and made our way around front where we could hear rock music blasting from the place. The Fort is surrounded by wood fencing like you'd expect from a military fort out west, back in the John Wayne movie days. Not that I'd ever actually seen a John Wayne movie, but I bet there was one that had some kind of fort in it. The wood planks were spaced far enough apart that you could peer between them, and there were plenty of people-sized openings to get through. But we always went in the front gate. I think of those other entry points as cheating, for some reason. The outside tables were full and we meandered our way into the crowded restaurant to find a double spot on stage left.

"That's luck," I said, taking a seat.

"Perfect," Vanessa shouted over the screaming lead singer.

"The sign out front said standup *and* improv," I yelled.

"Well, I'm here for the improv."

"It'll be local, you know. Like the little theater in the plaza with folding chairs."

"Holding hairs?"

"Folding chairs! Local. Like high school kids or something."

"That doesn't mean it won't be good."

"It can't possibly be like on TV."

"Just because it's not on TV," she shrieked, "doesn't mean it will—" and right there the band stopped playing. "—suck!"

"All right," the singer said, drawn out like...as if he was high as a junkie at a rave. "Okay, yeah. Thank you, thank you."

The smattering of applause from the now-deaf audience was drowned out by Vanessa's enthusiastic apologetic clapping.

"You totally don't suck," she said. "I was talking about the improv."

The guy was unplugged already and heading off the stage.

"Not that I think the improv will suck."

"It's okay, Vanessa," I said. "I really don't think he can hear you. It'll be a few hours before any of us will be able to hear again."

We had time. The band had to break down the drum set and haul the keyboard off stage. Finally, Dave Chesney, the guy who runs the place, got up on stage and winked at Vanessa.

"Thank you everyone for coming out tonight. This is our second week of Improv at The Fort and if last week was anything to judge by, it's going to be a big hit." Some cheers rang out over the applause. "Tonight I'd like to welcome back the company you got a little taste of last week. They've won Improv on the Beach two years in a row and took home a big trophy from the Orlando Improv Laugh Off last spring. Let's hear it for Died Laughing!"

I clapped along with the rest of the crowd as the group of men and women approached the stage from various places in the room, including behind the curtain.

"Wait…is that?" Could it be? On stage at The Fort? "It's Kaya," I said, grabbing Vanessa's arm. "I almost didn't recognize her. She looks so…"

"Lit up," Vanessa said.

It was true. I didn't realize how much stage lights enhance a person's face. Kaya was beaming as she waved at us.

There were seven performers in Died Laughing. Four men: Cole Harrington, who could pass for a shorter Idris Elba, although I admit I have no idea how tall Idris Elba is, but he seems really tall, doesn't he? I met Cole once at a party and if I replay the scene just right in my head I can sometimes convince myself he was flirting with me. But even I know that's wishful thinking. Seth Roberts, who looked vaguely familiar. The kind of guy you expect to be unkempt and foul-mouthed but turns out to just be adorably flustered and vulnerable. There was Kim Jeong, the guy who runs the bike shop just over the bridge, beachside. And their emcee, who called himself Monty, though I was sure that was a fake name, reminded me of that kid who played Payton in *The Politician*. (Somebody tell Vanessa I definitely do watch TV.) And there were three women: Fannie Carpenter, who I knew in high school and whose name is actually real. She was perfect for comedy, too, because she always had a Lucille Ball kind of wackiness about her. Eliza Wolf, who I'd never seen before in my life. And none other than the Divas' own Kaya Channing.

"Hi Kaya," Vanessa called, as if Kaya hadn't already seen us.

"Why didn't you tell us?" I said, acting just as silly as Van.

Kaya put a finger to her lips in hopes of shutting us up.

Everything went smoothly for a while. The group members took turns on stage, two, three, or more at a time, and Monty asked the audience to help set the scene with places, occupations, or props. It was pretty funny, I had to admit, especially the parts in which they had to pretend to be riding those weird bouncy animal things at playgrounds, or hula-hooping. Kaya was bonkers hilarious. Who knew? She's the sensible one. The one with all the sanity in the group. And there she was, at The Fort, doing somersaults across the stage and pretending to be a deranged stalker slapping her victim in the face with wet spaghetti.

I was prepared to buy Vanessa dinner next time out for suggesting such a fabulous distraction until, in what had all the grandness of a finale, with the entire group on stage, Monty took the mic and said ominously, "Attention, ladies and gentlemen. I've just been made aware that we have a situation on our hands. How many of you have heard of an incident that happened recently over at Café Flamingo?"

"What?" I whispered loudly to Vanessa. She didn't

look upset at all.

The crowd didn't seem to know what Monty was talking about, but made noises of encouragement, unfortunately.

"That's right. Downtown Strawbridge's newest landlord and celebrated star of his own 'local boy makes big' story, the dapper Ryan Duval—"

"Dapper?" I said with disgust.

"—was attacked by a tray-wielding waitress."

"Waitress?"

"The way I heard it, he had leftover sandwiches and chips dumped all over his head. On purpose."

"That's a lie!" I'd stood up and shouted and everybody laughed.

"Is it?" Monty said.

"That's not what happened at all."

"Well, why don't you come on up and show us how it all went down?"

And before I knew what was happening, Kaya and Fannie were behind me, leading me up the few steps onto the stage, to the audience's cheers.

"Ladies and gentlemen," Monty was calling like a carnival barker, "I give you the spitfire who did what every Strawbridge business owner has dreamt of doing at least once—sticking it to the landlord—Melissa Stathem. So tell us, Melissa. How did it feel?"

"It was an accident," I pleaded.

"An accident, huh?" Monty said, slyly. "Let's find out what Mr. Duval has to say." And to the crowd he shouted, "Come on up, Ryan. We know you're here."

"I really don't think this is a good idea," I said to Kaya.

"Just go with it," she said.

As Ryan climbed onto the stage smirking at me, I was handed an enormous blue plastic tray, so big it made the audience roar with laughter.

"Okay, Ryan," Monty said. "Show us what happened."

Grabbing Monty's microphone, Ryan said. "Happy to."

"How is this funny?" I shouted. "This isn't improv."

But before I could extricate myself from the bizarre situation, Monty, having retrieved his microphone from Ryan, said, "First, what'll we put on the tray?"

"Wait, what?" Ryan said.

Now it was getting interesting.

"It's not like you're wearing a fancy suit," Monty said to him.

True enough, he was in jeans and a button-up.

Monty turned to the audience, "What shall we put on the tray that gets dumped onto the landlord?"

As the crowd shouted suggestions that were as crazy as they were deafening, I watched with glee as the blood drained from Ryan's dapper face.

Chapter Nine

K etchup," Vanessa screamed. "Pour ketchup all over him!"

It was as if the entire audience was suddenly in on the joke—like they knew all about what had happened. Shouts of "Iced tea" and "French fries" flew about the room. It was moments like that, that made me want to move to New York City and get lost in anonymity.

"Ketchup could be arranged," Monty said with a sly smile. "But, to keep things safe, and so that we don't do too much damage—" with a wink at Ryan— "to the stage—"

"Thank you!" Dave called out from behind the bar.

"—we have some exciting choices for you, all approved by our host."

"With reservations," Dave said.

Kaya came onto the stage with a large silver colander up-turned on her head and carrying two platters piled high with cooked spaghetti.

"You remember the earlier bit involving a beating with a wet noodle," Monty said. "How about a dousing of noodles?"

Then Fannie came onto the stage struggling to carry a mop bucket filled with sand.

"Choice number two," Monty said. "Sand. But not

just any sand, mind you. This is one hundred percent parking lot sand dug up from out back a second ago."

"So, dirt," someone said.

"Very dirty dirt. And last choice." Monty gestured to Cole who came on stage with another bucket. "TP, folks."

Confused laughter ran through the bar.

"Not just any TP, mind you. But, wet TP."

"Who peed on it?" someone shouted.

"I don't think it's pee," Monty said. He turned to Cole. "Is it pee?"

Cole took a sniff to everyone's loud disgust and shrugged. "Could be," he said.

"Come on, guys," Ryan said. But he was smiling.

I could tell he was doing his best to be a good sport. And that, if you want to know the truth, made me mad. If he could play along graciously, then so could I.

"Okay, folks," Monty said. "Which is it going to be? Sand?" Cheers and whistles. "Noodles?" More cheers. "Or possibly-peed-on toilet paper?" Uproar, as you can imagine. "But wait, we have one more option. How about all three?"

The place was on fire. Monty took me behind the curtain to a back stage area about the size of a walk-in freezer.

"Okay," he said. "You're a waitress, got it? Just go with it."

He held me back for a while as Kaya and Cole were onstage with Ryan. There was a lot of banging and scraping and laughter from the crowd.

"What's going on?" I said.

"They're setting up, is all."

Finally I heard Kaya saying, "Here you are Mr. Hot Stuff Landlord, table for one." Then she shrieked. "Sally Waitress! Big shot at table one!"

Monty shoved me out from behind the curtain where I found the stage now set with a table and two chairs. Ryan sat in one, facing the audience. He looked scared, like we were planning to dump a bucket of fake pig's blood all over him. But, he'd been prepped, apparently, as he started shouting at me as soon as I sidled up to him.

"It's about time. I've been waiting for five seconds."

He got a bit of laughter with that one.

In my squeakiest voice, I said, "What do you want?"

"A little respect," Ryan said.

To which Kaya, backstage, responded, in falsetto song, "R-E-S-P-E-C-T."

Ryan looked up at me and said, deadpan, "Find out what it means to me."

For some reason, I was having trouble not laughing, even though I didn't find any of it funny. "I could look it up for you if you like," was all I could manage.

There was more mayhem between some of the improv troupe and Ryan, as they came and went from the stage, suggesting odd sandwiches and soups and I got in a few lines that are now just a blur to me, but the audience seemed to enjoy the antics.

Then Ryan held up a hand and shouted, "Manager! I demand to speak to the manager."

Before I could respond, Kaya was shoving me aside. "What's the problem here Mr. Huff-n-Stuff?" There was some back and forth and laughter and then Kaya shoved me back to the table. "I assure you, Sally here won't get your order wrong this time. Isn't that right, Sally?" She poked my nose with her finger.

"Sure, sure," I squeaked. "What'll it be Hot-n-Tot?"

"That's Huff-n-Stuff, pipsqueak."

"Okay Nuff-n-Gruff."

"How dare you?"

"Just tell me what you want."

"Fine." Ryan made a big show of perusing the non-existent menu. "I'll take the spaghetti." The audience, knowing what was to come, roared.

"Sauce?"

"None."

"Are you sure?" I said. "I could dump a whole lot of red sauce on you—er, your plate, if you'd like."

"Do I look like the kind of man who would defile perfectly good noodles?"

Having nothing to add to that, I said, "Will that be all?"

"Yes."

I stood there for a second or two, trying to figure out how I was going to get sand and toilet paper into the skit if he didn't order anything else, but Kim winked at me so I did what I was told and just went with it. I went back stage and got the huge tray. Monty dumped what must have been ten pounds of spaghetti noodles onto it, laughed at my struggles to hold up the tray, and said, "All over him."

So, I teetered on stage, veered this way and that under the load of spaghetti, screamed out, "Your entree Mr. Stuffed Shirt," and dumped the entire trayful onto his head. The audience roared with delight.

Ryan, feigning outrage, jumped up from his chair and screamed, "It's hot! I'm burning, I'm burning."

"Stop, drop, and roll," Kaya shouted. She gently pushed Ryan to the floor and yelled at me. "Quick, roll all over him to put out the fire!"

"I can do it myself," Ryan screamed, rolling around on the floor.

That was my cue. I knew immediately what to do. Monty handed me the bucket of sand at the curtain and I ran back to Ryan. "I'll put out the fire, sir," I said and poured sand all over him.

Ryan stood, letting sandy noodles drop from his head and shoulders to the floor. The cheers and laughter were so loud, I could barely hear him when he said, with all the dignity a Huff-n-Stuff could muster, "Do you have any wet wipes, perchance?"

I couldn't help laughing myself as I took the bucket of wet toilet tissue from Monty, carried it to Ryan and proceeded to take bits of soggy paper from it and wipe them all over his face.

"Thank you so much," he said loudly over the continuing laughter. "You've been so kind to me."

"But I dumped spaghetti on you," I said.

"It was no more than I deserved for trying to have you fired, my dear."

"Oh, Mr. Ruff-n-Fluff," I cried. "Does this mean...?"

"Yes, Sally Waitress, it does." He gathered himself

together, wiped himself off, and sat himself back into the chair. "I'll have dessert."

I didn't know what to do at that point, but luckily, Kaya stuck a can of whipped topping in my hand and, well, what else could I do? In the end, both Ryan Duval and I were decorated with whipped cream. We got to take our bows with the whole crew and then were ushered to the back stage closet where we found actual wet wipes to clean ourselves up as best as we could.

"You got some on your shirt," I told him.

"I have a washing machine."

And before I knew it, I was back at the table with Vanessa, having no idea what happened to Ryan.

"You set that whole thing up, didn't you?" I asked her.

"It wasn't me," she said. "I swear."

"Then who?"

Just then, Kaya joined us, the improv group having had a final bow without their victims.

"You!" I said.

She winked at Vanessa. "I was hoping Van would talk you into showing up. We even kept this table open for you guys."

"I hope it didn't make Ryan mad," I said.

"Why should you care?" Vanessa said.

Kaya said, "He seemed to enjoy it." She was sitting with her back to the stage, in a chair she'd stolen from a four-seater nearby, and she leaned to one side, peering behind me. "Oh," she said. "Looks like we pulled him from his date."

I turned to look, only to find Ryan Duval and his date, the same girl from dinner on Sunday. They were standing, pushing their chairs under the table, as if leaving.

"Does she look mad to you?" I said. "She looks mad to me."

"Maybe a little," Kaya said.

"Who cares?" Vanessa said. "If she can't take a joke…"

"Looks like she can't."

His date looked seriously unhappy. She glared at me, briefly, before turning away.

"Why should she be mad?" Vanessa said. "He was

just being a good sport."

I agreed. "She looks protective. Probably didn't like her date being embarrassed."

"She looks familiar," Kaya said, watching them make their way to the front door. "She works around here, I think. But that's not where I know her from."

"She's awfully pretty," Vanessa said.

I glared at her.

"What? She is."

"She's fraternizing with the enemy. We hate her."

"She can still be pretty."

"It's going to bug me until I remember," Kaya said. "Well, I've got to get back to the group. We're going to hang out and come up with all the funny things we should have said."

After waving her off, and before the music started up again, I said, "I was just kidding. He's not my enemy. But he's obviously dating someone."

"So?"

"So…you can't choose him to set me up with."

"Don't look so triumphant. I happen to have some-one else in mind."

"Who?"

"Not telling."

"Oh, come on."

But she wouldn't budge. "I will tell you that your first date is Saturday. Kaya's choice."

"Who'd she set me up with?"

"I'm not telling you that."

We sat there for a minute or two while the band set up for another round of noise. I tried my best not to appear frustrated.

"You're smiling," she said, finally.

"Am not."

"You are. I think you *want* to go on these dates."

"Well don't you want me to want to?"

"Not really."

"That's not nice." I was laughing though.

"You know it's supposed to be fun for us more than for you."

"I feel like this whole thing has strayed from its original intent."

"Your intent, maybe."

"You're no fun, anymore."

"Seriously, though. You should take some time to find a nice guy and think about settling down."

"Oh, my god, Van. You sound like my grandmother."

"It's true. You work so much. If you don't find your man soon, it'll never happen."

"What about you?"

"I don't work as hard as you do. And I'm dating."

She had a point. Not necessarily about everything. "I don't have to get married, you know. We don't all have to have that life."

"But you want it, don't you?"

I sighed. "I don't know. I like my life. I like my house and my restaurant."

"That's great, Mel. But at some point things will slow down and you'll be sixty and alone. What then?"

"Okay, granny, I hear you. I'll go on the dates. I'll have fun. But I'm not going to get married just to not be alone."

"You know, for someone who is so organized and prepared, you don't think about the future that much."

Luckily for me, the band started up and I didn't have to analyze my life anymore. We drank and danced and had a great time and when I finally got home at about two in the morning, my stray cat friend was waiting on the front steps for me. I said hello, poured some kibble into the bowl and put out a second bowl filled with fresh water on the bottom step, before heading off to bed.

Chapter Ten

How to Ruin a Scrumptious Recipe

Attempt Two: Add in Something Sticky

Ryan and I finished high school as friends, one of whom vomited on the other. Things are a little different when there's vomit between you. The whole school talked about it for weeks and while the teasing didn't seem to faze Ryan all that much, things were... quieter between us.

Once we graduated, I didn't see him again, other than across campus once or twice, until our second year of college. We both went to UCF, in Orlando. I drove over every day for classes while I planned my restaurant and begged my parents and grands for start-up loans. I think they played hardball just to make me feel like a good negotiator. That's not to say I didn't have a good time while I was in school. I met Vanessa as a freshman, when I took my mom into her salon—her stylist retired and I thought it would be a good idea for her to find one downtown, since that's where I planned to have my own business. And as a walk-in, Mom was lucky to get Vanessa. She and I hit it off right away and the next thing

I knew, I was out at The Fort dancing and drinking.

I'm petite, if I didn't mention it before, so not a really big drinker. Two is my limit. Three my extreme limit. I know that if I have three drinks and they're too close together, I'm going to be really sick the next day, so I've become pretty disciplined about it over the years. And I learned with Vanessa. Sip and dance all night and you'll be ready for classes or work the next day, no problem.

But one day in Orlando after a Principles of Marketing class, this girl, JoAnne, told me about a party going on that Saturday night over on the beach.

"You live over there, don't you?" she said.

"With my parents." I tried to stave off a request to sleep over at my place, in case it was hidden behind her question.

She said a lot of the business majors were going and I should go, too. "Trevor's dad has a little house right on the beach. It's going to be a blast."

I literally dragged Vanessa along with me. She said it was going to be a rager, a Fratfest, and she wanted nothing to do with it. But she gave in when I promised her that business majors were a tame bunch compared to the English majors. They were the ones you had to watch out for. I had no idea what I was talking about, of course, because I didn't live over there. I knew nothing about what went on after hours on or off campus.

"First," she said, as I looked for the house along a dark stretch of A1A in Floridana Beach. "If you're driving us home, you have two drinks max and stop by ten. Got it?"

"I promise."

"And second, if cops show up, I'm running. I am a business woman, you got that? I am not going to have a record."

I chuckled. "Can you imagine? A police raid? How cool would that be?"

"You were so sweet and mature when I met you. What have I done?"

"I'm Vanessa's Monster! Look, I'm going because it's supposed to be business majors. If it looks like a wild orgy of drinking and drugs, we'll leave."

For all of her worry, Vanessaended up rather disappointed. As much as she protested, the party was no rager. It was just what you'd expect of a bunch of up-and-coming CEOs. Drinks, yeah. Music, absolutely. A little dancing on the deck by the pool and some tabletop gaming in the rooms upstairs. It wasn't a huge house, but there was a dark path beyond the pool through the dunes that led to the beach and from the windows on the second floor, you could see a reflection of moonlight spread across the water.

"Wouldn't you love to live on the beach?" I asked Vanessa after we'd toured the party. I said hi to people I knew from my classes, but I was glad Van was with me. "You were hoping for a raid, weren't you?"

She lifted her shoulders with a sad smile. "I went to cosmetology school after getting an AA, so…maybe I was hoping for a taste of the college life. But this is nice."

I led Vanessa straight to where I figured she could find some cute guys to flirt with—the dining room off of a big, open kitchen. That was where most of the noise was coming from. There was a huge spread of food and a stocked bar with a guy I recognized from one of my classes making drinks for everybody. We got ourselves a boozy cocktail each, and took to a corner where we were immediately descended upon.

"You're Melissa, right?"

A young Stephen Colbert look-alike was the first to make contact. He wore thick-rimmed, square glasses and a collared shirt with rolled-up sleeves, finished with a loosened red silk tie. The entire outfit said, 'Please take me seriously.'

"Robert Allis," he said with a smile and nod. "From accounting class."

"Oh, yeah," I said. "You're a great numbers guy. Are you going into accounting?"

He glanced at Vanessa and his face pinked up. "Nah, my family's in liquor."

"I'm sorry," I said. "Let me introduce you to my friend, Vanessa. Vanessa likes to drink. And you're in the booze business. I bet you two have a lot to talk about."

They practically melted into each other, leaving me feeling like an appendage. I was too ready to leave when somebody tapped my shoulder. I turned to find Ryan Duval smiling at me.

"I'm surprised to see you here," he said.

"Why's that?"

"I've just never seen you at one of these things before. You still live at home, don't you?"

"Nothing wrong with that," I said, rather defensively, I admit. "I don't have the money for my own place yet."

"I mean, home. Like, Strawbridge."

"Oh, you don't?"

"No, I live in campus housing."

"Why?"

"Why not?"

"I guess if you're made of money."

He laughed. "I guess."

We stood there for a few seconds looking around.

"This is weird," I said, finally.

"What do you mean?"

"It's like we're not friends, anymore."

He turned to look at me and smiled. "You're right. That's weird. Come on. Hug."

"You got it."

As a group of friends, we hugged in high school—just two of us, trios, group hugs. We hugged hello. We hugged goodbye. We hugged whoever needed one in the moment. So I hugged him, just like we used to.

"Have you been out to the beach yet?"

I shook my head and he took my hand, leading me through the party. We ducked under balloons where there was some kind of game going on, passed by a few people chugging beers to chants from onlookers, and danced around what appeared to be some remote control car racing out by the pool.

We found the path to the beach and I had to take my shoes off to get through the thick sand. Music and laughter echoed behind us and grew quieter as the sounds of waves rolling up onto the shore got louder. A huge moon hung in the sky casting ripples of light along the edges of the waves, making it look as if the sea was alive with creatures.

We made our way to the wet sands where the ocean lapped at our feet and stood there looking out at the darkness. After a few minutes, it all started to feel a bit creepy.

"This would make a great scene in a horror movie," he said, as if reading my mind.

"Mutant fish zombies could crawl out of the sea and drag us in."

"Or aliens could land and use us as bait."

"That's awful," I said.

"Did you ever see that movie, *Jaws?*"

"No. I'm not a fan of swimming in the ocean, anyway. I don't need proof that it's a bad idea."

He lowered his voice and, mimicking a movie ad, said, "Don't go into the water."

Just then, voices chattered along the wind, startling us. He grabbed my hand, said, "Aliens, quick!" and we ran back to the dunes, stumbling, screaming, and laughing through the thick, dry sands near the path.

Once we were close to the beach house, we slowed and caught our breath, still laughing.

"We made it," he said.

He put an arm around me and stopped suddenly. I thought, for some reason, that he was going to kiss me…or vomit on me, and my heart raced. Was this it? Was Ryan Duval finally going to kiss me? But instead of leaning in, I panicked—so much time had passed. Would this be a real kiss? A meaningful kiss? Or just one of those spur of the moment college party kisses? Instinctively, I guess, I stepped backward, and stumbled in the sand. I tried to right myself by grabbing hold of him. At least, I thought I was catching myself. I was actually pulling him down with me, and as we were falling off the path, I thought to myself, at least we're not by the pool. And then he screamed.

"Aaaah!"

I scrambled to my feet. "What is it?"

He just screamed again. "Aaah!"

"Stop screaming. Tell me what happened."

He sat up, wincing, and lifted his left arm, the one he'd used to break our fall, and it was filled with thorns. And that's when I saw the huge prickly pear cactus he'd fallen against. I tried to help him up, but he wasn't having it.

"Just. Just. Wait," he said. He breathed in and out a few times and then pushed himself up with his other hand and turned around. His back was filled with cactus spines. "Pull 'em out."

"Let's get into the light."

I followed him as he hobbled back to the house where everyone screamed at the sight of him. His friends gathered around and took him into the master bathroom upstairs where, I guess, surgery was performed. I wasn't allowed in. Not that anyone blamed me for the scene, other than Ryan. It was just that he had friends there at the party and they stepped in. I'd done enough, after all. Did my part, so to speak.

Standing at the bathroom door, I heard one of the girls in the group ask about me.

"That was just Mel," he said. "A friend from high school."

I left the party as soon as I could pry Vanessa away from Robert.

When I told her what had happened, in great detail, all she said was, "Do aliens know how to fish? How would they know if they even like fish?"

Chapter Eleven

I was never sure about that cat. It was cute enough, gray with some pale striping. Didn't look streetwise. I imagined a stray cat would be brutish, tough, scarred, with a bit of one ear bitten off. But this cat was thin… maybe too thin. And dainty. I always put out food as soon as I saw it on the porch and then for a few days after, but the cat treated my house like a one-night stand every week or so. That's not technically a one-night stand, is it? No. It's an occasional foodie call.

But this time, when I got home Thursday night after a long day at the café and overseeing a catering event at the Chamber of Commerce, I found the food pretty much eaten from the bowl. Two days in a row! I was fearful and happy at the same time. Fearful that the cat was going to adopt me. And happy to see it was getting enough food.

On Friday morning, before I headed off to the café, I went to retrieve the cat bowls hoping to find the food I'd left the night before eaten as well. The bowls had to be cleaned after every use because, despite the cat being an obvious stray, and hungry, it was a bit particular. He'd leave bits of food in the bowl for the ants, or worse, the raccoons. After banging the food bowl on the concrete walkway—the only way I knew to get the ants off without smooshing them—and dumping out the water under my hibiscus plant, I took the bowls inside and washed them off, before heading to my bedroom to get ready for work. When I caught sight of movement on my bed, I leaped backward, screamed—just a little—and slammed the door closed. Whatever it was, I'd trapped it in my room.

"Now what?" I said to no one but myself. It was times like that, I wished for a roommate. But no. I am a strong, independent woman. I can call pest control and rat- or opossum-retrieval services as good as any man.

I then realized my front door was ajar. Apparently, something had crawled in while I was cleaning the bowls. Slowly, terrified, I turned the knob on the bedroom door and cracked it open to have a peek. There, curled up on my bed, one leg stretched out in front of him, was the cat, licking himself.

"Oh," I said, relieved. "It's just you. Well, come on. You need to leave."

I held the door wide open.

"Go on now."

The cat ignored me.

"Time to go."

Nothing.

I went to the front door and pulled it wide open.

"Feel the fresh air?" I called. "And the warmth? Don't you just love Florida in the fall?"

I went back to my bedroom and the cat had put its face under a paw.

"I can still see you."

It looked up at me, daring me to do something about its trespassing.

I walked over to the bed, put my hands on my hips and said, very sternly, "You can't stay here. I have to go to work. Where will you pee? Seriously. I can't leave my door open for you. You have to leave now."

He purred and put his head back down to go to sleep.

"Fine," I said. "Just until I'm ready to leave."

And the cat slept there on my bed as I showered, dressed, and had a bit of breakfast. I gathered up my purse and keys, went to the front door, opened it, and called for the cat.

"Time to go."

Nothing.

"Come on kitty."

Zilch.

Back to my bedroom I went, and darned if that cat didn't get up, hop to the floor, and crawl under my bed.

"Noooo!"

On my hands and knees, I peered into the darkness and yellow eyes shone back at me. I figured I could slither under the bed, but the cat could easily just run away from me. It'd take me longer to get back out from under the bed than it would for him to hide again. And even if I could get to him, what then? If I grabbed a leg, he might bite me. There was no way I wanted to get bitten by a stray cat.

"Well, this is just great," I muttered and left the house.

I drove recklessly across the highway into downtown and to the café, jogged to the door, ran inside and yelled for Lydia, my assistant manager.

"Cat," I said, breathlessly, when she came out from the kitchen, her curly brown hair—the shade of caramel—framing her round face. The café hadn't opened yet, but our employees were prepping for the day. Lydia shoved a sparkling headband onto her head and grabbed her apron from a bar stool.

"Cat?" she said.

"There's a stray cat under my bed and I can't get it out. What do I do?"

"There's not much you can do. Leave the door open and wait for it to leave, I guess."

"I can't leave my door open."

"Obviously, you'll have to be there."

"I have too much to do today."

She chuckled. "Well, then, add a trip to the pet store. First thing. Get the cat a litter box. Put it by the door so it can do its business until you get back."

That sounded like a good plan. "And what if it won't leave?"

"Then, congratulations. You have a cat."

"But I don't want a cat."

"Nonetheless. I've got to get back to work." She returned to the kitchen.

I stood there in the empty restaurant for a few seconds before accepting my fate. I drove to the pet store across town and, once back at my little house, hoped the cat hadn't already peed all over the place. When I opened the door, I didn't smell anything, so that was good. I set up the box by the door as instructed and went back to the bedroom where the cat was, once again, curled up on my bed.

"There's a box by the door," I told it.

It opened an eye and closed it again.

"Okay. I have to go to work now."

It settled deeper into the bed.

Back at work, Lydia started explaining cat parenthood to me. I'd need a flea comb, she said, because it probably had fleas.

"If I can hold it down to comb it, I can put it outside," I said.

"But it's chosen you. If it won't go out on its own, how can you force it to? That's just mean."

"Still."

"You'll need a cat carrier for trips to the vet. A variety of canned foods to try, because cats can be picky."

"Tell me about it."

"He probably had a long list of houses he visited for various special treats. They get used to being pampered. And don't forget the toys."

"It's a cat, not a kid."

"He'll need catnip mice and little fuzzy balls and things on strings for you to dangle."

"Wait...I have to dangle stuff?"

"You can get some that clip onto table edges and stuff, but if you want a relationship with your cat, you're going to have to play with him."

"Tonight is Triple F," I said. "How can I enjoy myself knowing there's a wild animal in my house?"

"It's not a wild animal. He probably had a home once or he wouldn't be so comfortable in yours."

I sighed. "Well, I'm still going out. But I feel like I'll be celebrating my last night of freedom." I desperately didn't want to be one of those people who claims parenthood when all she's got is a cat, but I have to say, I felt the weight of it. Imagine what it must be like to have a human to take care of!

Lydia nodded. "I'm glad to see you understand the gravity of your situation."

Chapter Twelve

Triple F, aka Friday Fun Fest, is a monthly festival in Downtown Strawbridge. When it was first proposed several years ago, I was sure it would die a sad slow death after the first six months. But what I failed to appreciate at the time was the enduring love the people of Strawbridge have for food trucks, live music, and shopping outdoors at night. While I was born and raised in Strawbridge, my parents are both from Minnesota, and they still sound like it. I grew up sheltered inside during the hotter months, with the air conditioning, and pushed outside as soon as the weather turned crisp sometime after Halloween. Generational Floridians are more heat hardy than that. They're out and about when it's ninety degrees, like sweat is nourishment, and then they wrap themselves in heavy jackets as soon as the temperature dips toward fifty. I think they're a bit nuts. But, they're great for business, because on the second Friday of every month, rain or shine, hot or cold, they swamp the Downtown section of Strawbridge Avenue for a street party.

I always walked from home, or from the café, wearing jeans and tennis shoes, and I typically went first to Glam it Up! to get Vanessa, sometimes having to wait while she finished up with a customer. This Friday she was waiting outside for me. Her shop was right in the thick of things. From Pubs' Sports Bar on the east end, all the way to The Fort on the west, booths lined the middle of the street, back-to-back facing north and south. Food trucks were parked at each side street, helping to block off the main thoroughfare to cars and many more got special parking, east side, in the lots across the railroad tracks. And just before the tracks, where Mangrove meets Strawbridge at an angle, a stage is set up where local bands play.

Vanessa was dressed in a tight-fitting small-print dress, making me look like her dorky teenaged sister, but you get used to that sort of thing with her.

"Come on," she said as soon as she saw me, taking my hand. "The Divas are waiting for us at Isabella's booth."

"This doesn't have anything to do with my mystery guy, does it? Because I already asked Isabella about it."

"You did?"

"After the BOMB meeting. She said I should just let love happen."

"Well, we're getting you another reading. It's already planned."

I started to protest but she cut me off.

"It's part of the Matching Melissa Challenge."

"That sounds so much better than The Pink Diva Man Hunter Plan. But, please tell me we aren't going on the radio with it."

"Why would we do that?"

She pulled me through the crowded street westward where Isabella had a booth—more like a tent—across from her storefront. There was a long line of people waiting to get in to see her—she apparently did readings for a discount at Triple F—but I caught sight of the other Divas just a few people from the tent opening. They squealed with delight when they saw me, pulling me into the group.

"Don't worry," Karen called out to everyone in line behind us. "It's just one of us going in and it won't take long."

And she was right. I was shoved behind the tent flap when it was my turn, leaving the Divas outside giggling.

Before I could take a seat, Vanessa poked her head into the tent and said, "We want to know if she's going to find love soon." And then she was gone, but not unheard.

"Sit, sit. Your friends have paid already." Isabella gestured to the velvet covered table at which she sat. Her tented sanctuary was dimly lit with fake candles that had a real candle-like flicker, and on the table sat a crystal ball on a gold stand and some cards. The tent smelled like new plastic. Isabella was draped in an airy gown that had the look of a lava lamp and moved like one whenever she raised an arm. Bangles on her wrists tinkled. Her earrings shook when she moved her head and her curls bounced. "Let's have a look, shall we?"

She laid her forearms on the table, palms up, and beckoned me to take her hands as she gazed wide-eyed into the clear ball.

"Yes, I see. I was right. Before. When you came to see me with your friends. It was only a feeling then. But I can see it clearly now, in the crystal."

"You see a man?"

"Don't be silly." She fell out of character for a moment, caught herself, closed her eyes to regain her aura, and peered again into my future. "I see love."

Hard as I tried, I saw nothing but clear glass and the distorted reflection of velvet on the other side.

"Tell me," I said, not completely certain I wanted to know.

"As I said before, this is a man you are very familiar with." As we both hovered over the ball, a tendril of hair fell over Isabella's face, but she didn't break our grasp. "This man…he has been watching you for a long time."

"That's why Pari called him a stalker."

"She's wrong. He doesn't follow you around. He just sees you. He wants to be near you, but I sense reluctance."

I shrugged. "He doesn't sound very committed."

"Neither of you put your own happiness in the forefront."

"I do so. I'm as selfish as they come." I have no idea why I said that.

"A bit defensive, aren't you? No. You are both wary of love."

"Well, that doesn't sound like a great start to a romance. How can we meet if neither of us really wants to?"

"Perhaps you won't. This could be a tragic love story. Two misguided souls who wander past one another again and again, never seeing what's right in front of them."

Now, I'm not one to pooh-pooh a psychic, but I did let out a decidedly pooh-poohish sigh. "Well, that's not nice. Why would you tell me about him if I might not ever find him? What kind of love guru are you?"

Isabella's hands left mine and she tossed them into the air. "I just describe what's in the ball."

"So, I should go up to every guy I know, even vaguely, and ask him if he likes me, or I'll miss my soul mate?"

She lowered her head and looked at me just like my mother does when I've said something stupid. "Just let it happen, Melissa."

"But what if it doesn't?"

"I was under the impression you didn't care if you found him or not?" She glanced behind me at the tent flap.

I sucked in a breath. "Maybe I do, maybe I don't. It varies from moment to moment."

"You may fool your friends, but not Isabella."

"You're talking about yourself in the third person now?"

She gave me a smirk. "Don't worry, dear."

"Who's worried?"

"I see love in your future."

"But I don't even know if I want love in my future. I mean, look in the ball again. How busy am I? Am I going to get married? How would that even work? What am I giving up to get involved with this guy? Do I still have a cat?"

Isabella sat back in her folded chair and laughed. "Why would you have to give anything up?"

"I don't know. Relationships take up a lot of your time. And then there's kids. I don't think I'm ready for all of that."

"You'll be ready when the time comes." She reached over and patted my hand. "Now, out. I have a lot of people to read."

And I was unceremoniously dismissed. I found the Divas on the sidewalk outside Isabella's storefront across from her tent and we all made our way to the east end, and across the street to where a group of food trucks were pumping out heady smells in the lot by the railroad tracks. They didn't ask me anything at first; I didn't know what to tell them, anyway.

"You look shocked," Vanessa said once we had a plate of fries to share.

We all sat at a fold-out table in the make-shift food court, listening to the sounds of the band playing nearby, with Karen, me, and Vanessa on one side and Sophie, Pari, and Kaya on the other. An almost cool breeze danced in from the lagoon a hundred yards away. I smiled to myself as I took a seat. The six original Divas, like a gang of gorgeous kickass business women, preparing to talk about boys. Boys are a curse.

"Basically, she said that I should let love happen. And I freaked out."

"Why?" Kaya said. "I thought you wanted to find this guy."

"Sure, I wondered who it was. But that doesn't mean I have to marry him."

We all turned to look at Pari and Sophie, our two most likely to marry Divas, who both looked back at us.

"I *just* met Sam," Pari protested.

"Don't rush us," Sophie said.

"We should all get married together," Karen said. "Like a…sextuple wedding?"

"Sextuple?" Vanessa shrieked. "That sounds dirty."

"It's a group of six," Kaya said. "There are six of us; there's nothing we can do about it."

"We could add Octavia," Sophie said, suddenly in the mood for a wedding.

"Or Trudy," I said.

"What about Noah and Carrie?" Vanessa said.

"Or," Pari broke in. "We could simply *not* have a sextuple wedding."

"Agreed," Kaya said. "We don't all have to get married, anyway."

"I'm getting married," Vanessa said.

"When?" Karen said.

"I don't know. I haven't met the guy yet."

"There's a guy over there," I said, nodding to a table nearby. "He's been looking at you since we got here."

"How can you tell it's me he's looking at?"

"When you went to get more ketchup, he watched you the whole time."

"Which one?" Kaya said.

We all turned to the table in question and the poor guy saw us, turned red, and looked away.

"You have to go over there now," I said to Vanessa. "You should at least apologize for our rudeness."

"Me? You're the ones who did it."

"But you're the one he's interested in."

Wiping her hands off on a paper napkin and plumping up her hair, Vanessa said, "Fine. I'll do it. But don't for a second think that fixing me up is going to save you from your blind dates."

"Isabella didn't say anything about having other people find the guy for me," I called after her as she approached the table.

We all sat and watched as she talked to the young man, pointed back at us—we all waved—and then sat down beside him.

"Well, this isn't fair at all, is it?" I said. "It's supposed to be my turn." They all knew I was joking. "So tell me. Who are you all setting me up with? I want to prepare myself."

"Oh, no," Pari said. "It's all secret."

"Uh, oh," Sophie said.

She was looking at Vanessa and her admirer. None other than Ryan Duval had joined them. The three of them spoke happily for a moment or two as we all stared, and then they got up and came over to our table.

Chapter Thirteen

D o you all know Ryan?" Vanessa said when she'd brought her new friend and Ryan to our table.

"I know most of you," Ryan said. He looked down at Pari and offered her his hand. "Ryan Duval."

"Pari Logan."

"You a business owner, too?"

"Psychologist. My office is in the Executive Suites." She nodded toward the building across the street behind Tracks.

"You haven't bought that one, have you?" I said.

Ryan smirked at me and then turned to Kaya. "It's been a long time," he said. "When did you get into improv? I suppose I should thank you for helping Mel dump wet noodles all over me."

"You're welcome," Kaya said.

"And this," Vanessa said, "is Sheldon Frasier."

"Call me Shel," he said. Shel was tall and thin with a square face, pale brown hair, and an uneven smile.

They pulled extra chairs over from the other tables to join us and Karen shifted closer to me so that Vanessa could sit with her new…discovery.

"Shel and Ryan here are friends," she said.

"Is that so," I muttered. "What a happy coincidence."

"From way back," Shel said. He was a sweet sort, on

first impression. Sweeter than I ever imagined Vanessa going for. But he looked like a young Colin Firth, so who cared if he was a bit on the sugary side?

Suddenly, I blurted out, "Shelly!"

Everybody turned to stare at me.

"Shelly Frasier, from high school."

"It's Shel," he said.

"I don't remember you and Ryan being friends in school."

"I graduated two years before you guys," Shel said.

"We've just been to the psychic booth," Vanessa cooed. She turned to Shel. "Have you ever been read?"

He laughed. "No. I don't think I want to know the future."

"Isabella was telling Melissa all about who she's going to fall in love with."

"Vanessa!" I said.

"So you're into psychics?" Ryan said.

"What if I am?"

"Couldn't she tell you something more important? Like, where to invest your money?"

"She's a psychic, not a broker."

Pari broke in, as if sensing a fight was looming, and said, "Tell us about the cat?"

"What cat?" I said.

"I heard it, too," Sophie said. "You asked Isabella if you would still have a cat when you got married."

"You were listening?"

"Of course," Karen said.

"You could have just come into the tent with me. I thought it was private."

"We didn't want to affect the spirits," Kaya said with a grin.

"Or the crystal ball," Pari said.

I turned to Ryan with a roll of my eyes. "They don't believe, either."

"I didn't say I didn't believe," he said.

"Back to the cat," Sophie, Strawbridge's resident cat lady, said.

"She's been feeding a stray for a while," Vanessa said.

84

"That's all."

"Well," I muttered. "There's a bit more to it than that. Now."

"Go on then," Karen said. "Spill."

So I told them about it. How the cat got in and I couldn't get it to go back out. Ryan was laughing at me. And I'm sorry to say, he wasn't the only one.

"I went home to check on it before coming here and I couldn't find it. But the bowl was empty and there was…business in the box. So, I guess it's still there. I told it to come out from hiding, but it ignored me."

"Haven't you ever had a cat?" Sophie said.

"You thought it would just do what you say?" Ryan said.

"My family had a cat or two," I protested. "But mostly dogs. And I admit, they didn't usually do what they were told, either."

"What I'd like to know," Ryan said, and his tone made me glare at him. "Is, why would you think you'd lose your cat if you got married?"

"I didn't want to know that. I wanted to know if the cat was going to leave. Or if I was going to have to keep it."

"Have to!" Sophie said. "Don't you want to keep it? I mean, it's a stray cat. It needs love and a safe place to live."

"Really, Melissa," Vanessa said. "You're going to make it live outside again?"

"Lots of cats live outside."

"Indoor cats live longer," Ryan said.

"And are healthier," Sophie said.

"All right, all right," I said. "I'll think about it."

"So what are you going to call it?" Karen said.

"I don't know," I said. "Cat?"

"You can't call it Cat," Kaya said. "That's so unimaginative."

"What kind of cat is it?" Sophie said.

I shrugged. "It's a cat. Kind of gray. A little stripey."

"Sounds like a gray tabby."

"I could call him Tabby," I said. They all stared at me. "It's better than Cat, isn't it?"

"How about something *avant-garde* and meaningful," Pari said. "Like, Rescue."

"I don't think Tabby's a dumb name," Karen said.

"Or Stripes," Sophie said.

"His stripes aren't that bold," I said. "Actually, now that I think about it. It might be a she."

"You don't know?" Ryan said.

"Oh, like you would know."

"It's not that hard to tell with a cat."

"Well, I didn't examine it, okay?"

"It'll be pretty obvious," Sophie said.

"Anyway, he's mostly just gray, really mild stripes, except for this cool geometric pattern on his head."

"Crop Circle," Shel said and we all looked at him. "For a name. It's a pattern…never mind."

"What about those patterns in the desert," Karen said. "What are those called?"

"Geoglyphs?" Kaya said. "Like the Nazca lines?"

"I don't know," Karen said. "Is that what I mean?"

Kaya laughed. "Yeah, I think so."

"I should call it Geoglyphs?"

"You could call her Nazca, but I'm not sure that's appropriate."

"How about Dust," Ryan said. "It's descriptive, a bit on the *avant-garde* side, and certainly appropriate."

"Ooh," Vanessa said, "I like that. Does he look like dust, Mel?"

"A dust ball, maybe. Dusty?"

"That's a good one," Kaya said.

"You've lost the *avant-garde*," Pari said.

"What is *avant-garde*, anyway?" Sophie said. "It sounds like 'advanced guard.'"

We all turned to Pari; she was the one who said it first. But she made a face. "I thought it meant…new and cutting edge."

"New and 'advanced' kind of go together," Kaya said.

"Here it is," Sophie said holding up her phone. "New, unusual, experimental. So, Pari's right."

"But that's just usage," Karen said. "What does it

mean, literally?"

Sophie scrolled. "Fore-guard or advanced guard. I am so smart!"

We all laughed.

Ryan said. "Maybe you should wait and see what her personality will be like, before you give her a name."

I noticed that we'd all suddenly stopped calling the cat an 'it' and were calling her a 'she.' I had the sinking, yet, not completely awful, feeling that I was definitely keeping the cat.

"Well, whatever his or her name is," Kaya said, "Melissa will need a cat sitter tomorrow. She has a date."

Ryan looked at me, as if to say, 'Too bad, you have a cat now. Your life is over.' But I had no idea what Kaya was talking about. And that's just what I said.

"I have no idea what you're talking about."

"Your first date in the Pink Diva Man Hunter Plan is tomorrow morning."

She said it! Out loud! In front of Ryan Duval and his friend. And of course, Ryan took the bait.

"Hold on," he said with a wide smile. "What's this about?"

"It's why we were at Isabella's," Vanessa said. "Like I told you."

"It's a long story," I said.

And so, the Divas told him the whole thing. About my ghost sighting, the ghost challenges, about Pari and Sam, the Ghost Whisperer. And about Isabella's prediction.

"Like a stalker?" Ryan said.

"That's exactly what I thought," Pari said with a laugh.

"He's not a stalker," I said.

"Oh, so you're defending him now," Vanessa said. "That's a good sign."

"Never mind all of that," I said. "I can't go anywhere tomorrow. Not if I'm going to deal with this cat thing."

"Uh," Kaya said, sarcastically. "Date."

"Uh," I said right back. "Cat."

"Don't be silly," Sophie said. "The cat'll be fine. It's not like a child. Just feed it in the morning and make sure it has a clean box. You did put a litter box out for it, right? It's not in your house having nowhere to pee, is it?"

"Of course," I said. "Lydia told me how to take care of it."

"You needed someone to tell you how?" Ryan said.

"Look, bud," I said. "Back off."

Everybody leaned back in their seats as if I'd smacked them.

"Whoa," Vanessa whispered.

"He has been aggressive," Shel whispered back.

"Sorry," Ryan said. His jaw stiffened and I could see he didn't want to apologize.

"Me, too," I mumbled.

"Mm hmm," Vanessa hummed.

"Just stop," I said. She was looking back and forth at Ryan and me and I knew exactly what she was thinking. Cute meets or meet cutes and sparks and all that. "This isn't a romance novel."

"I'll be the judge of that," Karen, our budding romance novelist, said.

"We need to get going," Ryan said, standing. "It was nice getting to know you all better."

"Can I call you?" Shel asked Vanessa.

"You sure can." They took out their phones and exchanged numbers and we all watched Vanessa gazing adoringly after Sheldon as he left with Ryan.

"She's a goner," Pari said.

"You see," Vanessa said after Ryan and Shel were out of earshot. "There's definitely something between you two."

"Yeah," I said. "War."

"Doesn't he have that girlfriend?" Kaya said.

"Just because he was out on a date or two doesn't mean she's a girlfriend," Vanessa said.

"You are *not* fixing me up with him, Vanessa. I mean it."

"I already told you. I have somebody else in mind for you. But I still think you and Ryan would be perfect together."

"Why? We have nothing in common. Except animosity."

"The meet cute, remember?"

"The what?" Pari said.

"A meet cute," Sophie said. "Like in a romantic comedy."

"Wouldn't that be a cute meet?" Kaya said.

"Here we go again," I said. "Forget it. Anyway, all these blind dates you guys are setting me up on will be cute meets, too. So don't worry about it."

"It's meet cute," Vanessa said. "And a blind date doesn't count."

"What crazy person called it that?" I said.

"That would be the French," Karen said.

"What?" several of us said.

"Damn to the depths whatever muttonhead thought up meet cute!"

We all stared at her, mouths open.

"Are you okay?" I said.

"Haven't you guys seen *Pirates of the Caribbean*? Do we need a pirate themed movie night? A Caribbean marathon! We can do it next spring."

"Speaking of movie nights," I said. "What do you say we combine the Christmas movie night you were planning with a Christmas Eve party at my house?"

"Seriously?" Vanessa said.

They all looked shocked.

"Totally serious," I said. "I've got my managers settled. And it doesn't look like I'll be opening a new catering storefront any time soon. So, I think it's time to have everyone over to my place."

"Like a well-rounded person," Kaya said. "Good for you."

"Look over there," Sophie said, motioning behind me. "It's Pat and Buddy."

We all watched as svelte and savvy Pat Willard, owner of Namaste, and frumpy Officer Palmer, the traffic cop, awkwardly exchanged greetings before turning away from each other.

"Buddy looks like a lost dog begging to be taken in," Kaya said.

"What happened there?" I asked.

Karen said, "She thinks he's too young for her."

"Is he?"

"Maybe," Kaya said. "I mean, maybe she's older than he is. But I don't see why she should care. He's so sweet."

"And they really got along," Pari said.

"For a week or two," Sophie said.

"Well, let's do something about it," I said. "And about Trudy and Mr. Cornell, too. They acted just like that last time I saw them acknowledge each other."

"Sophie and I could invite them on double dates with our guys," Pari said.

"I have a better idea," Sophie said. "Let's set them up on blind dates. Trudy with Buddy and Mr. Cornell with Pat."

"But what if that works out?" I said. "It's like, the opposite of what we want."

"We'll invite them on a huge quadruple date with us, Pari," she said. "But with the wrong partners. A little jealousy never hurt anybody."

"You think that would work?" Kaya said.

"It's playing with fire," Karen said.

"Let's do it," I said. "They could all use a little fire under their butts."

Sophie took charge of the Great Quadruple Date Conspiracy and was already trying to think of the best outing possible.

"And speaking of setups," I said to Kaya. "What's this about a date tomorrow?"

"Yep," she said, a huge grin on her face. "Your first fix-up."

"Thanks for the heads up."

"I told you about it on Wednesday," Vanessa said.

"Well, I forgot."

"Sure you did."

"You don't believe me?"

"I believe you're chicken to be fixed up. That's what I believe."

"Well, sure. Who wants to be fixed up. It's... embarrassing. At least give me time to prepare myself. Who is it?"

Kaya said, "You'll find out tomorrow."

"We're not giving you time to figure out who each of your dates is with," Sophie said.

"You're not going to tell me ahead of time?"

"Nope," they all said at once.

"How can I meet him somewhere if I don't know who he is? He's not picking me up is he? You can't send a guy to my house without me knowing who it is."

"I'll be picking you up," Kaya said. "Tomorrow morning at eight."

"Eight o'clock? In the morning? Are you nuts?"

"What?" Vanessa said. "Like you sleep all day?"

"But Zumba…"

"Zumba will have to wait," Kaya said. "It's all set with the café, too. They're not expecting you until well after lunch. So be ready at eight, wearing comfortable clothes."

"Ew," I said. "Where are we going?"

They all laughed!

"Not telling," Kaya said with a wink.

Chapter Fourteen

What sort of date starts at eight o'clock in the morning? Nothing good can come of that. For one thing, it's much harder to look relaxed, awake, and confident in the morning. Most of them are stumble-out-of-bed and find-a-hangover-cure affairs. Nothing will fix a boozy head better than a room full of Zumba fanatics and loud music. Other mornings are for preparation. Literally in my case, when I head over to the café to help prep for our lunchtime opening. Mornings are for frazzled brains making lists. They're never for dates. And comfortable clothes? Not that I'm fancy. I'd probably wear jeans anyway. But the word 'comfortable' and 'date' don't feel right together.

Kaya was at my door at eight sharp. She eyed me up and down, then insisted I put on dirtier shoes.

"I don't have dirtier shoes."

"You pull weeds, don't you?"

"I am not wearing my gardening clothes on a date."

"Just the shoes. Trust me. Bring a change of clothes and shoes with you for lunch afterward."

As I was digging around in my laundry room off the kitchen, I heard Kaya cooing. I found her on the sofa, the cat in her lap. "I don't see it for two days and it comes right out when you come over."

"And I'm not even a cat person. She's definitely a 'she.'"

I sat on a the easy chair by the couch and changed shoes, eying the cat suspiciously. "If she doesn't like me, why won't she leave?"

"Of course she likes you. She probably knows you're not completely sold on the idea of keeping her."

"She can read minds?"

"I bet she can read your body language."

I stood and approached them both carefully. When the cat looked up at me, I reached out to pat her on the head.

"Oh, my god, Mel," Kaya said as the cat jumped to the floor and sauntered into the kitchen to her food bowl. "You don't pat it. You pet it."

I stood there looking helpless. I'm sure I knew how to pet a cat; I've done it plenty of times…in my younger days. Apparently, it wasn't like riding a bike.

"Come on," she said and dragged me out the front door like a child.

I have to tell you: I was scared. Kaya drove us north in her little red Prius, past Rocky Water Boulevard, into a section of warehouses and lumberyards, to a small, old plaza that should have been condemned—if you asked me. The only words on the worn sign out front were: Pinky's Paintball.

"You're joking," I said as Kaya parked among several other cars and turned off the engine.

"I'm deadly serious."

"Kaya, I have to say…you are a woman of many surprises."

A devilish smile lit up her face.

"Please tell me you're coming with me. I don't want to do this by myself…with whatever guy you set me up with. I mean, I know it's not a stranger, but still."

"You're rambling. It'll be okay. And yes, I will be there."

Relief swept over me, but I was trembling. Paintball? As we got to the door of Pinky's—dark glass with the logo printed on it in pink—I stopped Kaya.

"Be avant-garded," I said. "This may bring out the worst in me."

A raucous laugh escaped her, along with her usual snort. Inside was a small lobby filled with people, many of them familiar. Karen and Vanessa were there, but Pari and Sophie were not. This did not surprise me.

"What's he doing here?" I said, much too loud, even for that crowd. I'd just caught sight of Ryan Duval.

He, along with several others, glared at me.

Not to be intimidated, I stomped over to him and asked, "Who invited you?"

"What?" he said.

"You heard me. Who invited you? Was it Vanessa? Tell me if it was Vanessa."

A suspiciously guilty look shadowed his eyes, and he said, "None of your business."

I raised my finger and was about to say "You listen here, bub," but Kaya was dragging me away.

"You're being rude," she mumbled and led us tumbling into another group of people. We both turned to find Steve Abbott regaining his footing.

"There you are," he said.

"Here I am?" I said.

Kaya said, "Steve's your date for paintball."

"Steve," I shouted. "Thank heavens."

Steve Abbott owns Pubs Sports Bar and was I ever glad he was my date. I was sure the Divas would fix me up with relative strangers, but I knew Steve very well. And I was ready to put it out there from the start—no way was he secretly crushing on me…I don't think. He wore a ragged, long-sleeved shirt and jeans. His hair, as usual, was sprouting atop his head, leaving his face to look a bit long and pointy at the chin. Steve was cute enough, in his hipster doofus way. You think a guy who runs a sports bar is going to be a college jock trying to relive his glory days, but Steve was more water boy raking in the beer-bellied has-beens' money, now that they had nothing left to live for.

"I'm glad to be your date, too," he said with a smile.

"But what is Ryan Duval doing here?"

"Jim invited him, I think. You got a problem with the guy?"

Kaya said, "He's Melissa's new landlord."

"You want him to be on our team?"

"No!" The room quieted and I shrank a bit. "No. It's a...a...conflict of interest. Or something."

Steve chuckled. "I get it. Landlords can be jerks. Have you ever done this before?" He looked at me, hopeful.

"Never. Why would you want to play paintball on a first date? I mean...not that this is the first of many. But not that it wouldn't be. I mean, you never know, right?"

"No worries. Kaya told me all about the fix-up bonanza and wanted to know what really odd things I'm into."

"I wouldn't call it a bonanza."

"You date a lot already, then?"

"Well, not exactly."

"Sure," he said. "Otherwise, they wouldn't need to fix you up."

"Well, it's not like I asked them to."

He threw up his hands. "Don't blame me. It wasn't my idea. Except for the paintball. That was definitely my idea."

"Right back around to my original question. Why?" Going around in circles is supposed to be fun and flirtatious, but I was just irritated.

"Kaya said the date should be unusual. And after the whole Ghost Challenge you put them through, I figured paintball was the way to go."

"Is there some kind of Diva News Network I don't know about?"

"Yep," he said. "It's called Downtown Strawbridge. Everybody knows everything."

There was a long counter at the back of the room and behind it must have been Pinky. She looked like a Pinky. Short and stout with a shaved head and a nose ring. She wore a t-shirt with the sleeves rolled all the way to her shoulders. And she watched us with a bemused look on her face as she led us through a series of stages: the waiver, long and filled with legalese—"sign or leave;"

coveralls, "light-weight so you can still feel the sting;" goggles "so you don't shoot your eye out;" colored vests and helmets—Steve and I were on Team Blue; and weapons of war, said with an evil laugh. Paintball guns are basically sticks with bottles attached to them. There was a trigger; that's all I needed to know. Aim and shoot. Nothing to it.

"We have to go through this rigamarole even when there aren't any newbs like you around," Steve said.

Pinky led us through the empty store fronts that had once made up the plaza, connected by crumbling doorways. On closer inspection, however, I noticed that the deterioration of the building was done purposefully, and so probably not as dangerous as it seemed.

"This is not your field of play in this morning's game," she shouted. Several pitiful "aws" rang out. "Anyone caught hiding inside during game play will be automatically sent to the dead-box."

We were led outside, behind the plaza, where a large lot sprawled before us, dotted with stacks of tires, large barrels, and some kind of weird tunnel system in the middle created out of huge ridged plastic tubes. There were stands of trees and shrubs here and there, a few large sections of wooden fencing, and quite a few hills of dirt. A set of rickety bleachers sat off to the right for people who just wanted to watch. That's where I really wanted to be. After giving us a general tour, Pinky led us to the center of the field, to a big blue barrel. Inside was a plastic pole with a large orange flag attached to the top.

"This is your goal. But you must get it back to your base and put it in the team's barrel to win. Refs in place," she yelled, and blew a whistle.

We were sent to our respective bases on opposite sides of the field of play. Ours was rather nice—a really big mesh canopy surrounded by piles of tires. Team Blue huddled there and Steve introduced me around. There were fourteen of us. And Ryan Duval wasn't one of them. I noticed that Kaya, Karen, and Vanessa were conveniently not on my team, either.

"Don't worry about remembering everybody's names,"

Sandy said. "Just don't shoot at anyone wearing blue."

"Got it, Sandy," I said, trying to impress her with my excellent name memory skills.

"This'll be a piece of cake," Joey said. "They've got three newbs and we've only got one."

"Okay, guys," Ally, our team captain, said. "Here's the plan."

"Have you played with these people before?" I asked Steve.

"Some of them. The weekends here are open, so Pinky just divides everybody up and lets us go at it. You have to clear out after each game and pay again if you want to play more."

"What if there are little kids?"

"It's adults only. There are certain kid times, but I think you have to reserve them."

"Do you always play here?"

He shook his head. "My friend Jim owns land down south a bit and we usually go there. It's a lot rougher and we can play all day. But this is cool, too. We get to play with people who aren't in our club here."

"Okay, get ready to head out," Ally said.

"I know you," I said. "You work at Ally's."

Ally's is the formal wear shop in town, best known for parading models through the streets in wedding gowns and tuxedos before their annual fifty-percent-off sale.

"Ally Barrister," she said with a nod. "Did you get the plan?"

"Sure," I lied.

As soon as the buzzer sounded and we all moved out, I asked Steve, "What's the plan?"

"Just stick with me. And remember, if you get hit, shout out 'hit' or 'dead man walking' and go to the dead-box."

"How nice." I was suddenly filled with a rush of terror and confidence, a very bad combination. Nonetheless, I was ready to paint some people, especially Kaya, Karen, and Vanessa. "Where was the dead-box again?" I had no recollection of being told.

"The bleachers."

"And I guess it would be bad form to sacrifice myself just to go sit on the bleachers with the non-players."

He turned to me and raised his brows. "Incredibly bad form."

We crept stealthily away from our base, separating from the other members of the team, and slithered over to some tire stacks.

"So, what do we do?" I said. "Just shoot the other guys?"

"No. We're getting the flag."

"Us?"

"Shh," he said. "Only shoot if necessary; we don't want to give away our position."

"Why would Ally put me on the flag team?"

"It's not because you can keep quiet."

"Very funny."

"She thinks the other team won't expect it. And she's right."

I followed him as he ducked and dodged through the stacks of tires and fences. Suddenly he held up an arm and hoisted his gun to his shoulder. I was shaking like Jello, but did the same and, my back against my rubber pillar, eased around it. Team Red!

"They've got us," he said. "Fire!"

I'd like to say I aimed and fired, but I just fired. And screamed a bit.

"Hit," Steve said laughing. "Not bad."

We'd knocked out a small group from Team Red and skulked about some more, heading toward the center of the field.

"Keep an eye on our flank," Steve said. "The flag station is straight across there."

"We could make our way over to those palms," I said.

He led the way. Shots echoed all around us and I realized that the rest of our team was leading everyone away from us so we could sneak up on the flag.

"Okay," Steve said once we'd snuggled into the palm shrubs, getting scratched by thorns. We didn't care; we were warriors.

The flag was still where Pinky had put it, on a stick, in

a barrel, in the middle of a series of tubes on the ground.

Steve said, "I'll cover you while you crawl into that tube. Then, if I'm sure no one saw you, or if I can hit everyone who did, I'll give the word and you crawl out the other side and grab the flag."

"You don't expect me to take the pole back into a tube, do you? 'Cause I don't think that'll work."

He chuckled. "You ever see those videos with the little dog carrying a huge stick, trying to get through a gate or something?"

"Exactly."

"Don't take it into the tube, throw it in and I'll be on the other end ready to get it. Then hightail it that way, to the nearest bunker. I'll meet you there and we'll make our way back to base."

Sure, it sounded like a great plan. But it would never work. And for some reason, instead of telling Steve that, I just sat there until he said, "Now!" Then I jumped out from behind the shrubs, skittled between two tubes, grabbed the flag stick out of the barrel and ran like the devil. I think I was screaming and shooting too. Yes. I was definitely screaming and somehow shooting, holding my gun with my right hand, the flag stick in my left. I made it behind a fence, still aiming for anyone who might come at me, and waited for Steve. Once he was beside me, we checked for paint, saw none, and started running again.

We were going to win! I, a complete paintball newbie, had captured the flag! I was going to lead my team to victory! Until I heard Steve call out, "Hit." I turned to see him grimace and frown at me. Then his eyes went wide. I turned and ducked behind a stack of tires just in time. A ball ricocheted off the rubber as I fell to the ground and rolled over. I sat up, grabbed at the flag stick and fumbled for my rifle. I knew I was vulnerable to another round of fire. But it was too late. I looked up to see Ryan Duval standing over me, his gun raised.

Chapter Fifteen

Any last words," Ryan said, aiming at my chest.
He was so close, I was sure the paintball would sting when it hit. I closed my eyes and winced.
"Let not poor Nelly starve!" I shouted.
He laughed and shot me.
It stung all right. "Ow."
"You're supposed to say 'hit.'" He knelt down beside me. And for the tiniest split second, like one millionth of a millionth, I thought he was going to kiss me. It's possible that in that millisecond of a millisecond, I might have turned my face to him to…like, kiss him back. But, just as my hands left the ground to wrap around his neck, he reached down beside me to grab the flag stick. Without another word, he ran off with it, leaving me to catch up to Steve as we both dead-walked to the bleachers.
"Who's Nelly?" he asked.
"You heard that?"
"I think everybody did."
"Last words of King Charles the second."
"Let not poor Nelly starve? Was Nelly his horse?"
I laughed. "His mistress."
"Sure. Makes more sense now."
"I imagine the mistress of a dead king would have a

hard time in the world."

"What, no Kings Mistresses Guild?"

"Savages," I said.

We climbed to the top of the bleachers to watch what we could of the game. I thought it would be over right away, but nearly a half hour later, Ryan Duval showed up in the dead-box, along with several others from both teams. In the end Team Blue won and we all headed over to Pubs for lunch. I rode with Steve in his black Santa Fe; the back of the car was filled with paintball equipment: gloves and vests; goggles and masks; jugs of paintballs. And a set of golf clubs were tossed in as a sporty after-thought.

"For all your crap," I said, "your car is surprisingly neat."

"Neatly cluttered. That's how I like it."

"So, how often do you play at Pinky's?" The state of his car was the extent of conversation ideas in my head, so I was grasping.

He shrugged. "Maybe once a month. Her place is kind of touristy. There are a lot of limits. Only so much time; only so many people can play."

"Tell me about Jim's place."

"Down south. You know Jim Spencer?"

"No."

"It's several acres out there where they haven't developed yet. We scatter our debris after every session and each time we have to rebuild our own bunkers and cover. There's an old bus out there, some tents, we built a couple of forts. It's really cool. You should play with us sometime."

"So, why Pinky's today?"

"Because it's a date." He took his eyes from the road to grin at me for a second. "When we play out at Jim's, we're there pretty much all day. And it's nice to do a simple game now and then." He parked in the lot behind Pubs—on the east end of Downtown, the opposite of my café. "Look at this spot," he said with a wide grin. "You must be good luck. Sometimes I have to park in the garage across the street."

102

"Tell me about it. I should just walk to my place from home."

"I hope you don't mind eating lunch here," he said once we got out of the car. "I'll look a lot better to you, with employees falling over themselves to please the boss."

"I don't believe they're afraid of you for one second."

He chuckled. "You're on to me. Anyway, we usually gather here after paintball."

"Jim's got the land; you've got the restaurant."

We made our way through the south-side mall—really just an indoor corridor with shops on each side—past the Flower Power booth and Octavia's Closet, also a booth, to Strawbridge Avenue and west a bit to Pubs.

"Dang," I said, before he opened the door for me. "I was going to change clothes. I left them in Kaya's car."

"You look great."

"But these shoes," I muttered.

"No one else is going to be any cleaner."

The cold air hit us as we walked in and Steve put an arm around my waist.

"You go ahead," he said with a nod to the back of the restaurant. "I'm just going to check in."

"No problem."

I supposed the paintball gang in the back was mostly players from Steve's club. They'd gathered in a spot separated by the main seating area by a half-wall. When they all saw me, they shouted, in unison, "All hail King Charles!"

"Great," I mumbled.

The Divas pulled me to their table, one of six four-seaters, an extra chair tucked in here and there. They had all changed into normal clothes, eating-out clothes, and shoes meant to be seen. I hadn't even combed my hair.

"Ryan says there's a story there," Karen said.

"Where?" I said, pretending ignorance.

"With King Charles and what you said."

"Did I shout that loud?"

"Not everyone heard you," Kaya said. "But there was a lot of talk about it."

"Apparently," Karen said, "Last words are something of a badge of honor among the local clubs."

"Maybe you'll get a plaque," Vanessa said.

"So what's the story?" Kaya said.

Everyone started shouting at me to explain and I glared at Ryan who was sitting at a corner table with members of Team Red. Steve hadn't lied. Everyone but Kaya, Vanessa, and Karen looked as if they'd crawled through dirty plastic tubes and rolled down hills made of rubber tires.

"How do you even remember?" I said to him.

"Seriously?" he said. "How can you not remember?"

"Oh, I remember."

The room quieted a bit when Steve showed up and took a seat next to me. "What's the noise all about?" he asked.

Ryan said, "Either you tell it, or I will."

"*Your* version," I said. "Go ahead."

He stood and scanned the room, looking as if he were going to make a dire speech. "Ladies and gentlemen."

"Good grief," I said.

"I give you Mr. MacNamara's world history class, sophomore year, Strawbridge High."

Applause.

"Every couple of weeks, MacNamara would divide us up into groups and give us these silly assignments, just for fun."

"We were graded," I said.

"One time, Melissa and I were in one group and our assignment was 'famous last words.'" An "oooh" ran through the crowd and teasing glances were exchanged. "He gave us a big list to choose from and I took Charles the Second."

"*I* took Charles the Second."

"Melissa thought she had Charles the Second," Ryan said with a smirk. "But she didn't."

I wanted to scream "did so!" but I managed *some* dignity, combing the stringy hair from my face and back into a pony tail holder with my fingers.

"So we lined up in front of the class, Melissa to my right, and when it was my turn, I flopped onto the floor, raised my hand to my invisible brother and said—"

Everyone yelled, "Let not poor Nelly starve!"

I was red as a radish; I could feel it.

"And then…" Ryan motioned to me.

I pouted, my hands folded across my chest, seething. "I kicked him."

Roars of "whoa" and "you go girl" echoed through the restaurant and I was offered many high-fives.

"And what did you shout at me?" Ryan asked, once the group had calmed down.

By this time I was well aware that the entire restaurant was listening in.

I shrugged. "I might have called you a jerk."

To the crowd now engrossed in my shame, Ryan said, "She said, 'you big stupid jerk.'"

The laughter was impossible to sit out, so I just let it go. It was pretty funny almost ten years later.

"I had to go to the principal's office," I said. "For assault."

"She might have been arrested, for all I know. But I went and pled for leniency."

"Tell them what you told Principle Dobson." I had him now. "Spill it."

Ryan's cheeks pinked up a bit. "I told him you didn't kick me all that hard."

"That's not what you said."

"I don't want to," he whined.

Everybody started chanting, "Tell us! Tell us!" until Ryan raised his arms in surrender.

"All right, all right," he said. "I told him she kicks like a girl."

The uproar was probably heard all the way to my café. I'm surprised Ryan Duval made it out of there alive. Okay, it wasn't that bad. We ordered and yakked through lunch and I forgot all about being on a date with Steve.

"So," he said nudging me with an elbow as we were finishing up the last of our fries. "You eat."

"Of course I eat."

"I just mean, well, you don't look like you eat very much."

"Ew. Are you calling me skinny?"

"No. But a—let's change the subject."

"Oh, no. I know what you're saying. You think I'm one of *those* girls."

"Maybe."

"Is that why you chose paintball? Hoping to see me squirm or see a bug and scream?"

"Nah. You can't be too fussy and run a restaurant. But if I'm being totally honest, Kaya pushed for the paintball."

I looked at Kaya across the table from me and she winked.

"I'll bet she did," I said. "I hope you don't mind this whole setup thing."

"Not at all. I don't date much, either."

"Who has time, right?"

"Exactly. What we need are people who aren't in the restaurant business."

"Do you really think so?" Vanessa said. "Wouldn't it be better to date someone who knows what you're going through?"

"But we'd never see each other," I said.

"You saw each other today," Karen said.

I looked at Steve and he looked at me and we both nodded.

"I guess they have a point," I said. "If we dated someone with more time, they'd always be pestering us."

"Why didn't you call me today," Steve mocked with a high-pitched twang.

"Where have you been?" I gruffed like an angry dude. "The game started an hour ago."

Kaya shook her head and smiled. "You two are perfect for each other."

Chapter Sixteen

The Divas left after lunch, leaving Steve and me to flail awkwardly for several moments looking for conversation material. Finally, he said, "So, you've got five friends. Does that mean five fix-ups?"

"Unfortunately, yes."

"And then you pick one?"

"Not at all. We're looking for the one Isabella said I'd find."

"But how will you know?"

"Easy. She said my soul mate—I'm not sure she used those words exactly—"

"But that's what you're looking for."

"Well, sure. When you go to a psychic, you want to know where your soul mate is and when you'll meet them. Anyway, it's someone who likes me already. Someone who's been watching me from afar."

"Like a stalker."

"Why does everybody go to stalker? I think it's romantic." I looked at him and he looked at me. I raised my brows, expectantly. "Well?" I said.

"Well, what?"

"Is it you? Are you my stalker?"

He thought for a moment, holding his breath. "I'm going to say no, and here's why. One, I'm not stalking you.

Two, while I like you plenty, I hadn't thought of you as girlfriend material before now."

"Before now?"

"I'm just saying, if we dated, who knows? But three, and three is the most important reason: if I say yes, you'll be finished with the fix-up thing and your friends will be very angry with me."

"We can't have that."

"Come on, I've got to see a man about a stapler. I'll walk you as far as Morgan's Office Supply. Unless you want me to drive you."

"And risk you losing that fab parking spot? I don't think so."

"I don't know, Melissa," he said as we stepped out of the restaurant into the Downtown Strawbridge Saturday shopping crowd. "I think you may be the one."

We both laughed. After I left Steve at Morgan's, I stopped into Kaya Vintage Clothing and waited for her to finish up with a customer. Kaya's store was just this side of thrift shop. It was neat and orderly, but no two pieces of clothing were the same. It was a well-known secret that she had stashes of stuff in the back room and in her own home because she didn't want the shop to look too cluttered. Once the bell on the door tinkled, signaling her customer had left, I came out of the dressing room in a knee-length turtle-neck A-line.

"Cute," Kaya said.

"I have a feeling it's meant to be a mini."

"But it still looks good on you."

"I'm not sure I can carry a paisley." Not only did it look like I was wearing an oversized tie, it was orange, brown, and green.

Kaya stood at the door while I changed back into my jeans. "So, how'd it go?"

"Well, I realized that all I really have to do is go up to every guy I know and ask him if he's been worshiping me from afar. It'd save me a lot of time."

"Where's the fun in that?"

"For you guys, you mean."

"So I'm guessing Steve wasn't the one."

I carried the dress back to its place on a rack in the front of the store with Kaya following behind like a puppy. "I like Steve. But, yeah, he's not the one."

"But what does that mean? Are you going to see him again? Or are you holding out for Mr. Stalker?"

"The whole point was to find out who Isabella was talking about, right?"

"But when you do, if you decide you don't like the guy, you might go out with Steve again?"

"First," I said as I swiped through the hangers on the rack. "I *have* to like him. Isabella said he was the one. And second. Does it matter?" I looked at her, curious. "Do you want me to date Steve Abbott for some reason?"

She opened her mouth and closed it again and after a second or two said, "No. It's no big deal."

"You're invested," I said. "Maybe you like Steve."

We meandered through the store to the counter.

"I just thought you two seemed like a great couple today, that's all."

"Well I won't discount him completely, if it'll make you feel better."

She smiled. "I can't ask for more than that." She'd walked around to the employee side of the counter and leaned on it, folding her arms. "You work harder than any of us. When you made Lydia manager of the café, we really thought you'd slow down a bit and work some regular hours. Honestly, we don't know how you do it. All the partying and all the working. When do you relax?"

"I spend an hour or so a week on my garden."

"Is that enough?"

I shrugged. "It's calming. I like gardening, and cooking. But at the restaurant, there's so much going on that cooking isn't as joyful as it should be."

"So cook at home."

"Cooking for one? I don't think so."

She smiled. "How have things been going with the cat?"

"I'm getting the feeling that my fellow Divas think my life is missing companionship. I think I might prefer the cat to a man."

"You should go home and spend some time with her now, so she'll get used to you."

"And do what? Sit on the sofa watching TV?"

"I'm going to give you some really good advice, so pay careful attention."

"Sounds serious."

"It is. If you aren't comfortable being alone with yourself, you'll never know for sure."

"Know what for sure?"

"You'll never know if the guy you're seeing is right for you. You'll never know if marriage is what you want. And you'll probably never really know yourself. Look at you! You're so lucky. You have a great business that allows you free time. You have your own home. Your own space. Maybe you work so much and party so hard because you're afraid to be alone. And you can't make decisions about your future out of fear."

"I don't think my strong work ethic is born out of fear. But you're right that I don't spend a lot of time at home, with just myself."

"Well now you have a cat to take care of. So you won't be totally alone."

Another customer came in and I told Kaya I'd see her later. I walked to the café thinking about what she'd said. It was true enough that when I made Lydia the manager of Café Flamingo and Lucy the manager of catering, I'd planned to spend more time at home, hence, my stab at a garden—not an easy feat in Central Florida. But I ended up working just as much, just not managing. I'd become a stand-in employee for whatever needed to be done. Maybe Kaya was right.

Having a restaurant is like having a baby. You have to make sure it's taken care of when you're not around and you're always thinking about it, even when you're trying to have a good time. The only time I don't really worry about it is when it's closed. And even then, I'm thinking about it. Is it okay all by itself? Is it locked up tight? Did I remember to turn off the fan in my office? You can't break a habit like that easily.

As soon as I walked through the door to the café that

afternoon, I knew everything was fine. The key to owning a business is great staff.

"Melissa," everyone called out when they saw me. Even some of the customers waved a hello. I went immediately to the back room to stash my stuff, grab an apron, and change shoes. I was still filthy from paintball and wearing unsafe shoes for restaurant work. Luckily, I always had a pair of hard-toed ankle boots stashed away in my office. I'd washed my hands and was prepared to go out front to clear tables, but before I could get back out to the floor, Susanne pulled me aside.

"Beardsley's here again."

"Oh, no."

Lionel Beardsley was Strawbridge's resident critic. He wrote opinion pieces for everything, from movies to shoe stores. He was basically a curmudgeon with a platform. And he'd been to my little café three times now. Thus far he'd stuck to the more expensive places around town when it came to food.

"He's definitely writing a column, then. But why? Why would he start reviewing cafés? Isn't he a fine dining horror?"

Susanne looked as baffled as I was. "Maybe he just wanted to apologize for last time."

I looked at her, my face askew and we both laughed. The last time Beardsley was in the restaurant, he called me over to complain that one of my waitresses was "as slow as molasses on ice" and I said, "How did complaining work on the molasses? Because it won't work with busy waitresses."

"Is he alone?"

She shook her head, nervous. "That guy is with him."

"What guy?"

"The one you spilled a tray on."

"What? You think Beardsley knows about that? Is he interviewing him? It's going to be in the papers!"

"Everybody already knows."

I felt a little sick. "What did he order?"

"Apple Crisp Salad, a side of potato salad, a Berry Berry Smoothie, and a Double Brownie Ice Cream-o-palooza."

I groaned. "He's definitely writing a column then."

"You don't know that."

"Who would order a Berry Berry Smoothie and a Double Brownie Ice Cream-o-palooza together?"

"Maybe one was for the other guy."

"Maybe." Ryan had just come from Pubs, like me. He might have skipped dessert there so he could ice-cream-o-palooza here.

"It'll be okay," she said. "The food's good. The service is good."

"But Beardsley's bad."

She couldn't argue with that. Lionel Beardsley liked to pretend he was unbiased and fair in his criticism of everything around Strawbridge, but his victims would say otherwise. And I'd dumped a tray of trash all over Ryan who was now sitting with him.

"I'll stay in the back until he's gone," I told Susanne. "Let me know if you need anything."

She nodded and went back to work. As much as I enjoyed being out front, I imagined it would be better not to remind Beardsley of our last encounter. Plus, I was still pretty dirty from paintball. I wasn't dressed for much more than wiping down tables. And I didn't really want to see Ryan Duval again, either. But before I could settle in loading dishes into the dishwasher, Susanne was back.

"He asked to see you." She was pale and her eyes wide.

"Did he yell at you?"

She shook her head, fast, like a frightened child. "No, but then again, he always sounds angry."

I wiped my hands off on a towel and followed Susanne to the front of house. I could see them in the front corner booth. "If things start to get out of hand," I told Susanne, "pull me out."

She squeaked, but I took that as an 'okay.'

"What can I do for you?" I asked Beardsley.

The table was cleaned off, just coffees in front of them. Beardsley sat like a large, bearded toad, his balding, freckled head downward as he perused his cup, black-rimmed glasses perched on the edge of his nose.

"I wanted to ask about your cat," Ryan said, pulling my attention from Beardsley.

"Huh?"

He frowned. "The cat," he said, rather aggressively, if you asked me.

"Oh, right. The cat. Why would you care about my cat?"

"As it turns out, my niece is looking to adopt one. So, if you decide not to keep it…"

"Oh." It came out defensively, but he started it.

"Her name's Penny," Beardsley broke in. "She's a sweet enough girl."

"How old is she?" The fact that Beardsley knew Ryan's niece made the hair on the back of my neck tingle.

"Eight," Ryan said. "She's going to want to get one soon, so I was just wondering…"

"About what?"

An exasperated 'pft' escaped him. "About wanting the cat."

"Well, I—" Pointing at Beardsley, I said, "How do you know Ryan's niece?"

"She's my great granddaughter."

"So—" looking at Ryan now, "He's your…"

"Grandfather. I'm sorry, do you not know Lionel Beardsley? I should have introduced you."

"Oh, no," I said, rather too sarcastically. "I know Mr. Beardsley very well."

Beardsley laughed and it sounded like a grumpy old British man's *harrumph*. "Indeed she does," he said.

"Anyway," Ryan said. "I didn't mean to put you on the spot. I just got the impression you weren't exactly a cat person."

"I'm not, really. But I'm going to give it a try. I'd hate for you to make your niece wait on my account."

"Sure," he said.

"So, is that all?" I turned to Mr. Beardsley. "Was your meal satisfactory?"

"As expected," he said.

I rolled my eyes as I turned away. "I'll have your check

to you in a sec."

"Oh, one other thing," the old man said.

I turned back to the table, ready to defend myself against some criticism.

"I've just been speaking to Madaline Richards. You know her, I'm sure."

I nodded.

"She's asked me to help judge the Holiday Baking Contest."

"She…she did?" How could she?

"And I understand you will also be a judge."

I was, to say the least, taken by surprise. "That's right."

"Why?"

"What do you mean, why?"

"You're not a certified chef."

I sputtered. "Neither are you." Okay, so I can't always think on my feet.

"But I make my living judging food."

"And I make my living serving it, what's your point?"

"Simply that if either of us is best suited to the position, it would be me."

"If you want to be a judge, be a judge. I'm not stopping you."

"I shouldn't have to do it with you. You're rude and unprofessional."

"Grandfather," Ryan mumbled.

"What?"

"You were very rude to me last time I was here."

"Then don't be a judge. I can't imagine why you'd be invited to be on the panel, anyway, if you want to know what I think."

"I don't have to be invited, my dear girl. If I want to be on the panel, I will be on the panel."

"Wow," I said. "You really are something."

"Grandfather," Ryan mumbled again.

"Be a judge. Don't be a judge. I don't care."

I turned and left before he could say any more. What an arrogant, grouchy man. Maybe I didn't want to be a judge with *him*. Did he consider that? But I wasn't backing out now.

I was almost through the door to the kitchen when I heard Ryan call my name. Ugh. Why wouldn't this guy leave me alone?

Chapter Seventeen

I turned to find Ryan standing by himself, his grumpy gramps back at the table leaving a tip that was probably the bare minimum.

"Sorry about that," he said. "My granddad is used to having his way."

I smirked. "And that's supposed to mean anything other than he's a spoiled octogenarian?"

"You could cut him some slack, is all I'm saying."

"Look, dude. Just because you're obligated to kiss his ring doesn't mean the rest of us have to."

"He takes a lot of flack because of what he does. It's his job."

"Oh, so he was on the clock just now when he acted like that?"

"I'm just saying that it's not easy being the critic."

I chuckled. "Did you not just hear what he said?"

Ryan held up his hands, "I'm just saying...okay, I get it. He's got a bit of an attitude."

"That's the truth. Is he going to write about me dumping that tray on you? Because that has nothing to do with the food."

"It sort of has to do with the service."

"So he is?"

"I don't know."

"But you told him about it?"

"Not directly. I mean, I didn't intend to. He saw my suit that day."

"Great," I mumbled.

"He told me what you said to him last time he was here. It's not like you don't have an attitude, too."

"Oh, no. You're not going to blame me for your grandfather being a jerk."

He put up a hand and shushed me as the old Bearded Beardsley joined us, huffy and cranky as ever. I realized that my employees and most of my customers had been listening to us. But I was on a roll.

"Don't shush me," I said. "If you want people to stop complaining," I said to the old man. "Stop being unfair to them."

Beardsley grabbed Ryan by the arm. "What did you say to her? Don't try to defend me, Ryan. Don't let any of these people push you around."

They seemed to argue while paying the check as I watched them from the back room.

"So…" Susanne said as she brought a tray of dirty dishes into the kitchen. "That didn't go very well."

I shook my head. "The other customers like my snarky attitude."

She looked at me, confused. "I guess."

"I admit I was kind of rude to Beardsley. I just get really defensive when people complain about something that's no one's fault. Petra had a dozen tables to handle last time he was here. We were swamped and under-staffed."

"You know I heard that he wrote some books a long time ago?"

"Beardsley?"

"Yep. Novels, or history, something like that. Anyway, he seems to think he's special."

"Still, I should be nice to him. Not just because he's a customer, but…you know."

"You can't suck up to him just so he'll write nice things about you."

"It's not about me. It's about the café. But he just…

he's so pompous."

"Exactly." Susanne put an arm around my shoulder and gave me a squeeze. "And yes, your customers love your snark. Now go on. We've got things covered. Plenty of staff today. And I hear you've got a critter in your house."

Oh, yeah. The cat. "Maybe when I get there, I'll find she's clawed a window open and ripped a screen to get out."

She laughed. "Not likely. You've got a cat, honey. Go make friends with it."

What was I going to do with a cat?

That night, back at home, as I was getting ready to go out with Vanessa, the cat sat on my bed watching me.

"Dusty?" I said, figuring I should let her know she had a name. "I'm going out tonight, okay?"

She didn't answer. She wasn't the friendliest cat, considering I'd let her stay in my house. A little gratitude would be nice.

Vanessa and I had a standing Saturday night date at The Fort that was rarely interfered with. Come to think of it, we liked Friday nights at the Fort as well. And the improv was a big hit, so Wednesday nights would be a regular outing, too. The Fort was our place. We found a table for two on the balcony overlooking the stage and dance floor and a few minutes after our drinks arrived, Van held up a hand and said, "Melissa, just stop."

"Stop what?"

"I don't want to hear about the cat all night."

I honestly hadn't realized I'd been yakking about it. But thinking back on it, it had started as soon as I met her out front.

"You're nervous," she said. "I get that. But if you become a cat lady like Sophie, it'll be me next and I don't want a cat."

"It's not contagious."

"Yes, it is! Pari would never have a cat if she wasn't friends with Sophie. And now you have one. Oh, I'm probably going to end up with a cat, anyway." She sighed and pouted.

"What's that supposed to mean?"

"Everyone else is pairing up. And I'm not, like, the kind of woman that has to have a man—"

"Right."

"I mean, a man to marry. But it looks like Pari and Sophie are on their way to the next stage in adulting."

"It's like a magnet, isn't it? Pulling us in."

"Like cats."

"Well, I can't put her out now."

"Don't be that way. If you feel like it's too much, you should find her a new home. There's no shame in it."

"Never. I will not give Ryan Duval the satisfaction."

"What's that?" Ryan said from behind me.

He'd come up the stairs and sidled over to snoop! And Vanessa must have seen him and didn't warn me.

"Nothing," I said.

Sheldon Frasier was with him and I got an irritating headache on the spot.

"Mind if we join you?" Sheldon said after he'd already pulled up a chair next to Vanessa.

At least Vanessa looked at me before answering, but with a 'please, please' beg to the eyes.

"Oh, all right," I said.

Ryan grabbed a chair from another table, too, and sat down next to me. "Sorry," he said lightly.

The place was filling up fast and I was relieved when the band started up because I wouldn't have to make conversation with Ryan. But then Sheldon and Vanessa left us for the dance floor.

"I'm not much of a dancer," Ryan said.

"That's true."

"Oh, I see how it is."

"There are some memories we can't get out of our heads," I said.

"Anyway, I can leave if you want. I mean, if you're hoping someone will ask you to dance."

"If I want to dance, I'll dance. Girls don't sit around waiting to be asked anymore."

We sat in silence for a minute or two until he said, "So, you were talking about me."

"You were mentioned. That's all."

"So you aren't going to tell me?"

"Fine. You were making fun of me last night at Triple F. About not knowing how to take care of a cat. And then today you wanted to take it from me—"

"I'm not planning to kidnap it."

"I was just telling Melissa that I'm going to keep it."

"To spite me?"

"Exactly."

He laughed. "Well, I'm happy to be a part of helping out a stray cat."

I rolled my eyes and saluted him. We both went quiet again, watching the throng down below.

"Shel's not much of a dancer, either," he said.

I tried not to smile. "No, he's not."

"He reminds me of that Peanuts Christmas movie my parents always watch."

"He's doing a mix of the Marionette and the Armpit."

"What?"

"Somebody named them," I said. "The different dances they do in that show. It's online, hold on." I dug my phone out of my little purse and Googled it.

He laughed when he saw the page. "I can't wait to show him this."

"He may never dance again."

"We can't have that," he said, handing me back my phone. "I'll take this secret to my grave."

"Is your grandfather going to write about my café?" It just sort of fell out of my mouth. I suppose I'd been wanting to ask him as soon as I saw him.

"I think so."

"Isn't that unethical?"

"How so?"

"You're my landlord now. And I dumped a tray of dirty dishes all over you."

"So you admit you did it."

"I never said I didn't do it. I said it wasn't my fault."

"Semantics. It doesn't matter, anyway. My grandfather wouldn't trash a business for revenge. He'd already picked your restaurant to review."

"But now that you own the building, isn't it, like, a conflict of interest?"

He peered at me. "Maybe. But I don't think it would be right for me to interfere with his job."

"Of course you'd take his side."

"What does that even mean? What side? And, yeah, he's my grandfather. What do you want me to do?"

"Tell him not to review my restaurant."

"Is that how you want things to go? You want to avoid a review by pulling strings? How is that fair to the other restaurants downtown?"

Suddenly I felt very small and stupid. "Excuse me," I said and left the table. I grabbed a guy on my way down the stairs and pulled him to the dance floor. Luckily it was UPS Pete and not a stranger and he was happy to dance with me, though he did look a bit nervous, probably because I was dancing out some rage. Rage dancing, while not necessarily unattractive, can be scary to those nearby.

We danced through the whole set and when the music finally stopped, Pete told me I looked tired and dragged me back upstairs. When I saw that Ryan was still there, I asked Pete to join us. He already knew Vanessa and I introduced him to Sheldon.

"And this is—"

"Ryan," he said, shaking Ryan's hand. "Good to see you, man." Pete pulled up another chair from a half empty table nearby to sit between Ryan and me.

"You know him?" I said.

"We're on the same trivia team."

"I have no idea what that means."

"How's Charlemagne?" Ryan asked him.

"Ruling the house as always," Pete said with a chuckle. "Charlemagne's my dog," he told me.

"You're a dog person," I mused.

"I bet you're a cat person."

"Not at all."

"She is now," Ryan said.

"Does having a cat automatically make me a cat person?"

We chatted for a while but Vanessa and Sheldon

carried the conversation. Finally, Pete stood, saying he had to get home.

"I'll go too," I said.

"No," Vanessa said. "It's still early."

"I really should get back to Dusty…or whatever her name's going to be."

"I'll walk you out," Pete said.

Once we were outside of The Fort, with the band's guitar and drumbeat echoing in our heads, and heading around back to the parking lot, Pete said, "I thought you were on a double date, there, and I was intruding."

"Not at all. It was supposed to be just me and Vanessa."

"It was sort of awkward, though."

"Sorry about that. I guess it did look a bit weird for me to ask you to join."

"No, no. I get asked to join double dates all the time."

I laughed. His dry wit took me by surprise. I stopped at my car and said, "You're not, like, secretly in love with me or anything, are you?"

He looked at me as if I'd just sprouted teeth on my forehead. "What?"

"Sorry…again. It was just something Isabella said."

"The psychic?"

"Yeah."

"She told you I was in love with you?"

"No, not you. Someone. It was stupid to ask. Maybe I'm a bit tipsy."

"Are you okay to drive?"

"I'm fine. I'm not really tipsy. Just weird."

He smiled, if warily. "Okay, well, I'll see you around town."

I called after him, "Sorry…again."

Well, I was going to have to tell Kaya that the plan of just asking every guy I saw if he was worshiping me from afar was a definite no-go.

The next morning I woke up with a cat on my chest and Vanessa banging on my front door.

Chapter Eighteen

How to Ruin a Scrumptious Recipe

Attempt Three: Just Throw Things at It

The summer after college graduation Vanessa and I headed out west of town to Regional Park to watch the guys we'd been seeing play baseball. We'd been out with them a few times, double dating, and both agreed that they were guys' guys. Into sports and the outdoors, beer, boating, and dogs. They didn't seem to mind that we were not into any of those things. Still, we decked ourselves out in jeans, sports jerseys, and baseball caps, ready to eat hot dogs and cheer the boys on.

They played for a local league that pitted businesses and industries against each other. Our guys were in construction and their team was the Circuit Breakers. They were playing against Madeline's team of realtors, the Handyman Specials. We slathered ourselves in sunscreen and learned to yell 'batter' over and over again in quick succession. We just needed to remember when we were supposed to do it, having found ourselves, more than once, apparently rooting for the wrong team.

At some point during the very long game, I caught

sight of Ryan, standing near home plate in a Handyman Specials uniform, swinging a baseball bat. I sucked in a quick breath, and was surprised at my own reaction. It wasn't as if I hadn't laid eyes on him in decades. I'd watched him walk across campus at UCF several times, always finding myself lost in some ridiculous memory of our days as friends. But I imagined he'd stay in the Orlando area after graduation and now, here he was, back home again. *Near me* again. Then I pinched my left arm and mentally scolded myself to stop with the Ryan nonsense, already. I tried to ignore him and stopped shouting so loud, hoping he wouldn't notice me.

"Do we have to stay to the end?" I asked Vanessa after an hour and a half.

"I suppose not. We're meeting them later. Just a little longer."

It was the fourth inning and the Breakers were ahead two runs to zero when the Specials were at bat with bases loaded. Ryan was up and part of me was rooting for him and Madaline's team. I did know her and some of the other players, after all. But I was supposed to be cheering on the guys we were dating. Ryan's first attempt was a strike and the crowd cheered and groaned. He took a good swing at the second ball and the 'thwack' rang out all around us as the ball went straight up and over the fence to our left. For a brief few seconds, the crowd was silent. Then there was a loud cracking sound before the ref called, "steeeerike!"

"Wouldn't it be just my luck if it hit my car?" I said to Vanessa as Ryan readied for his last attempt. "I mean, what are the odds?"

A few people left the stands, probably checking their windshields.

"I guess it depends on how many cars there are in the parking in a spot that could possibly be hit."

She had no idea, though, that I knew Ryan. Sure, I told her about the cactus incident, but she never saw him. This made the odds, in my opinion—the number of guys I knew in high school, who went into real estate, who decided to play in the local league, and happened to hit my car with a fly ball?—astronomical. Ryan struck out.

An announcement was made over the loudspeakers, with the license plate number of the car that was hit. Vanessa and I looked at each other.

"Is that yours?" she asked me.

"Who remembers their tag number?"

"Well, let's head out now, anyway."

We exited the gate into the parking lot and when we got to my car, of course, my windshield had a huge circular crack, like a giant spider spun a glass web on it.

"I don't believe it," Vanessa said.

"It figures." I'd forgotten about the universe and it's delightful irony.

There was a man leaning against my trunk who introduced himself as a park employee; I didn't quite catch the name. He was basically there to tell me that the parks department wasn't liable and I'd have to talk to the guy who hit the ball. And that guy was Ryan Duval.

After the man left, I turned to Vanessa. "What should I do?"

"You gotta let the guy know. He should pay for this."

"Is it his fault?"

"Of course it is."

"But, isn't the park at fault for not putting up enough netting? Am I at fault for parking here?"

"Everybody else is parked here."

"But should I have known this was a possibility?"

"You should still talk to the guy who hit the ball."

I didn't want to. I wanted to just leave, but I wasn't even sure I should drive my car. I could try at least. But I was in the middle of gathering funds from my family to help me lease a building and open my restaurant. How much was this going to cost? We were just about to go back to the bleachers and wait for the game to end so we could ask the guys about it when I saw Ryan jogging toward us. I stopped, a little too quickly, grabbing Vanessa's arm absentmindedly. The closer he got, the better he looked and the younger I felt until I was back in high school by the time he saw me.

"Melissa?"

"You know him?" Vanessa said, nudging me.

I shushed her. "Hey, Ryan."

"Oh, man," he said looking at my windshield. "I'm sorry."

No 'How long has it been?' No 'You look great.' No hug. Nothing.

"What are the odds?" I laughed nervously.

"Let me give you my number. Call me when you know how much it'll cost."

So business-like. I looked at the windshield and back to Ryan. It was all so awkward.

"Go on, Mel," Vanessa said. She started digging in my purse, nearly pulling it off my shoulder.

"Okay, okay." I found my phone and took his number.

"I'm going to get back to the game," he said. "Call me, okay?"

"Sure," I said.

He took a few steps away from us and turned back.

"You do know you're wearing football jerseys, right?"

I looked down at my Kirk Cousins shirt with a giant eight on the front. "So? This is the extent of my sports wardrobe."

"I had to borrow this one," Vanessa said of the Brett Favre I'd lent her.

He smirked and ran back to the field. I stood watching after him a bit too long, causing Vanessa to say, "So, who is he?"

"I knew him in school."

"He's gorgeous. Did you date him?"

"Nope." I moved to get in my car.

"That's too bad. So, we're leaving?" She got in the passenger seat next to me and I started the engine. "Why didn't you date him?"

"I guess I'm just not his type. You think the glass will shatter and fall out before I can get you home?"

"Oh, no. We're going straight to *your* house. You can borrow your dad's car to take me home, can't you?"

Of course I could. And when I got back home from dropping her off, my dad had already called the windshield people. Almost a thousand dollars for a new one.

"Did you talk to the guy who did it?" he asked me. My dad wasn't a big man, and neither was his voice. He had one of those kind faces, and it only grew softer and sweeter the older he got.

"Yeah."

"Did he offer to pay?"

"Yeah."

"You don't want to take his money, do you?"

That's my dad. He knew me too well. "He's just a realtor." It was the first excuse I could come up with.

"I guarantee he makes more money than you do, honey. Ask him for half, then."

A few days passed as I tried to get the nerve to call Ryan, but didn't succeed. I was at the location where Café Flamingo would be. At the time, it was still a taco place, but the owners were moving north. Mr. Jenkins—stooped and gray—and I were standing on the sidewalk along Strawbridge Avenue, trying to work out a deal when Ryan showed up out of nowhere. And as if I was a mouse, trained to salivate whenever I saw Ryan Duval, my heart raced and my cheeks burned. He greeted Mr. Jenkins and they shook hands, then he turned to me.

"Your dad told me I'd find you here."

"How'd you get my home number?" I stuttered a bit on the first H, but I don't think he noticed.

"I found it in my old black book from school." He grinned. "I bet you didn't know you were in it. I figured you still lived at the same place."

"I do, for now." No, I didn't know he'd put me in his little black book. What a joke we all made of it. A literal *little black book* with the words "Little Black Book" printed on the front in white. Ryan had thought it was so clever.

"Who are you going to put in it?" Josh had asked him.

"Every girl I like."

"You really think Jane Larson is going to give you her number?"

"I have ways of making girls talk."

We all laughed and pretended to try to steal his stupid little black book for days afterward until we moved on to other nerdy things to get silly about. I always imagined—not that I'd thought about it very often—that he'd forgotten about the book or even threw it away.

"What?" I said, coming back to reality and seeing Mr. Jenkins and Ryan staring at me.

Ryan said, "There's no shame in living at home."

"Of course not," Mr. Jenkins said. "Once you get this restaurant going, you'll be on your own before you know it. Your parents must be very proud."

"They'll be proud if I don't lose all of their investment."

"Nice spot," Ryan said, looking at the building. "What kind of restaurant are you planning?"

"Sandwiches and smoothies."

"You didn't go to culinary school, did you?"

I cringed. "Didn't you ask me that years ago?"

"I'm sure I didn't."

"So, what do you say, Miss Melissa," Mr. Jenkins said. "You like the price?"

I took a moment, not wanting to be rushed into my decision just because Ryan was there. "I do. Let's sign some papers."

"My wife will call you when we get the lease ready. You've got a bit of work ahead of you."

Mr. Jenkins said goodbye, leaving Ryan and me standing on Strawbridge Avenue looking awkwardly at each other as downtown traffic crawled past.

"That's your car?" he said, nodding toward it parked in front of the building.

"Yep."

"It's a Jetta. I didn't really notice before. Pretty new?"

"Just got it last year."

"And I wrecked it. But the replacement looks great."

"Yeah, we got the factory standard windshield."

He whistled. "Okay, then. What's the damage?"

"I feel bad making you pay."

"You aren't making me. I'm offering. I broke the windshield; I'll pay for it."

"My dad said you could maybe just pay half."

"Your dad paid for it? Now I'm definitely covering all

of it."

"What difference does it make?"

"I don't know; it's just different."

"My dad can afford it. He's helping me start this restaurant."

"I can afford it, too. And it was my fault."

"Maybe I shouldn't have parked there."

"So I'd be standing here with somebody else—"

"Why would they be *here*? Are they renting my restaurant space now? Who are these people?"

He chuckled, shaking his head. "The point is, they'd be taking my money without hesitation."

"Are you saying I'm stubborn?"

"A little, yeah."

"When you park at a ball field you take a risk."

"Oh, please. Do you know how bad of a ball player you have to be to do what I did?"

"So, you expect me to make your being a lousy ball player that much worse by taking nine-hundred dollars from you?"

He whistled again. "Ouch."

"You don't have to pay it."

"We can do a mobile transfer thing."

"Are you sure?"

"Come on; get your phone."

Grudgingly, I dug my phone from my purse and he transferred the money to me. "I'm really sorry."

"Why are *you* apologizing to *me*?"

I started laughing. "I don't know. Are you sure you can afford it?"

"I'm one of the top selling realtors in town. Didn't you know?"

"I thought you'd go into finance or something."

"I've got bigger plans."

"I'm glad. I mean—not that there's anything wrong with real estate. I just meant…I don't know what I meant."

He chuckled. "There's the Melissa I remember."

"Ditzy is how you remember me?"

"Always trying to be kind."

131

He started backing away toward the side street next to my new restaurant location and my first thought was, *Wait, aren't you going to try to kiss me?* Thankfully, I didn't say it out loud.

With a smile and a wave, he said, "I'll be looking for your grand opening."

I nodded and watched as went around the corner. He was chopped in horizontal bits through the front and side windows of Harvey's Tacos, slatted with blinds, until he was out of sight. Part of me was happy he was living in town. But another part of me wished he was still far away. Never mind, I told myself. I've got a restaurant to open.

Harvey's Tacos, I thought. No wonder they're leaving town.

Chapter Nineteen

W hat was up with you last night?"

"Good morning to you, too," I said, letting Vanessa into my little living room.

"Why'd you leave so early?"

I stumbled into the kitchen to get some water. "You want anything?"

She plopped herself down on my the sofa. "Where's the cat?"

"She's the cutest thing." I stood at the table eating a banana. "When I came home last night, she was peeking out from my bedroom. You know, I think she belonged to somebody before. I think she was an inside cat. She's got this relieved vibe going on, like, thank goodness I'm inside. Not that she's being all that nice to me. But she slept on my pillow last night, so…progress."

"Are we going to be talking about the cat all the time now?"

Tossing my peel into the trash, I grabbed my glass of water and sat next to her on the sofa. "You set me up, Van. I didn't want to be on a double date, especially if my guy is Ryan Duval. Why won't you stop trying to push him on me?"

"I didn't know Shel was going to be there."

"But you went off with him, leaving me with Ryan."

"What's so bad about Ryan Duval?"

"I told you I don't like him."

"But why?"

"I don't want to talk about him."

For a while we both sat, fuming.

"Well, I gave you a chance," she said.

"What's that mean?"

She looked at me slyly. "Shel told me what happened."

My face burned hot. Was Ryan Duval telling people about us? "What did he say?"

"He said that you two were good friends in high school and even went out once. Why didn't I know about it?"

I felt some relief, but was still wary. "That's not exactly true."

"Then spill."

I rolled my eyes. "We didn't go out. We just…went to a party together."

"Ooh, sounds romantic."

"It wasn't."

"So, what happened?"

"Let's just say, it was a disaster, the likes of which no romance could ever survive and leave it at that."

"I don't get it, Mel. We tell each other everything. How do I not know about this?"

"It's humiliating. Stuff you don't tell anyone."

"So no double dates for us, then."

"I was right. You were trying to fix me up."

"I just thought you two would be great together."

"I think Ryan Duval and I are like chlorine and ammonia. We do not go together. You better not be fixing me up with him for the Matching Melissa Challenge."

"I told you I wouldn't." She was frowning. Even when Dusty came out of the bedroom and rubbed against her calves.

"You can date Sheldon," I said. "I don't have to be friends with Ryan for that."

"It could get uncomfortable. I don't want to have to worry about keeping you two apart."

"It'll be okay."

"Sheldon's probably not the one for me, anyway."

"Don't say that, Van. Don't let me ruin something good."

"Well, I can't play interference the rest of my life if I were to, you know, get serious with him."

"You won't have to. I'll deal with Ryan Duval. I have to get ready for work." But I sat there.

"Well, what are you waiting for?"

Dusty hopped onto Vanessa's lap and purred at her.

"I don't know what I was thinking, taking in a cat. I live at the café. I don't feel right, leaving her here all by herself all day."

"She's a cat; she'll be fine."

"You don't think they get lonely?"

"I don't know. Ask Sophie."

"I can't have her at the café."

Dusty put her paws on Vanessa's chest and rubbed the top of her head on Van's chin.

"That's for sure. You're going to have to change your routine now that you're a proper cat lady. Come home more often. Or better yet, take more time off."

"And do what? Play with the cat?"

"Find a hobby. There's more to life than your business, Mel."

"Is there?"

"There is now. Dusty. So find something to do at home."

"Knit?"

"There's nothing wrong with knitting. Why did you make Susanne manager of the café and turn the catering over to Lucy this year, if you weren't planning to slow down?"

"I have slowed down."

She looked at me as if I were crazy. "You're lying to yourself. You were ready to lead a normal life. You told me how lucky you were to be able to have these great businesses that you could oversee instead of having to work yourself ragged every day."

I grudgingly remembered.

"And we were going to go on a vacation together. To

the Rockies, or Maine. But you just kept working. Worse, instead of running the businesses, you're just showing up and doing everybody else's work. What were you doing bussing tables last week anyway?"

"I don't need a lecture, Van."

"Maybe you do. It's Sunday. Why are you even going to work today? Your crew can handle it."

"I don't know what else to do, okay?"

She stared at me and I glared at her. But her eyes softened.

"I know, Mel. I get it. But try to remember why you decided to relax a bit recently."

I turned to look around my little house. Dusty had run from our heated exchange and was in the kitchen munching on kibble I'd left in the bowl.

"That's just the thing," I said. "I can't remember why I did it. If feels like a stupid decision now."

"It did seem impulsive when you told me about it."

"Why didn't you say anything?"

"Because I thought it would be good for you."

I said nothing as she stood, wiped cat hair off her shirt and gathered up her purse. "I have a few appointments today myself, so who am I to talk? But why don't you stay home? Just this one day, stay home, and think about what you want to do with your life."

"Too scary," I muttered.

At the door, she stopped and said, "Oh, yeah, Your next date is Saturday. I'll pick you up at eight."

"Thanks for the advanced notice."

"I don't like the idea of springing them on you. That's Kaya's thing. Anyway, this date is a full Diva thing."

"I don't like the sound of that."

"The Divas got your back."

"More like the Divas will be laughing at whatever you have in store for me."

She pursed her lips, then said, "Yeah, maybe. And that's eight *in the morning*."

Before I could protest, she closed the door behind her.

For a few seconds I thought she was telling the truth

about giving me a week's warning, about being nice and all. But then I realized she did it so I'd be wracking my brain all week wondering what kind of humiliation I'd be suffering. I had no idea my ghost challenge had turned my friends so vengeful.

Chapter Twenty

It was the last full week before Thanksgiving. Not a good time to change my work routine and definitely not a good time to be away from my businesses. But there was the cat to consider. There was no way I was going to give up that cat and prove Ryan Duval right. Maybe that's not the most loving way to adopt a cat, but that was where things were. I'd just have to figure out a compromise.

"I'm going to have to go home a few times a day from now on," I told Susanne later that day when I finally showed up at the café. It was a typical Sunday afternoon, busy, but at least we had enough staff.

I did spend some quality time with Dusty. We played with a feather on a string and I batted some toy mice around with her for a while. I learned that there's nothing on television on Sunday mornings, except *Columbo* reruns, which aren't that bad. And I thought a little bit about what I might do if I didn't work so much. I could take up a hobby, like Pari with her photography. Or volunteer, maybe at an animal shelter, like Sophie. But nothing in particular inspired me. So, annoyed with myself, and having bored Dusty into a nap on the bed, I went in to work.

I found Susanne in the office doing last week's paperwork and piddled about with the radio stations until she dropped her pencil and swiveled the chair around to face me.

"Fine," she said. "I'll stop."

I did my best to look innocent. "Whatever do you mean?"

She chuckled. "What's up?"

I rolled my eyes. "It's stupid."

"I'm sure it is."

Leaning against the tall filing cabinet in the corner, I crossed my arms. "I've decided to really try to take more time off."

"Oh, no," she said, mocking me. "What will we ever do without you?"

"I know I've said it before; but this time, I mean it. I just need a hobby."

"I thought you had a garden."

"Another hobby."

"Don't you do Zumba?"

"That's not a hobby."

"Teach it, then."

"That sounds like a job."

She nodded. "It is. Okay. I'm sure something will come to you. I have to get back to work. Stop bothering me."

"You love me. Anyway," I said, as I grabbed an apron, "I guess I'll start eating lunch at home and going home in the evenings like a normal person."

"You're not sick or anything are you? Please tell me you're not dying."

"Hah, like you could get rid of me. No, it's just... I think it's either get another cat for my first cat, or be there more often."

"Sometimes a cat comes into your life and forces you to look at things differently," she said, pulling a wisp of hair behind her ear.

"I'm not going to marry it and move to Asheville."

She winked at me as I left the office and headed back out to the front. I stood for a while, just looking at my smoothly running restaurant and felt a bit silly. What was

I doing? They really didn't need me. But what else would I do? I'd spent the past five years building this business into a success—adding the catering three years ago. What else did I want to do?

"Melissa," somebody called.

Quinn was sitting in a booth at the window along Woodplum Street waving at me.

"I said hello, like, four times," he said when I took a seat opposite him, facing the front of the café.

A small plate with the crumbly remains of one of our chocolate cookies sat to one side and he had a finger looped through the handle of a thick white coffee mug, half full.

"My brain's working overtime, as usual," I said. "I'm just not all there, lately. Listen, I can't remember if I ever really thanked you for the cheap tickets to the Halloween party for me and the Divas. So, if I didn't, thanks. I owe you a few."

"We restaurateurs gotta stick together, right?"

"Sure." The truth is, next to guys like Quinn and his place, I didn't think I stood out as a restaurateur. I ran a café. A successful café, sure. But the extent of my cheffing skills is sandwiches and soups. Lionel Beardsley popped into my head, telling me I had no business being a judge this Christmas. "Take it easy on yourself," I mumbled.

"What's that?"

"Oh," I waved a hand. "I was thinking about the Holiday Baking Contest."

"You're still judging, right?"

"Lionel Beardsley complained about me—"

"What does he have to do with it?"

"Suddenly he wants to be on the panel with us. Well, without me."

He looked at me, questioning.

"Turns out, he's Ryan Duval's grandfather."

"No kidding. And I suppose he doesn't want to sit on a panel with Ryan's assaulter." Before I could protest, he said, "I'm joking. So, if he doesn't like it, he doesn't have to be a judge."

"My thoughts exactly."

"Damn straight. You're too tough to let someone bully you out of an opportunity."

"Why do I hear a sales pitch coming?"

He laughed. "Not a sales pitch. A gift. You remember The Salty Shanty?"

"Bill Myerson's place, sure. He died last year."

"We went to the funeral together, so I know."

My turn to laugh. "That's right. And you were bothered that I didn't wear black."

"And it turned out you weren't the only one."

"I swear I didn't know there was a tropical theme. Who has a theme at their funeral?"

"Myerson, apparently. Anyway, the guy owned several restaurants, if you recall, and had quite a big will full of first parties and third parties and bequeaths of the second and fourth parts."

As Quinn went on murdering the language of estate law, my brain wandered to his face. Quinn was very good looking. He wasn't Reese Fuller gorgeous—let's face it, Sophie struck gold. And he wasn't Sam Preston adorable —I didn't think Sam would be Pari's type at all. Life's funny that way, isn't it? No. Quinn was somewhere close to a Reese—regular build, a bit too tall for me, dark brown hair, brown eyes, nice brows, not too bushy, but not straight across the forehead like Ryan Duval's. Ugh. Why did Ryan Duval pop into my head while I was getting dreamy about Quinn? Quinn… Do you suppose he's the one Isabella was talking about?

"Booth five to Melissa. Are we reaching?"

I suddenly popped back into the world. "What?"

"I said, what do you think?"

"About what?'"

"You really are out of it today. The food truck."

That's right. He was talking about a grant that Bill Myerson's will set up for after he bit the seafood bucket.

"You really think Bill would have wanted me to have one?"

"The executor of his estate set up a committee and we voted. You're first on the list."

Suddenly, it was as if the universe had answered the question I'd been struggling with. It wasn't more leisure time I was looking for. It was a new outlet.

"You can start small," Quinn was saying. "The grant covers the cost of the truck, the set up, and painting with your logo. Your café would be perfect. Think about all the greasy food we get at Triple F. You can offer smoothies and sandwiches as an alternative. People will love it."

"What a great idea, but…" Something told me this could be the dark side of the universe speaking. Hadn't I been resolved to live like a normal person, have a home life of some sort? And here was another business opportunity being handed to me on a cake plate. But I could probably never manage to adjust to being normal. So, perhaps the gods of ambrosia were telling me I was wrong, and working was my heart's true desire. But then the universe threw me a cat, as if it was saying, slow down, enjoy yourself even if you don't know how. So, this could be the gods of Marmite tricking me out of a well-deserved life of ease. I felt dizzy.

"Oh, my," I said.

"Oh, my? You sound like Dorothy Gale."

We'd both watched *The Wizard of Oz* at Karen's the month before.

"I'm okay," I said. "I just can't decide where the gods stand, that's all."

"You mean, their opinion on food trucks?"

"More like life and the universe."

"And everything?"

"Exactly."

He shook his head with a smile. "Give it some thought. I'll check back with you at the end of the week."

"A whole week. Gee, thanks."

"No rush."

In the end, it didn't matter which side of the universe was calling to me. Before Quinn was out the front door of Café Flamingo, I'd already made up my mind. A food truck was just the thing the brand needed. I glanced out the window, across the street, to Mabel's with all the 'Going Out of Business' signs in the window. If only Ryan would let me lease that space. It could be headquarters for all three of the Café Flamingo businesses.

"What if," I told Susanne back in the office just inside the kitchen area, "I also sold some food out of Mabel's space?"

She looked up from the order form she was working on and squished her face into a frown. "What are you talking about?"

I sat in the padded folding chair next to the desk and leaned toward her, excited. "Ryan Duval won't let me lease the space as just an office for the catering business. But I could sell some kind of food, too."

"You're going to open up another restaurant just so you can also use the space to run the catering out of? Isn't that what you already do here?"

"But this would be a much smaller operation than Café Flamingo."

"And you said Ryan wanted something quaint and clever to enhance the downtown vibe. Is he looking for another food joint?"

"I bet he would be open to a quaint, cutesy food joint. Like meat on a stick, or—"

"Are you high?"

"Macarons!"

"You'd just be adding another business in which to house the catering business. Melissa, this makes no sense. You've got two food businesses already. You can't possibly want to open yet another."

"Well, now that you mention it..."

"What have you done?"

"What do you think about a Café Flamingo food truck?"

She pursed her lips. "I knew it."

"What?"

"I knew you would never be able to turn your businesses over to me and Lucy. Instead of relaxing and enjoying your success, like you said you were going to do—and recommitted to it not two minutes ago!—you're adding wheels and racing toward more work."

I started to deny it, but truthfully, taking on the food

truck would mean hiring and training a new set of staff. It'd take me at least a year or two to get it running on its own. "You're not completely wrong."

"And what about Dusty?"

"I told her I would be there for her and I will."

"You're talking to it already?"

"Is that bad?"

"Next step is four cats and a poodle."

"No way. And the food truck proves it."

"I suppose you are too young to retire."

"Of course I am. What was I thinking, anyway?"

"I don't know. Something about not wanting to be so obsessed with work. Wanting a normal life. What happened there?"

"Oh, yeah. Now I remember. My Uncle Bob died."

"That was it. You told me all about it. Never took a holiday; rarely saw his kids."

"I guess I come from a family of workaholics."

"No. Not workaholics. You're driven, that's all. Ambitious. You like your work. And there's nothing wrong with that. As long as you try to have a life outside work, too."

I sighed. "Oh, Susanne. You're so wise. And right, as usual. I should just admit to myself that I love to work and go with it."

"With a food truck?"

"Yes!"

And so, it was official. I'd made myself the CEO of a major—well, three-part—corporation. Café, catering, and food truck. I was going to be a Strawbridge Icon. I could work as much or as little as I wanted. And there was nothing Ryan Duval or Beardsley the critic could do about it.

Like a yoyo, I was up and then flung down again. Beardsley. How much damage could he really do to my restaurant? And to my catering business by association? So far, he hadn't put any restaurants out of business with his snarky reviews. None that I knew of. But he'd hurt a few. Sales drops and whatnot. I heard one guy over beachside had to revamp his entire menu after a Beardsley takedown. A few local plays had closed up shortly after the grouch panned them, and that was pretty bad. And people say his review of a film had people protesting outside the cinema a few years ago.

"Are you okay?" Susanne pulled me from my panic.

"Sure, sure. We're going to be fine."

That Wednesday, after the now weekly HDS BOMB meeting, I met up with the Divas at Café Flamingo for a late dessert. We filled the back booth that overlooked Woodplum Street, Sophie sandwiched between me and Kaya, leaving Pari, Karen, and Vanessa with their backs to the front door.

"I always feel like someone's going to sneak up on me when I sit on this side of the booth," Karen said. "That's why I like to keep a pencil behind my ear." She yanked it out and threatened us. "Office Ninja."

"Do you have enemies we should know about?" Kaya said.

"I don't think so."

"A disgruntled customer," Sophie said with a sly smile, "might come at her with a stapler."

"Or hit her with a three-hole punch."

"A hole punch sounds like an anti-punch," I said. "Like…a sci-fi punch in the vacuum of space."

"No," Kaya said, looking at me with pity. "A hole punch. One of those things that punches three holes in a stack of papers all at once."

"I know what a hole punch is," I said. "I was making a joke."

"Are hole punches still a thing?" Vanessa asked.

"Not only are they a thing," Karen said. "They're heavy. I could get a concussion."

Pari said, "You don't really think someone's coming after you with a hole punch do you?"

"What on earth could you have done to make someone angry?" I said.

"Exactly," Kaya said. "Karen couldn't make a customer mad if she tried. Melissa on the other hand…"

They all laughed.

"Very funny," I said, as I caught sight of Quinn Norris approaching the table behind Karen, "I'll let you know if anyone comes at you with a deadly office supply."

"Hello, ladies," Quinn said.

Karen shrieked. "You scared the bejeezus out of me." Then she turned on me. "You said you'd warn me."

"And don't call us ladies," Kaya said.

Quinn scooched into the booth next to me. "Sorry about that. What should I call you?"

"Do you have to call us anything?" Pari said.

"Could we not discuss feminism in social situations right now?" I said. "I invited Quinn here to make an announcement."

Karen squealed. "Really?"

"Not that kind of announcement." Was everything going to be about love with the Divas until I got hooked up? "Quinn made me an offer the other day—"

"Really?" Karen sang.

"Not that kind of offer," I said. "Can I just get through this?"

"Okay, I promise no more outbursts," she said with a sly grin.

"I've been awarded a grant from Bill Myerson's will."

"You mean he left you something?"

"Were you related to him?"

"An heiress!"

Trying to control a Diva conversation was pretty much useless. "Not exactly. No. And Not really. The guy left money to help local restaurants and, to cut to the chase, I'm getting a food truck."

"I'm glad to hear it," Quinn said.

"What's Quinn got to do with it?"

"Are you and Quinn going to do it together?"

"Really?" Karen gasped.

"A Tracks/Flamingo sort of thing?"

"Would that even work?"

"What does 'cut to the chase' mean, anyway?"

"Quiet!" The entire restaurant fell silent and I shouted, "Not you," so they all went back to talking. "Quinn is…what are you?"

"I'm on the committee that the executor set up, that's all."

"So why aren't you getting a food truck?" Kaya asked him.

I turned to Quinn. "That's a good question."

He grimaced. "It's not really on brand with Tracks."

"What's that supposed to mean?" Sophie said.

"Tracks is too fancy for a food truck?" I said.

"I don't mean anything against Café Flamingo."

"Don't you?" Pari said.

"Look, ladies." He threw his hands up in surrender.

"There's that 'ladies' again," Pari said. "You don't look like an octogenarian."

"Ok," Quinn said. "Women, listen—"

"Hold on to your corsets, girls, here comes some mansplaining," Kaya shouted.

We all stared at poor Quinn for a few seconds as he whimpered helplessly and stammered a bit. Then we broke into laughter.

"They always look so pitiful," Kaya said.

"We're just teasing you," I told him. "And he's right that, around here anyway, people tend to like their food trucks to smell like fried food."

Quinn let out a sigh and said, "That's what I meant. I mean…Café Flamingo can freshen up the food truck scene in Strawbridge."

"I think it's a great idea," Pari said.

The rest of the Divas agreed.

"But don't think it'll get you out of the Pink Diva Man Hunter plan," Karen said.

I glared at her. "I'm sure it won't."

"Ah, yes," Quinn said. "The Matching Melissa thing. Don't worry. It'll be at least a few months until we even get the truck," Quinn said.

"Anyway, I wanted to celebrate my new acquisition with all of you. And Quinn. Dessert is on me."

"There ought to be champagne," Sophie said. "Or is that too fancy?"

"It'll have to be Diet Cokes, I'm afraid."

Sophie lifted her glass and scooted out of the booth. She shouted, "Café Flamingo is getting a food truck, everybody!"

This was so unlike Sophie that I wasn't the least bit surprised when she turned red and quickly sat back down. But the whole restaurant—well, the crowd that tends to hang out for smoothies or dessert in the early afternoon —toasted a new way of pigging out at festivals.

And naturally, who should wander over to the booth but Ryan Duval and that girl he was always hanging out with. I'd been so excited about my decision to complicate my life further that I hadn't noticed they were there at all.

"Congratulations," he said.

All the Divas were looking at me. "Thanks," I muttered.

"Mel, you remember my sister, Alicia?"

"Oh, sure," I said. I searched her face looking for hints until I found them. "You were a few years behind us in school."

"That's it," Kaya said. "I knew I'd seen you before. I went to school with Ryan, too."

Alicia nodded with a slight smile. She was a quiet, shy girl. Ryan introduced her around and suddenly all the Divas were thrilled. She was nice enough and we all chatted for a few minutes, then Quinn got up to leave, taking the Duvals with him.

"So, it's his sister," Vanessa said. I was shaken out of my reverie. She'd been awfully quiet this whole time and now she was smiling coyly at me. "Not his girlfriend."

"Don't you think it's odd that he hangs out with his sister so much?" I said.

"She just got into town," Sophie said. "She was in vet-erinarian school in Colorado."

"Why do you know so much about the Duvals?"

She shrugged. "She's works at my vet's office now."

"How many times a week are you bringing a cat to the vet?" Kaya asked her.

"I get a feline charity discount."

"Well," I said. "I don't need to know about his life. Or hers."

"There's history there," Vanessa whispered, like it was something sinister.

Pari nodded. "Love drama. The worst drama there is."

"Is that a psychology truism?" I asked.

"Nah. Just my experience."

We all chuckled a bit.

"So, tell us what happened at that high school party Kaya told us about," Karen said. "You can't have such strong feelings against somebody without a good reason."

"He's my new landlord, remember? And he won't let me lease Mabel's space."

"That's not history," Pari said.

"Of course it is. Last week counts as history."

"She went out with him in high school and it just fizzled out," Vanessa shouted. "That's it. I'm sorry I made a big deal out of it."

I gave her a relieved and thankful look. But if she hand't brought it up in the first place, she wouldn't have had to rescue me from the Diva interrogation.

"She's right," Kaya said. "Let's stop with the Ryan nonsense. We're celebrating a Diva accomplishment. Well, the first step toward a Diva accomplishment."

We joined her in raising our glasses.

"To food trucks and smoothies," Kaya said.

We toasted with cheers.

"We didn't celebrate when you got a cat," Sophie said to me.

"To the cat," Pari said.

"Hear, hear!"

"To Melissa's date this Saturday," Vanessa said.

I was forced to drink to my own humiliation.

Chapter Twenty-one

By the time Saturday morning arrived, Dusty and I had established a cat/human routine that seemed to satisfy us both. She needed some play time at lunch and in the evening, but in the mornings she was content to lay about somewhere in my bedroom while I prepared for the day. After evening play she had her dinner and didn't seem to mind that I spent most nights out with Vanessa.

But that Saturday morning, she had other ideas in mind. It was as if she knew I was anxious about my mystery date. She didn't sit on the bed or the chair at my desk and watch me. She followed me everywhere. Into the kitchen for some water and a banana. Into the bathroom where she sat outside the shower meowing the entire time. On my dresser as I tried to find some casual clothes to wear, not knowing what to expect. And then to the door when Vanessa knocked. For a few seconds, I was afraid she'd try to run out when I opened it. Thankfully, she didn't.

"You can't wear that," Vanessa blurted out as soon as she saw me.

"Well hello to you, too" I was wearing jeans and a white t-shirt with daisies embroidered on the neckline and hem. Not my typical date attire. But I'd been told to dress casually.

Vanessa was wearing the cutest yoga pants and strappy top I'd ever seen on her.

"What is that pattern?" I said. "Is that…?"

"It's sloths."

I peered closer at her chest. "It is."

"I hope Sheldon is as curious as you are."

"Sheldon's going to be there? Does that mean Ryan will be there, too? Why is he everywhere I am?"

"Small town," she sang. "Go put on some stretchy pants."

"I don't like that sound of that," I grumbled. But I did as I was told. I ended up with my dull black bell-bottomed Zumba pants, a black sports bra covered partially with a black mesh tee.

"You don't expect Zumba to be such a dark activity," Vanessa said when I appeared from my bedroom, Dusty at my heels.

"It's not, typically. But I'm in a dark mood today. It matches my awareness of what's going to happen to me."

"Oh, don't be silly. I won't let any harm come to you." With a head scratch for Dusty, she was out the door beckoning me to my doom.

As she drove us north on US1, along the lagoon, I said, "Why was I supposed to wear something stretchy? Are we doing yoga? 'Cause I don't think that's a good date idea. Can you even talk during yoga?"

"You'll be fine."

"So it is yoga? It's not that hot yoga is it? Oh, I can't do that. In a hot room with a bunch of sweaty bodies, butts in the air."

"It's not yoga."

"Why are we going north? The paintball place was north. Is this like paintball?"

I only then realized that she was wearing sandals. "Am I wearing the right shoes?"

"You'll get shoes when you get there."

"We're going bowling? I didn't need stretchy pants to go bowling. Is it some crazy kind of stretch bowling? Am I going to be bowled?"

"You ask too many questions."

Well, she didn't take us to Pinky's Paintball—or to a bowl-your-friends alley—but just a few doors down to what looked like a gym. A metal building, three stories tall, at least.

"Dear god of spaghetti, no," I mumbled.

It was rock climbing.

Vanessa was laughing as she led me to the front door of Climber's High where a blast of cold air hit us as she pushed me into the lobby—a small area separated from the main floor with seating for observers, and what looked like parents, completely blasé about their children's fate as they scaled fake rocks, dangling high above the floor in the next room—a sight we were all treated to as there was only a glass barrier between us and the…danger zone.

As the kids' class was apparently ending, and children were running screaming into the front room, Vanessa and I met up with the group of adults waiting their turn. My date was Diego West.

"Oh, thank goodness," I said when he hugged me. I don't know who I was expecting, but just then, Diego seemed like the perfect choice for Vanessa. We saw him all the time and he was one of the nicest guys we knew. And not bad to look at. Dark hair and almost black eyes, a slightly smirky smile with dimples. And, I should add, not too symmetrical.

"You were expecting Sly Stallone?"

"Why would I?"

"That movie, *Cliffhanger*. Where he drops that girl into the canyon."

I stared at him, my stomach churning. "Why would you say that?"

He laughed. "It was just a movie."

"You'll be gentle, won't you?"

"Of course. I'm belay-certified."

"Delay sounds like a good plan."

Just as Vanessa had promised, everyone was there. Sophie and Reese, Pari and Sam, Karen and Kaya. Vanessa was already hanging with Sheldon, and Ryan was with a group of friends, some of whom I recognized

153

from around town. At least he didn't bring his grandfather. Although, wouldn't that be fun? Grumpy old fart Lionel Beardsley, helmet on his big ole' fat head, clinging to the side of a fake rock. I'd love to see that.

Somebody paid and we were all moved into the main room to another area where we got harnesses and shoes. The harness was basically belts and loops that you strap on and walk around in. Diego helped me put it on and I told him it felt like I was wearing a diaper. And the shoes! I told him they were too small and he just chuckled and shook his head.

"Newbie," he said.

At least the shoes were flexible. I could see where that might come in handy. Then Diego belayed me. And I told him to belay me really good. I didn't want to tumble to my death, or become a pile of broken bones. Apparently the belaying apparatus was the rope and anchor thing that would hold me up if I slipped off the doodads. And about those doodads. When I looked up at the huge rock I was about to climb, it looked like trash was stuck all over it. Colorful trash to be sure, but it was a mess. Turns out it was those little colorful knobbies, or holds, and tape. I was told to follow the green ones and I did my best.

First, I climbed up a few feet and fell off. Just for practice.

"So you don't get to the top and freeze," Diego said. "You got to know it's okay to fall. When you're ready to come down, you shout 'take.'" Then he put his hands on my shoulders and looked deep into my eyes. It would have been romantic if I hadn't been so terrified. "I got you," he said.

"You got me," I said, more to convince myself than anything.

I'll just say this, climbing up a few feet and falling a couple of times doesn't stop you from freezing when you find yourself a hundred feet up a fake wall getting ready to slip off a blue knobby that you didn't know how you managed to get onto, with Diego yelling "butt to the wall, butt to the wall" because you apparently weren't properly responding to "keep centered," when he was screaming that.

"How can I keep my butt to the wall when I'm facing it?" I shouted.

"I'm trying to speak your language," Diego said with a laugh.

It was all going so well. Sure, after a while the sounds of the gym combined into a dizzying hum and my arms were beginning to feel like jelly. I was doing everything I'd been told to do. Keeping my center of gravity over my feet—the butt to the wall position—and using my feet to guide my way up. But at some point, the sound clapped back loud in my ears, echoing around me like thunder, and when I looked at my foot, to find my next move, I realized how high off the floor I was. Diego looked like a Lego man and all the other little Lego people gathered around him were looking up at me. He was shouting something, but I couldn't make it out.

I froze. I froze like a Thanksgiving turkey. Talk about butt to the wall. I hugged that fake rock like I'd never let it go. And I was prepared to stay there. They had to send over a rescue team, one climber on each side of me, to gently talk me into falling. And I would only do it if they held on to me as I let go.

Not my proudest moment.

Once down, my knees buckled and I crumpled to the mat like a kindergartner. Diego and some of the instructors made everyone stay back, like they do when someone's having a heart attack. I caught sight of Ryan, looking at me as if I was going to die and it was his fault.

"Why was everyone staring at me?" was all I could manage to say.

"I was asking you if you were ready for me to take your weight," Diego said. "You'd just stopped. I guess I was shouting."

"I didn't hear anything."

"It happens," he said. "I think you're going to make a great climber."

"Oh, no," I said. "I'm never doing that again. How high was I? A hundred? Two hundred?"

Diego laughed. "Twenty feet, tops."

We all met for lunch at Burgers, in a back room I didn't even know existed. It was our first time rock climbing for all the Divas and we swapped stories.

"I thought you knew what you were doing," Sophie told me. "You looked so confident."

"And so fast," Pari said. "You were up the wall in just a few minutes."

"It's a blur," I said. "Honestly, I think I was just trying to get it over with. I had no idea I was that high up."

"Obviously," Diego chimed in.

Once everyone was wrapped up in their own conversations, I turned to him. "So, rock climbing is your thing?"

"It's one of my things."

"How many things do you have?"

He looked confused. "Many things. I enjoy the gym, the beach. I play ping pong in a league."

"There's a ping pong league?"

"At the community center. You should join us sometime."

"Why didn't we do that for our date? That would have been so much easier."

"But," with a nod to the Divas, "not as fun for them. Why have you let them do this to you? It's not really about finding your *amor verdadero*, is it?"

"*Amor* I know, but…"

"Your true love. The one you are meant to be with."

"In the beginning, it was about finding the guy that has supposedly been waiting for me to notice him. Isabella the psychic says he's out there. But, now it's more like retribution for my ghost challenges."

"The great Diva Ghost Hunting Adventure, as I've heard it called."

"The people of downtown sure are into each other's business."

"Blind dates as revenge," he chuckled. "Our date makes sense now. Well, am I the one?"

"You tell me? Have you been watching me from afar, waiting for your chance?"

He gazed at me with the smoldering eyes of a dashing

romance book cover model. "I can assure you, I'm not the waiting type."

"I see."

"That doesn't mean we couldn't be great together."

"I'll keep that in mind."

"And the ping pong invitation stands. You're welcome to come along with me anytime you like."

"Where do you find the time for anything outside your restaurant?"

"Please," he smiled and gestured to his domain. "This is a smooth machine. It gives me all the time I need for pinging and ponging."

"And rock climbing. Have you ever climbed a real rock?"

He laughed. "No thank you. Watch that movie. Only pretend rocks for me."

We left Diego to his restaurant and the Divas dispersed in the parking lot.

"So, Diego's not the one?" Vanessa asked as we walked to her car.

"He's a great guy."

"But no sparks."

"You'd think there would be some kind of bond after a guy harnesses you and sends you up a fake wall, but no."

"I heard him ask you to play ping pong with him."

"Somehow ping pong and rock climbing don't go together. You'd think his other pastimes would be cave diving and jumping out of airplanes."

"That's for people with a death wish. You should join him. There may be something there, you know. If you give it a try."

"Why do you care? This is just a game for you guys."

She said nothing as she unlocked her car. I climbed into the passenger seat and begged for the air conditioner.

"It's just a game, right?" I said once it was blowing warm air onto my face.

"Sure," she said. "I'm just rooting for my choice, that's all."

"I didn't think you were that invested."

"He's always flirting with you, even if you don't see

it."

"Well, we talked and we both agree that there's nothing there at this point."

"But there could be."

"Yeah there could be, Van. But Isabella said this guy already liked me. And I thought that was what this fix-up was all about. Not just about getting revenge on me for the ghost challenge."

"It can be a little of both."

"Anyway, I've been thinking about it. And with the holidays just around the corner, and the new food truck, and the cat, I really don't have time for a relationship."

"Not this again. Fine. If you don't want to relax and have some fun, I can't force you."

"We go out all the time. I have lots of fun."

"That's not relaxation. When we go out, you're just blowing off steam. It's like you party as hard as you work. When are you going to give yourself a break?"

We were both quiet until she pulled into my driveway and as I pushed open the car door, I said, "I play with the cat now. That's relaxing."

She laughed, shaking her head. "You'll never change."

Dusty meowed at me from the bedroom as I entered the cool house. I found her standing on the foot of the bed as if expecting some attention. So I sat beside her and gave her head some scratches.

"I've changed enough," I told her. "Now, I've got to get some work clothes on and head over to the café."

The cat made a *hmph* sort of noise, jumped to the floor, and walked out of the room.

"Not you, too."

Chapter Twenty-two

The week of Thanksgiving was always tinged with anticipated panic. It was as if everyone in Strawbridge was on edge, bouncing about in the holiday buffet line, waiting for the waiter to remove the velvet-covered rope so they could charge the pans full of turkey and cranberry sauce. People were planning their Black Friday shopping routes, deciding which store to storm at opening, and which store could wait until evening. And all of those people were aching to get into the holiday spirit early by coming out to Downtown Strawbridge.

Café Flamingo steadfastly refused to start serving peppermint smoothies or turkey and stuffing sandwiches —which I, through fiat, determined to be Christmas fare—until Black Friday and there were some lighthearted complaints. And not one holiday decoration would be put up until Thursday, when we were closed. It was a Downtown Strawbridge rule. The streets would be nearly empty on Thanksgiving Day while busy employees left their homes to sneak in back doors and deck their stores with green and red, inside and out.

Every year, one store was awarded the Best Holiday Decor ribbon. We'd won it three times in our five years of being in business. Once with our flamingo Santa, little flamingos on his lap and waiting in line to see him. Once with Flamingo Santa in a sleigh on the roof. That was when I was dating the owner of a roofing company; it was all his idea. And last year, we won with our flamingos dressed up as ballerinas with music from *The Nutcracker* playing all day. But last year, we flopped by rerunning the 'flamingos on Santa's lap' theme. Not even an honorable mention. Downtown Strawbridge demanded innovation.

This year, I had a new idea. And I was going to need at least one tall person. The tallest person I knew was Karen. But I didn't want to bother her. She'd be decorating the front window of Morgan's Office Supply and she was competition, after all. Morgan's didn't have the advantage of a sizable concrete space in front of their store, so they could only set up scenes in their window displays.

"It'll have to be Dean or Doug," Susanne told me on Monday morning as we were making our holiday plans, along with Lucy, my catering manager. We were sitting in the back booth, our usual meeting spot. "And a step stool."

"We have no other choice, I guess."

Catering orders had to be organized and prepped, with a schedule for setups and breakdowns. And our store was at the beginning of the parade route, set for the Saturday before Christmas. Unlike the City of Strawbridge, and the rest of the county, Downtown Strawbridge held its own parade late in the season, giving Strawbridge citizens yet one more reason to party.

We wanted to give out candy canes to the spectators who would watch the parade and then follow it down the blocked-off road to the other end of Strawbridge Avenue where Santa would climb out of his sleigh and take kids' gift orders from a gold throne on the usual Friday Fest stage.

"We only got half our candy cane order," Lucy said. "I've called them and they promised to have the rest by December fourteenth."

"That's cutting it close," I said. "Let's send someone out to the local stores with petty cash."

Seeing Pari, Karen, and Sophie entering the café, I scooted out of the booth. "Let me know if you need anything," I told my managers, and greeted the Divas at the front of the restaurant.

"You want a booth?"

"We just stopped by to give you fair warning," Pari said.

"Okay, but I was just talking to Susanne and Lucy and they reminded me that I can't do anything this weekend; the whole of downtown will be packed with shoppers and starving people."

"We know that," Sophie said.

"Your date is on Thursday," Pari said with a smile.

"We're all off on Thursday," Karen said.

"But what about Thanksgiving at your place?" I asked her.

"That's still on. It'll be lunch after your date."

My mind ran like mad through schedules and menus. "I guess that will work. But you know I have to decorate that evening."

"We all do," Sophie said.

"Not me," Pari said. "But my building's having a Thanksgiving party I have to go to. Anyway, I'll pick you up at eight."

"Can't one of you make me a date for the afternoon?"

"Not this time." Pari's smile was filled with laughter and I tried to think of what sort of horrible event might be happening on Thanksgiving Day that would make an awful date.

"Any hints?" I asked her.

"Nope."

"I suppose I have to wear casual clothes again."

"Definitely. Prepare to get dirty."

"Please tell me they don't do tractor pulls on Thanksgiving."

"Oh, they do," Sophie said. "But that's not it."

They ordered smoothies to go and we chatted while they waited, but I couldn't get anything more out of them. A Thanksgiving Day date. And I couldn't even dress up for it. What fun could that be? As I saw them to the door with their smoothies, I caught sight of Ryan Duval across Woodplum Street at Mabel's. She was standing in front of her little shop talking to him. I practically shoved the Divas out of the café and waited by the door, watching Ryan. If he came this way, I could talk to him without them seeing me. But if he headed the other way, I'd have to chase after him and it'd be all over the Diva network. Just my luck, he motioned a goodbye to Mabel and headed east, right in front of Pari and Karen. Sophie had apparently gone to Bookish. What choice did I have? I suppose I could have waited to talk to him another time, but I was stupidly determined. So, I bolted out the front door of Café Flamingo and ran. I crossed Woodplum without looking both ways, but it's a side street so I felt I could get away with it.

When I got close enough to Ryan, just past Bead It! next door to Mabel's, and right behind Karen and Pari, I called out to him. All three of them stopped and turned around. I pushed between the Divas and charged at him.

"I need to talk to you about Mabel's place," I said breathlessly.

Ryan glanced up at Karen and Pari and nodded a hello. "We've already settled it."

"No, we haven't. I really need a location close to Café Flamingo. And I'm going to be adding a food truck. The business is growing." I beamed like a little girl wanting validation.

"Where are you going to park a food truck?"

My mouth fell open slightly. I hadn't thought about that. "Well, I don't know."

"You're not parking it on the street in front of Mabel's space."

"It probably wouldn't fit, anyway." Parking along Strawbridge Avenue is notoriously tight. I didn't think that was the right time to mention my catering van. It would be great advertisement sitting out in front of the store.

"And I told you already," he said. "I'm looking for a shop. Not a business office."

"But it's perfect for me."

"It's not perfect for me."

"What if I sold something there, too?"

"Like what?"

"Macarons?"

He shook his head slightly. "You want to open a macaron shop so that you can operate a catering and food truck business out of it?"

"Yes?" I squeaked.

Looking up at the sky as if to ask the clouds why he found himself standing in front of a crazy woman, he said, "That's nuts."

I took a defiant step towards him. "It's really rotten of you not to honor my agreement with Mr. Jenkins." I'd obviously lost the battle by that point.

He looked down at me, put his hands on his hips, and nearly growled. We stood there like that for a few too many seconds and I can't speak for him, but I felt ridiculous. Unfortunately, I wasn't going to stop just because I was making a fool of myself. That's just not the Melissa, Strawbridge Business Icon, way. And, once again, for the tiniest second, I thought he was going to kiss me. Why was I always thinking that? Just before he vomited all over me. Just before he fell into that cactus. At paintball. When would I learn?

Breaking the spell, he nodded at Karen and Pari, still standing behind me, watching my humiliation. "Good seeing you again." Then he turned and continued on his way.

"Macarons?" Pari said.

"It was worth a try," I said.

"What's a macaroon, then?" Karen said.

We both looked at her.

"Is macaron a fancy way of saying macaroon?"

"You explain it to her, Pari," I said. "I'll see you two later."

Dejected, and somewhat flushed, I returned to the café. Where *was* I going to park a food truck?

Chapter Twenty-three

On Wednesday, Vanessa and I went to The Fort for Improv Night to watch Kaya and her group perform. I couldn't enjoy it; I spent the whole time fearing they'd drag me up onto the stage again. Vanessa made me leave early because, and she said it like a mother hen, "Tomorrow's a big day."

I was ready at eight o'clock the next morning when Pari showed up looking cute in brightly colored yoga pants and an oversized tee. Her long, black hair was pulled back into a pony tail and a garment bag was slung over her shoulder.

"Gobble, gobble," she said as I let her in.

"Not a turkey shoot! I won't kill a turkey."

She laughed so loud Dusty ran back into the bedroom. "I would never make you kill anything. But you might wish you were dead when we're finished with you."

"But it's Thanksgiving."

"Exactly. You'll be so hungry once we eat, you won't think twice about how much you cram in."

"Do I need to put some dirtier clothes on?"

"Not dirtier," she said looking me up and down. "Just stretchier. Like me."

"I don't like the sound of this," I mumbled as I went to my bedroom to change.

"I need to store my fancy clothes here," she said after I'd got my proper clothes on and we were ready to leave. "I figure we can change here after, and then head over to Karen's for Thanksgiving lunch."

"Is it lunch if it's at two o'clock?"

"Linner, then."

Naturally, she drove us north of town, where all the best torture happens. But when she pulled into the plaza where Climber's High was, I started to protest.

"I already did rock climbing."

"But you didn't get to see what else they have there. There's a whole other section on the other side of the building."

"Great."

She parked outside Ninja Play, a bright blue and yellow spot painted with cartoons of people jumping, swinging on what looked like chandeliers, and getting punched in the face by boxing gloves on sticks.

"How can they make that look fun?" I said. "Am I going to get hit in the face?"

"Not if you're good."

"Good at what?"

She pulled open the front door and let me into a brightly lit, air conditioned cavern filled with… contraptions.

"No," I said. It looked like a huge course of obstacles. People were jumping over things, falling into pits of foam and balls, leaping from one spot to the next over pools of…goo?

"How is this place open on Thanksgiving?"

"The holidays are the best time to come. Much less crowded. Tildon," Pari said when he joined us. "Tildon Frakes, meet Melissa Stathem. Mel, I've told him all about you."

"And me nothing about him." I looked up…way up. If I stood on my tiptoes I could kiss his chest.

"Is that so?" Tildon said. He had lovely pale green eyes that I'd only be able to see when he looked down at me, unfortunately.

"She knows a little." Pari turned to me, scolding. "I've

166

told you about Tildon before."

I shrugged. "If it's not restaurant related, it doesn't stay in my brain."

Tildon laughed. "I know exactly what you mean."

"You run a restaurant?" I followed him to the counter where Pari paid our entrance fee.

"I'm an attorney."

"And this is how you unwind between cases?"

He smiled and led me to the lockers where Pari and I stored our purses. "This is my first time, actually."

"So it was Pari's idea."

"Yeah, but I'm game if you are. It looks like a lot of fun. And I'm told there are showers if you get into the goop."

"Nice."

There were, as it turned out, four different courses that ran from the front of the building to the back. No walls or coverings were between them so while you were struggling to, say, jump from one platform to another without getting hit with the huge, soft—but not as soft as they make it out to be—hammer that keeps popping out to slam into you, you had to be careful not to get distracted by the person hanging from a swinging twirly thing next to you, even if they were screaming like a madwoman.

The ultimate goal of Ninja Play was to, at some point in your Ninja Play membership, make it through all four courses without an error. Apparently, only three people had managed to do so since the place opened. Judging by my performance on level one, someone like me would take about thirty years to master every course. And probably a few more to do them all consecutively without falling into a goo pit. And to make it more exciting—yay! —it's timed.

On the baby course that we started on, the goal was to do it within five minutes. But there wasn't a buzzer, and we didn't get booted off the course if time ran out, like courses three and four—which I pledged never to attempt. We were given all the time we needed and that was pretty much why, Pari told me, a lot of people avoided it. The other courses boot you out as soon as your time is up. Only one person is allowed on the course at a time. So Pari and Tildon waited while I went first.

Obstacle one, jump onto a moving merry-go-round of spinning foamy upright tubes, and jump off again at the opposite side onto a slide. But don't slide to the bottom, or you'll end up in a tub of goo. Instead, slide just to the middle, grabbing onto one of the rings dangling from above as you pass underneath. Then—as the rings are moving—let it drag you off the slide, and let go over a tall cylindrical post about two feet wide. Did I say just let go? Well, sure. You just let go. And drop a few feet onto this post, landing in such a way that you don't fall right off it, into a huge bin of foamy balls. If you manage to stay standing on the post, there's a rope, the end of which is hooked over the edge at your feet. And if you get that without falling off, you use it to swing over to a ledge. The struggle goes on and on.

On my first try, the foamy upright tube of the merry-go-round flung me off into the foam pit below. I had to get to the side of the course and walk alongside it, all the way to the end and make my way back up front to stand in line and try again. The second time, I slid right into the goo. An employee wiped the excess goo off me and let me leave, only to do the same thing on my third attempt. On go four, as the ring dragged me off the slide, I fell into the ball pit. On my fifth time, I made it all the way to the rope swing, grabbed hold and swung. Back and forth, back and forth. Until I dropped into the ball pit.

Meanwhile, Pari made it all the way through on her fourth try and Tildon, like me, gave up on his sixth attempt. Because it was time to go.

"Do you want to shower?" Tildon asked me.

"What?" I must have looked startled because he quickly apologized.

"The goo, I mean. If you're going to shower, I will. Otherwise, I'll do it at home."

"I, uh…"

"It's not together," he said, still flustered. "They're individual."

Finally I laughed. "Of course. What do you think, Pari?"

Tildon and I weren't entirely covered in goo. There were towels at the end of the course that we dried off with when we fell into it.

"I've got a big towel you can sit on," she said.

"That was amazing," Tildon said as we gathered our things from the lockers. "Thanks for suggesting it, Pari."

"I'm glad you had fun."

Back out into sunlight, the strange echo of sounds from Ninja Play still in our heads, we stood in the parking lot.

"So it's off to Karen's now?" Tildon said. "After we change clothes, of course."

"We'll see you there," I said. There was an awkward second or two where it seemed neither of us knew the appropriate behavior at that point. Do we shake hands? Hug or kiss? None of them felt right, so I just waved as Pari and I headed to her car.

"You didn't get any goo on you," I told her. "But you can shower at my place, anyway."

"Appreciated," she said. "I don't think I realized how sweaty I was going to be.

We made it to Karen's, Pari in a pretty floral wrap-around and me in a peach sundress and a lacy bolero— one of the bonuses of Florida living is wearing light clothing during much of the holidays. Karen lives in a condo across the street from the beach. From Downtown Strawbridge, after leaving my house, Pari drove us over the huge causeway bridge and through the swanky little beach town, then south on A1A. We made it there by two o'clock where Tildon and I were pushed together for a tour of the place.

"I've been here before," I protested.

"Tildon hasn't."

I couldn't argue with that. The entire home was decked out in oranges, browns, and yellows, down to the throw pillows. The girl must have a storage locker somewhere just for her seasonal decor. We walked through the spacious living room already filled with guests, then bypassed the kitchen for the bedrooms. Karen had one set up as a den or office, very comfy, and the guest bedroom had a sofa and chairs with a TV and bookshelves.

"So, no sleepovers for Karen, huh?"

"The sofa is a pull-out," Pari sniped. "Master bedroom is off limits, but you can peek in."

"Seen it," I said.

"I haven't," Tildon said. "Nice."

We stood at the door ogling Karen's gorgeous queen-sized, shell-themed comforter, her beautiful oak furniture, but mostly, the French doors leading out to a balcony from which she must be able to view the ocean.

"Okay, back to the kitchen," Pari said.

We said hi to all the guests again, most of whom I already knew—the Divas, of course, Pari's Sam, Sophie's Reese. Some downtown folks. We were given plates in the kitchen and filled them with Thanksgiving foods inhabiting not only on the little round table, but all the countertops, as well.

"Karen must have spent all day yesterday on this feast," I said.

Tildon and I were starving and as we'd not been there for the *hors d'oeuvres*, we were first in line for turkey, dressing, mashed potatoes, Brussels sprouts, candied carrots, sweet potatoes topped with brown sugar and pecans, and yes, I also put two spoonfuls of old-fashioned green bean casserole, gloopy with Campbell's Cream of Mushroom soup and topped with crispy onions, onto my huge platter.

"Are you really going to eat all of that?" Tildon asked.

"Watch me."

As we left the kitchen to find a place to sit in the dining room, Karen, wearing an apron that made it look like she had a turkey—in a top hat, no less—plastered to her body, came up behind us and forced us out onto her little back porch, another balcony from which we could gaze out to the Atlantic, and where there was a table for two set up, covered with a brown and gold plaid cloth.

"They don't want us to forget this is a date," Tildon

said when she left to grab us some drinks.

A cool breeze wafted in from the ocean and a group of seagulls somewhere out of sight squealed, as a flying V of brown pelicans glided by.

"Do you go on many blind dates?" I asked him.

"I went on one when I was first out of college. It was a disaster."

"What happened?"

"When I showed up at the restaurant, it turned out that we knew each other. She'd been in my torts class."

"Those cakes with a bunch of thin layers?"

"No. Torts, like civil wrongs."

"As opposed to civil rights."

He laughed. "Pari didn't tell me you were so funny."

"So, it wasn't really a blind date."

"And we hated each other."

"Why?"

"I'm not entirely sure. You know how some people just rub you the wrong way? They take one look at you and think they know you and everything you say just makes them mad?"

"I'm not sure I do."

"Well, that's how it was with me and Rachel Platte. I almost married her, though."

"Now who's the funny one?"

Pari showed up with a Diet Coke for me and an iced tea for Tildon. "How's everything going?"

"Just fine, thanks," Tildon told her.

"You can join the party for dessert," she said.

"You mean you won't lock us out?" I said.

She rolled her eyes and disappeared again.

"This date isn't totally blind, either," Tildon said in between bites of turkey.

"That's true, I guess. I've seen you at the café."

"And there was that other time. A few years ago. At a party. Ben Ward's I think. We were introduced."

"You have a great memory."

"It helps with the job."

"Did Pari tell you what this whole blind date thing is about?"

"Yeah, no worries. She was sure to explain that it was all in good fun. Not that you or I couldn't find dates on our own. Not that I *can* find dates. I mean, I could. But I really don't."

"You don't have to explain it to me. Who has time to date?"

"Right. Or even the predilection."

"Predilection?"

"The desire."

"You don't want to date?"

"Honestly, if I could just skip to the marriage bit, I would."

"I hear you can have them mailed in from faraway."

He laughed. "I guess I mean that...I find dating tedious. We spend time getting to know someone and then have to do it all over again with someone new until we find the one we want to spend the rest of our lives with, often to find we were wrong and have to start the process all over again. There's got to be a better way."

He had a point. "And who has time for all of that? I'm not sure I'm the marrying type, anyway."

"Are your parents divorced?"

"No."

"That's usually why people don't want to get married, isn't it? Poor role models."

"I just work too hard."

"But work can't be everything, can it?"

"It is for me. I love it."

"Have you talked to Pari about this?"

"Why would I do that?"

"I have an idea she'd tell you that you're working all the time to avoid something."

"There's nothing to avoid. I have no other interests."

"So, you're avoiding yourself."

"Huh?"

He chuckled and stuck a forkful of mashed potatoes into his mouth. Finally, he said, "I heard something a long time ago. If I'm remembering it correctly it goes, 'The most important relationship in your life is the relationship you have with yourself.'"

"Was that Freud or Socrates?"

"Diane Von Furstenberg."

I nearly spit Diet Coke on him when I laughed. "You are so funny."

"But it's true. If you can't spend time alone, doing nothing but being with yourself, how can you really know what you want?"

"So, you spend time alone?"

"I meditate every morning and bike to work to clear my head, inhale the nature all around me, and prepare for the day."

Ick. Thank goodness we didn't have a meditation date. I'd never have made it through.

Chapter Twenty-four

When we carried our nearly empty plates back into the kitchen, there was a flurry of cleaning and organizing going on. Trays of food and plastic storage bins with lids were being placed on the dining room table for everyone to take home leftovers while desserts were displayed on the kitchen table along with small plates. Pumpkin pie, apple pie, cherry pie.

"Karen, you've got every pie possible here," I said as my plate was taken from me, cleaned off and put into the dishwasher before I realized what had happened.

"Into the living room," Karen said. "You're up for karaoke."

Tildon, standing beside me, laughed. "I can't sing."

"Neither can I."

"Doesn't matter." She turned us around and gave us a little push.

The living room was packed with guests and I caught sight of Ryan Duval. "Great," I muttered.

"What is it?"

"Why is Ryan Duval everywhere I am?"

"You think he's stalking you?"

I looked up at Tildon, just to make sure he wasn't serious. I didn't want anyone making a police report. "I think it's more like sabotage."

His face twisted up in confusion.

"Okay, everybody," Karen said, wiping her hands on her turkey apron. "It's karaoke time."

"Karaoke with a twist," Pari said.

"Ugh," I said to Tildon. "I don't like twists."

"You get the music," Karen said.

"But not the words," Pari said.

"We have to sing from memory?" Sophie said.

"Nope," Karen said. "You have to make up your own words."

Everybody loved the idea, if you want to call groans and laughs and anxiety love.

"And there will be prizes," Karen said.

Tildon and I hung back, neither of us wanting to be first…or participate at all. There were three acts before I was forced to the front of the room. Vanessa, always up for humiliation if it meant fun, was first. She sang to the tune of "Island Girl" by Elton John. She started out really great with "I'm a girl, who likes to party all over the world." But from there, she went off the rails with singing stuff about cutting hair that didn't rhyme, until she was shouted off the makeshift stage—the spot in front of the room where the karaoke machine and microphone were.

Reese Fuller was second. I never thought of Sophie's guy as a singer, but he had a good voice. And standing there, with the mic in his hand, he kind of looked like a smoldering crooner. But he chose that Eurythmics song, "Sweet Dreams," singing "My pants are way too tight, I won't make it through the night," and then he too started muttering nonsense and was booed back into the crowd.

Next was Ryan. As soon as he stepped up to the mic, my heart raced and my face grew hot. It was as if, suddenly, he wasn't Ryan Duval, landlord or Ryan Duval, the guy I hardly ever spoke to anymore. He was my friend from school. That guy I loved hanging out with over lunch, joking around with in English Lit class. We used to curl up under blankets on the bleachers during December football games and share a hot chocolate. And there he was, the guy I had a secret crush on, in Karen Morgan's living room, singing to the tune of Right Said Fred's "I'm

Too Sexy."

"I'm so hungry for dessert, so hungry for dessert, so hungry, it hurts. I'm too hungry for that pie, too hungry for a pie, I cannot lie." Then he trailed off with "I'm running out of words, I don't know what to sing, I…"

He looked up at me, smiling, as he was booed back into the crowd and it seemed as if he saw me as that girl in school always cheering him on, telling him he could get an A in Trig even though he hated it. Or helping him practice for speech class.

With that weird, hollow, nostalgia making me tremble, it was suddenly my turn. I'd already been handed the song list and chose "I Shot the Sheriff" by Clapton. I gathered all my nerves and sang, "I ate the turkey, but I did not eat the Brussels sprouts." Applause. I was on a roll. "I ate the turkey, but I did not eat the Brussels sprouts. Karen told me to eat my veggies. And I put some on my plate. But when it came time to put them in my mouth, I spat, I spat them out. I said. I ate the turkey, but I did not eat the Brussels sprouts."

Needless to say, I won the Golden Turkey Karaoke Award, which was a dozen of Karen's famous chocolate chip cookies, and all the leftover Brussels sprouts. Tildon bombed trying to come up with words to "Maniac" from *Flashdance*. But he did the little tippy-toe dance the whole time so it went on much longer than it should have. All in all, while it was embarrassing, and a little scary, the whole experience was a good one.

After everyone had pie, the party settled into its ending. Tildon and I found Pari and Karen in the kitchen and thanked them for setting us up.

"No offense to Tildon, Pari, but I'm glad it's over."

"Was it that bad?" Karen said.

"Not the dinner part. This was great. Even the karaoke was pretty fun."

"And you won."

"But the obstacle course thing. Never again. I'd rather go skydiving."

"Skydiving, huh?" Karen said. "Mental note."

"I was joking," I said, panicked. "Please, I beg you. I

don't want to die."

She laughed. "Is there any skydiving around here? How would I even set that up?"

When they found out Tildon would be driving me home, they giggled like four-year olds. When I told Tildon to drop me at the café because my staff and I were decorating for the holidays, he volunteered to help out.

"That'd be great," I told him. "We actually need a tall person."

"Alas, you only want me for my body. And you're admitting you don't hire tall people. I feel a discrimination lawsuit pending."

"It's harder to boss around tall people when you're five foot two."

"Anything you say can and will be used against you in court."

We found Café Flamingo hopping with activity. Susanne, Petra, and Lydia had brought in trays of cookies and snacks, while Doug supplied eggnog, spiked and tee-totaled. The store's sound system blasted out holiday tunes and everyone was jolly hard at work. Out front, they'd already loaded up the tables and chairs into Dean's pick-up truck and driven them over to our little storage unit uptown. We needed half the space out front for our sidewalk sale tomorrow, and the other half would house our seasonal display. Luckily, the café's overhang had gutters already outfitted with hooks for holiday lights. They'd provide the perfect way to attach the plastic sheeting that we planned to drop down every evening after closing, in hopes that no one would mess with our display overnight. Downtown Strawbridge wasn't known for rowdy after-hours behavior, but we'd had a protest or two, so you could never be too careful.

I'd sent Riley off the night before with petty cash to find us a tall fake tree and he didn't disappoint. We placed it on the slab in front of our store at the corner of Woodplum and Strawbridge. Its stand was weighted with bags of sand so it wouldn't topple over if we got a strong wind from the lagoon.

Lucy had already ordered, and received, more plastic

lawn-ornament flamingos. This design would require more than our usual of nine. Tildon helped us stack the flamingos atop each other so that it looked as if they were towering ants, working to hold up the highest one as he, or she—it's hard to tell with plastic—attempted to put a mini flamingo on the top of the tree, like a star. We had the mini flamingo pinned to the tip of a fake pink wing made out of popsicle sticks, it being glued to the flamingo. I could only hope it held all season. We attached all the flamingos together as best we could with stick-on Velcro and twisty ties, and the base was made sturdy by strapping them together—they looked like a gaggle of nutty birds facing this way and that—with pink tape and sticking their legs into a slab of Styrofoam covered with glued-on sand. It looked like a beachy flamingo pyramid gone wrong. Thirty-nine flamingos in all.

"We forgot to decorate the tree," Dean said, shoving two round, green-iced cookies into his mouth at once. "We beffer be kefful."

And so, as Tildon held the flamingos steady, we first layered the tree with twinkle lights and then covered it with balls and trinkets.

"I brought my old tree skirt," Lydia said. "I'll get it while you guys wrap boxes."

We'd been collecting empty boxes for a few weeks and everyone donated some holiday wrapping paper and bows. In the end, we had a fantastic holiday display, as long as nobody punched the tower of flamingos, we were all set. And anyway, one of us could just run outside and stand them back up again—we figured, hoped, *prayed*.

As we all stood in the street that early evening admiring our handiwork, other store employees around us were doing the same in front of their shops. We turned to look across at Bookish to find they'd put Santa in their window display, reading books to dolls and teddy bears. Old Geezer's antiques next door to Sophie's place had Santa hanging halfway off the edge of the roof and two reindeer up on their hind legs pulling off the icon's red trousers.

"Reindeer don't have opposable thumbs," Tildon said.

"That just wouldn't happen."

We all laughed.

"Hey, Melissa," Sophie called from the door of Bookish.

I waved.

"Did you know that a group of flamingos is called a flamboyance?"

"Seriously?" I yelled.

"I just looked it up. Happy Thanksgiving!"

"What's all this?"

I turned to find Ryan Duval standing on the sidewalk looking at our display.

I gave him a 'duh' look. "A flamboyance of flamingos, obviously. You like it?"

He pointed to the overhang with the plastic tenting rolled up and tied along the edge. "What's that?"

"We can't bring our display in every night," I said. "So we're going to lower the sheeting to hide it. The whole front and side of our store will be covered.

He shook his head. "That's not gonna fly. Your store's got to be accessible if there's a fire or something."

"Oh, and the fire department will never get through that thin plastic tenting. Not those burly guys."

"It's a code violation."

"Like you know the code."

"I'm the landlord. It's my job to know the code."

"It's no problem," Tildon said. "Hi, Tildon Frakes, attorney." He and Ryan shook hands. "We can rearrange the sheeting so that it only covers the display. That whole side on Woodplum and this side here in front, along with the door, will be exposed."

Ryan looked peeved and I smiled sweetly at him.

After a curt nod, he said. "Do that."

"We will," I said.

"Then get on with it."

"You're going to watch? You don't trust me?"

"I'm the one who gets hit with the fine if you don't."

"Okay, fine."

He laughed.

"What?" I said.

"You said fine."

I looked at him. No emotion. Oh, I got the joke. But I wasn't going to give him the satisfaction. "Go inside and get some eggnog and cookies." I'd practically yelled at him to enjoy himself and as I watched him enter the café, I caught sight of Susanne. She winked at me, conspiratorially.

"All right then, flamingo stackers," Tildon said. "Let's see if we can figure this out."

It was almost dark by the time we'd reconfigured the sheeting. It required our very tall ladder and our very tall volunteer to get hooks along the inner parts of the overhang that angled upward toward the building. The angled parts would remain partially unfurled all the time, making them even with the outer edge of the overhang, and easier for us to lower and raise as needed.

"I don't think I thought this through completely," I told Tildon as he was preparing to leave. "We have our work cut out for us."

"But think of the glory if you win the contest."

"When we win."

"I like your confidence. So, despite my not being—" air quotes—"the one. I had a great time today. I've never had a date that lasted all day before. Except when I was six and I went to spend the day with Patty Hamilton…or Nixon?"

"One president or another."

"The day was memorable, but alas, she was not."

"I still remember my first date. Petey Something-or-other. His mommy took us to the park."

"Perhaps this is why we are both so against dating in general. Started too young."

"Burned out too soon. Yes."

"Well, I have to ask…did your other dates kiss you goodnight? Is that appropriate?"

"In today's litigious environment, I appreciate your asking."

"Your face says otherwise."

I chuckled and said, "I think a light, friendly kiss will be acceptable, your honor."

"That would be 'counsel.' Only the judge is honorable, I'm afraid."

"I should have known."

"Well, I'll see you around, then." Leaning over, he kissed me. Light and friendly, just as I asked. And with a smile, he turned and walked away.

"Your new boyfriend is really tall," Ryan said from behind me causing me to jump.

I turned and shot him a glare. "He's not my boyfriend."

"You've been seeing a lot of people lately."

"It's really none of your business."

He sighed. "Look, I'm your landlord now. I know it's awkward—"

"It is not."

"—but maybe we should call a truce."

"I'm sure you'd like that."

"I would. I'd like you to stop complaining to people about Mabel's storefront."

"If the people of downtown don't mind—"

"That's not the point, Melissa. What the other business owners want is irrelevant. I'm doing what's good for downtown. They'll thank me when I find a great new shop for that space and it brings in more business. It'd mean more business for you, too."

I let my eyes drop from his face to his shoulder. He had really great shoulders. God, I hated it when he was right.

"You know I'm right about this," he said.

And he could read my mind.

"I need a space close to the restaurant to run the catering and food truck out of."

"An office space."

"No, Ryan. A place where customers can come and sample food for their events."

"So, an office with seating?"

"And a kitchen."

"There's no kitchen at Mabel's."

"Sure there is. It used to be a bakery."

"That was years ago."

"The plumbing's still set up. I could build a kitchen. I need one so I don't have to use the café for catering. I want to expand beyond sandwiches and fruit plates." To be honest, I hadn't considered that until recently and certainly wasn't committed to the idea. But now that I'd said it, I was all for it. I'd still want to stick close to the Café Flamingo brand, of course. But think of the possibilities.

"Earth to Melissa," Ryan said. "I can almost literally see the wheels turning behind your eyes."

I hadn't realized I was staring at him again.

"Look," he said. "Let's just move past this."

"Okay," I said, giving in.

"Truce, then?"

"You are my landlord. I don't have much choice."

"I was hoping…"

"Mel," Lucy called. "The flamboyance is falling!"

I stumbled past Ryan as the few of us still hanging around outside rushed to right the leaning tower of flamingos. By the time we moved a bag of sand from under the tree to hold down the flamingo's foam base, I turned to look for Ryan. But he was gone.

Chapter Twenty-five

Black Friday was exhausting. With a quick neck scratch, I said good-bye to Dusty, promising to check in as soon as possible, and was at the café by eight o'clock. Shoppers were already meandering the streets on both sides of Strawbridge as store employees were dragging their sales tables out front and loading them with deals.

We rolled up the plastic tenting to reveal our flamingo display and Dean brought extra sandbags from his truck that he'd spray-painted ingeniously to look like boulders. We used them to hold down our flamingo base and returned the other one to under the tree. Then we hauled out two six-foot foldout tables, bedecked them with pink and green cloths and brought out our boxes of goodies. Croissants, cookies, and muffins. And we had all of our Café Flamingo logo items on sale: Flamingo key chains, mugs and insulated cups, hats and tees, and our new Café Flamingo Christmas tree ornament, a flamingo in a Santa hat with our logo at the bottom.

We were packed from nine in the morning until nine that night—the minimum required closing time for all stores downtown on Black Friday. Some stores stayed open until eleven, but nine was as long as we were willing to serve food and still get our employees out and home at a decent hour. Black Friday was probably the only Friday night of the year that I didn't go out after work. It was back home to Dusty and bed because I had to get up and do it all over again on Saturday. And Saturday night I was meeting up with Vanessa at The Fort.

Dusty didn't seem to mind that I'd spent so little time with her on Friday, and on Saturday morning, as I got ready for work, I told her it would be another long day. She meowed a bit and let me scratch under her chin. But I was worried. Maybe another cat *would* be a good idea.

"You want a friend?" I asked her.

She purred.

"I'll think about it. But it won't mean I'm going to be a crazy cat lady. Just so you know."

Having a cat was so much more wonderful than I thought it would be. I could talk out loud when there weren't any other people around and not worry that I was going crazy. As I left, I promised her I'd visit a few times to check in and she ignored me. She was the perfect pet.

The day at Café Flamingo went smoothly. The flamingo tower only toppled once and it fell against the front window, rather than onto the sidewalk and street, so that's a plus. And after a quick break at home and a change of clothes, I drove over to The Fort and found Vanessa on the second floor at our favorite table overlooking the dance floor, with Kaya and Sophie. There wasn't a band that night, so the music was loud enough to dance to, but not so loud we couldn't hear ourselves think.

"Where's Reese?" I asked Sophie as I sat down next to her, opposite Vanessa who sat next to Kaya.

"Well, hello to you too," Kaya said.

"Sorry, hi all."

"I mean," Kaya said, "the girl can go out without her man attached."

"Really?" I said. "It happens so rarely."

Sophie laughed and ran her fingers above her right ear, tucking her short hair behind it.

"Ready for a trim?" Vanessa asked her.

"Maybe. Or maybe I'll grow it out. I've worn it super short for so long."

"I'd go short," I said. "Except that I'd look like an elf."

"Not me," Kaya said. "This is the perfect length for me. I will die with shoulder-length hair."

"Aren't we all supposed to go shorter as we age?" I said. "Seems like I read that somewhere."

"Same place you read we can't wear midriffs after thirty?"

"Seriously," Vanessa said. "Remember that poem about wearing purple. Sophie what did you say it was called?"

"I don't remember."

"It was like, two weeks ago."

"That was a month ago, at least."

"Anyway," Vanessa said. "We can do what we want."

"But that poem was about doing what you want once you get really old," I said. "We need a poem about doing what we want right now. Any time. At any age."

"Karen wants to be a writer," Kaya said. "Tell her to write one."

Sophie said, "I'm not sure novel writing and poetry use the same skill set."

"Of course they do," Kaya said. "You write out what you want to say and then just keep chipping away at the words until you're left with a poem. Doesn't seem that difficult to me."

"You write one then," I said.

"I can't write," she said with a laugh.

"So, how's the Pink Diva Man Hunter Plan working out?" Sophie said, probably desperate to change the subject.

"Well, on the one hand, none of the guys you've picked so far have been the one Isabella was talking about."

"Or they just won't admit it," Vanessa said.

"Nah, I think I'd know," I said. "But on the other hand, I've been shot with paint balls, carried down from a wall, fallen into goo, and forced to sing karaoke with my squeaky voice. So I'm sure the plan's going great for you all."

"There's the one that got away," Sophie said.

I turned to find her looking over the railing to the dance floor. I stood a bit out of my chair and, following her gaze I saw Ryan Duval dancing with a girl.

"Why is he everywhere I am?" I said, plopping back down in my seat.

"It's Downtown Strawbridge," Kaya said. "Everybody's here."

"And he's not the one that got away," I said. "I never had him."

"But did you want him?" Vanessa said with a wink. "I wonder if Sheldon is here."

"You're not going to look for him are you?" I said. "This was supposed to be our night out."

"I heard he's found someone to lease Mabel's store," Sophie said.

"It better not be a doctor's office or anything like that, or I'll sue him."

"Wow," Vanessa said. "Not Saturday night vibes, Mel."

"It's called Poppin' Shop. Gourmet popcorn, popped and kernels. And some other specialty stuff like nuts, I think."

"Like we need another food venue," I said.

"You'd think he wouldn't want a place that would compete with Café Flamingo," Kaya said. "Seeing as he's your landlord, too."

"This stuff is more like you'd buy as gifts," Sophie said. "I don't think you can get popcorn to go."

"Still," I said. "I don't like it."

Vanessa said, "You wouldn't like anything in that space."

They all laughed and I let a smile touch my lips. "Maybe not."

"Hello, Divas," Ryan said and I jumped.

"We were just talking about you," Vanessa said.

I looked around for the girl he'd been dancing with, but he was alone.

"Is that right?"

"We hear you're renting Mabel's space to a popcorn shop," I said. "Another food place, right across from Café

Flamingo?"

"It's not a restaurant," he said. "And you don't serve popcorn."

"Maybe I'll start."

"Anyway, it's not a done deal."

"Where's Sheldon?" Vanessa asked with a glare at me.

"You wouldn't believe it. His company set up for a wedding over on the beach for some millionaire, and some of the guests took the canopies apart and used the tenting to toss people up in the air or something crazy like that. They lost a bunch of them in the ocean and Shel—"

"They lost people in the ocean?" I said.

"The canopies, not the guests. Anyway, Shel and his guys rented boats to try to get them back."

If you asked me, Ryan was a little drunk.

"Seriously?" Vanessa said.

"Yeah, they also threw all the chairs into the host's pool. Those nice padded chairs, too. All ruined."

"I had no idea the chair and table rental business could be so exciting," Sophie said.

"I could tell you some stories about catering," I told her.

"I actually came up to see if any of you would like to dance," Ryan said. But he wasn't look at all of us; he had his eyes on Kaya.

"No thanks," I said, anyway. "I've seen you dance."

"I'd be happy to," Kaya said.

As soon as they left, Vanessa scolded me. "That was mean."

"It's a joke. He knew I was teasing. If he even heard me. Anyway, there's your proof. The guy does not like me."

"Or," Sophie said, "he's trying to make you jealous."

"That's real mature," I said.

"Isn't that what we're trying to do with Pat and Buddy, and Trudy and Mr. Cornell?" Vanessa said. "What are we calling that again?"

"The Quadruple Fix-up Conspiracy," I said.

"The *Great* Quadruple Date Conspiracy," Sophie said.

"Whatever, if it works for them, it could be working

for you, Mel."

"How many times do I have to tell you? The guy's not into me. If anything, it looks like he's into Kaya."

"Eh," Sophie said. "Maybe."

I couldn't see Ryan and Kaya dancing without standing up and towering over Sophie to get a good look. And I wasn't about to let anyone know I cared.

Chapter Twenty-six

That first full week of the holidays that follows Thanksgiving flew by in a whirlwind. This time of year was always my favorite. The air started to turn cool and there was the promise of a really cold day here and there. Downtown smelled like cinnamon and chocolate. And holiday music rang out, echoing back and forth across the street as people strolled along, window shopping.

In years past, I'd work from seven in the morning until ten or so at night, then go out with Vanessa for a drink or two, dance wildly, and then flop into bed only to get up the next day and do it again. I felt as if I thrived when I had dozens of things to do at once and millions to do in a day. I think I often defined success as the ability to multi-task like nobody else. But this year, while I loved being at the restaurant and helping out with catering, I was relieved to have Dusty as an excuse to work regular hours and spend more time at home. I had food in my refrigerator for the first time and started baking cookies and holiday breads.

A simple call once or twice a day to check in was all I needed to feel confident that business was running smoothly. I was beginning to think of success in terms of my team, not just myself.

The Wednesday after I watched Kaya and Ryan take

to the dance floor at The Fort, she placed an order for lunch and specifically asked for me to deliver it. She'd done that a few times. Once when she had a dress in stock that she wanted me to try on. Once when she wanted to talk about our five-year high school reunion. And once to help her get gum out of her hair—she'd held somebody's toddler while they tried on clothes.

But this time, I think she wanted to talk about Ryan Duval. We were all seniors together, after all. She and Ryan hung out sometimes, because he was one of those guys that was friends with everybody. But she and I only had a few classes together; we were friendly enough, just not technically friends—until we became Downtown Divas.

I waited in Kaya Vintage Clothing, relishing in the relative quiet, as Kaya finished up with a customer and sent her on her way with a new old dress in a garment bag before handing over the sandwich and chips in a white paper bag with a pink flamingo on it.

"Been busy?" I said.

"Like crazy. I might make a dent in my inventory this season."

"Still piled up in your spare room?"

"Neatly hung on racks. I'm not a monster."

She hopped up on her stool behind the register and I leaned on the glass case full of vintage jewelry and hair accessories.

"So," she said unwrapping her BLT. "Ryan Duval."

"You gonna start seeing him? I always thought you two were cute together?"

She scrunched up her face as if I were nuts. "We were never together."

"Just as friends, back in the day."

"I'm not saying he's not nice to look at, or nice to talk to. But he's not my type."

"What is your type?"

Suddenly her face got all dreamy as she chewed for a moment. "Taller, for sure. More muscles."

"Ryan's muscular enough."

"More." She popped open her bag of ridged chips.

"Like, linebacker muscles."

"You like to feel protected. I thought you were an independent woman."

"Not for protection." She leaned forward and eyed me seriously. "To run my hands over."

I gasped, happily. "You are so bad."

"The girl knows what she wants. But seriously. Ryan's the past. I have this weird thing about dating people from school."

"That is weird."

"Yeah. I'm not sure why I feel that way. Maybe I'm superstitious or something. Like, anyone I knew back in the day, they knew *that* me. Not the me I am now."

"That makes sense. Anyone from back then will come with all the baggage of the past. Good rule to follow."

"But it isn't."

"Then why are you following it?"

"I told you. I'm superstitious. That doesn't make me smart. It makes me weird." She smiled broadly and took another bite. "You couldf dathe him."

I laughed, but I understood her well enough. "Nope. Honestly, Kaya. Ryan's not into me. He only asked me to that pool party because he was scared to go alone."

"Ryan? Scared to go to a party alone? Did we know the same guy?"

"We were friends, that's all."

"Maybe. But I talked with him Saturday and I'm just saying, it wouldn't be the end of the world if one of the Divas paired you two up."

But, luckily for me, both Karen and Sophie, the only two picks left, promised not to fix me up with him. And neither of them really knew him well enough to want to.

The next Saturday promised to be a long and exhausting day...and it delivered. The restaurant was packed from opening until I left at five, to get ready for the big to-do—the Downtown Strawbridge Tree Lighting Festival. The event had been discussed at length at the weekly HBOMB meetings, not that I'd attended them all, and the schedule was emailed to every business owner and manager. We were to dress for the holidays and were given the lyrics to the holiday song we'd be performing. Everyone would bring a tree ornament to hang on the tree. Naturally, I was bringing our Santa flamingo. After we hung them, and after much fanfare, and a short speech by the mayor—if that's even possible—the tree would be lit. Then it was food and partying into the night. Downtown Strawbridge really knew how to throw a festival.

I wore a red, sleeveless dress with a full flouncy skirt, a puffy bit of crinoline underneath for extra pouf, and a faux-fur-lined red jacket. Sophie picked me up after she'd gotten Vanessa and Kaya, and drove us over to her apartment building. Pari had already picked up Karen from beachside and we all met up there to walk the short distance to the party. Pari and Sophie lived in the Creek Overlook Apartments on Manatee Road just south of downtown. It's a short walk from there to Mangrove, which intersects Strawbridge Avenue in something of a Times Square-ish corner. There's a building there, though it doesn't come to a point, and in front of that building there's a tiny, triangular park. And in the middle of that little squat of land, the Downtown Strawbridge Christmas tree—a twenty-footer, at least—was planted in a huge pot—the poor thing. Some years prior, someone started a petition to purchase a fake tree for the annual tradition, but nothing came of it.

The square—triangle?—was blocked off to traffic like it is on Triple F. A choir stand was set up for us to sing on and next to that a bandstand where one of our local groups was tuning up. Food trucks filled the little lot across the railroad tracks just east of the park, pumping out the smells of cinnamon and butter. And people were milling about excitedly. While the air had a chill to it, if it had been twenty degrees cooler, the evening would have been perfect.

The Strawbridge Elementary School chorus was singing as Sam found Pari, Reese found Sophie, and Sheldon found Vanessa, with Ryan Duval tagging along. I tried my best to ignore him, huddling with Kaya and Karen like we were orphans at a family reunion. But he joined us with a clueless smile.

"You all look festive," he said.

"You don't look so bad yourself," Kaya told him. Kaya was decked out in a vintage Fifties dress, not unlike mine, except hers had three-quarter cuffed sleeves, a sweetheart neckline and was green satin.

"He's just wearing a suit," I said.

"But I've got a tie with colorful Christmas lights on it."

"They don't light up."

Karen laughed. "That would be fun."

"I'm saving my light-up tie for the big day."

"Sure you are," I told him.

"Karen," he fake whispered. "Where can I get a light-up tie?"

I couldn't help but laugh.

When it was time for the Downtown Strawbridge managers and owners to take to the stands, Ryan made a big deal of escorting us to the platform. It was a rickety, tiered, metal contraption with steps on one side leading all the way to the top. There were only four levels, but, if you want my opinion, the last row was still too high. I was ordered to the front because, as realtor extraordinaire Madaline Richards said, "Shorties got to be seen." The others carefully took their places behind me, standing as still as possible in hopes of avoiding a minor catastrophe. If the kids could handle it without toppling the whole thing over, surely we adults could do it.

I jumped a bit when I realized that Ryan was standing next to me.

"Why are you here?" I said.

"Shorties got to be seen," he said with a smile.

"You're not short."

"I'm no Tildon Frakes."

"He could win a local contest."

"He's much too tall for you."

"I'm sure we could make it work."

"Is that something you're thinking of doing?"

"I'm open."

"Sure, sure," he said. "But I remember you telling me you would never date a guy over five-eight."

"I did not."

"I remember it like it was yesterday. Tall boys with short girls is hilarious, you said. And you never want to be hilarious."

"When did I say that?"

"You were giving us a speech, out behind the band room. You were going to be taken seriously, you said. Something about being short and everyone treating you like a child."

"Sounds like I had too much sugar that day."

Suddenly Pari piped up from behind us. "This is all very interesting."

I turned to give her a mind-your-business glare. "Anyway," I said to Ryan. "I meant, why are you singing with us? You're not a store owner or manager."

"Neither am I," Pari said.

"You're not helping."

"Shh," Madaline said, as she motioned to the band on the stage next to us to begin, and took her place with us on the bottom row.

Having missed the relevant HBOMB meeting, I was unprepared for the accompanying props that would be running across the stage during our performance of "The Twelve Days of Christmas," and singing our first line, let out a very loud snort of a laugh when a little kid appeared in a bird costume.

"What are they going to do for the milking maids, I wonder," Ryan said in my ear over the singing and music. And I laughed again.

Madaline leaned forward and caught my eye, giving me a motherly scolding look, but that only made me giggle all the more. And Ryan wasn't helping.

Before each day of the song, the kids, dressed as gifts, ran off the stage only to show up again as they were mentioned in the next round. It was organized chaos and I'm really thankful because by the end of the song *everyone* was laughing, even the kids who were having a wonderful time, so I wasn't in trouble with Madaline anymore.

The kids were dressed mostly as birds, of course. The partridge; a couple of turtle doves who managed to get their wings stuck together every time they ran onto the stage; some French hens—depicted as chickens with "moi?" signs pinned to their fronts; calling birds which were crows who cawed louder than we were singing; geese carrying eggs—thank heavens they weren't laying the eggs all over the stage, but boy would that have been a hoot; and the swans who spent their stage time hitting one another with their necks. Of course, by the time the song ended, there were seventy-eight elementary school kids both on stage and down in front doing what you'd expect kids to do—playing and wrestling, and some doing cartwheels over their swan necks. Milkmaids throwing up their skirts and twirling. Kids lassoing each other with golden hula hoops—the five golden rings. Drummers drumming to their own beats. Lords leaping and tumbling. It was fabulous.

"Well, at least they didn't multiply them, like the song says," Ryan said as the kids were taking their bows. "There's not enough room in the square for that many kids."

Our part of the show was over, so we moved away from the stands to let those behind us climb down.

I said, "I never really thought about it. I mean, what a horrible Christmas that poor person must have had. How many French hens would that have been?"

"But think of the five gold rings."

"I suppose. And at least the partridge wouldn't be lonely for his kind."

"Speaking of the partridge, where was the pear tree?"

"Stage fright," Vanessa said as she and Shel joined us.

We milled about between the stage and the little park with the Christmas tree in it, waiting for Madaline to move the festivities along. She was on the stage behind us, tapping on the microphone.

"Hello," she said. "If we could get the ladders set up by the tree now, thank you. I'll say 'when' but let's not all rush at the tree at once. Take your time, it's a big one—there's plenty of room."

"The ornaments," I said, digging in my purse.

"Okay," Madaline's voice echoed around us. "We now

invite the owners, managers, and workers of Downtown Strawbridge to place an ornament on our grand holiday tree."

The band played a hard rock version of "O, Christmas Tree" and we all moved forward like lions stalking a zebra. It was as if we were each plotting the best spot for our decoration and waiting for the perfect time to pounce so as not to lose it to a bigger, stronger cat. I knew just where I wanted my flamingo, so I stepped faster and got to one of the two twenty-foot stepladders by the tree before the mad rush was let loose. I climbed to the top and leaned over, a lovely *arabesque* remembered from ballet class when I was four, to loop the little golden thread over a branch. A risky move, I know, but I'm still agile, I figured. I do Zumba. I was stretched out like a windsock, and just as I managed to get the string over the limb, somebody—quite a few somebodies I think—bumped into the ladder and it fell away from the tree. There was a long, drawn-out "Oh!" from the crowd as the people who were likely to be crushed beneath it, pushed the ladder back again. As I clung desperately to it, the ladder went right past vertical and fell toward the tree. In an instant, I was flung into the thing, still clinging to the edge of the ladder. Finally it was set right again, but I hung there, my arms and legs wrapped around the rungs. I froze. Red skirt and crinoline be damned. I was not letting go.

And the band played on.

Chapter Twenty-seven

Everyone called me to come down off the ladder, but my legs were trembling and I couldn't seem to make myself move. It was the strangest thing. In my head, I knew the ladder wasn't going to move again—people were holding it steady beneath me. But, I was terrified anyway. In the second that the ladder had swung toward the ground and I felt my body start to slip off, one of my arms reached out, instinctively, I guess, to stop my fall. It seemed like such a long way down. I could have broken my arm, or hit my head on the cement. That's all I could think of, clinging to the ladder—how close I'd come to really hurting myself. Afterward, I realized that I was more likely to have landed on a soft pudgy pile of people, so the danger seemed less serious.

Finally someone came up the ladder to get me. He put his arms around me, gently unwrapping mine from the ladder and placing my hands on the sides.

"Now your feet." It was Ryan.

Of course it would be Ryan. But I didn't have the energy to be angry or embarrassed about it at that moment.

"Good," he said. "Step down. One foot at a time. I've got you."

"I need to sit down," I said once I was safely on the

ground.

Madaline showed up beside me with her motherly scowl. "Shorties shouldn't climb the ladder," she said.

I nodded. "Got it." Though, honestly, *my* height really had little to do with it. I was clearly in shock or I'd have told her so.

Ryan led me away from the tree and the crowd, telling everyone to give me some breathing space, and sat with me on one of the little wrought iron benches along the sidewalk facing Strawbridge Avenue some distance away.

"Are you okay?"

"I think so. I panicked, I guess."

"Understandable."

"Is it, really?"

He smiled at me. "Of course."

"You were there when I was rock climbing, right? I panicked then, too. I thought I was really high up, but it turns out I wasn't."

"Maybe you're afraid of heights."

"Well, I sure went up the ladder without worrying about it."

"Anybody would be afraid of heights when they're getting ready to fall. I wouldn't worry about it, if I were you."

It had quieted down a lot and I realized that everyone was gathered around the tree listening to Mayor Hawn's speech. I turned to watch as the lights of the tree came on and the crowd cheered.

"We should go now," I said. "The Divas were going to get hot chocolate and cinnamon sticks after."

He stood and offered me his hands. As I reached up to take them, I realized I still had my flamingo ornament clutched in my left hand. "Oh," I said.

"Let's get that on the tree."

I gratefully took his hands, but wobbled a bit when he pulled me up.

"Still shaky, I guess," I said.

I looked up at him and he was looking down at me and everybody in the world was walking away toward the food trucks. A hint of "All I want for Christmas" wafted through the air.

"Steady now?" he said.

I nodded. We walked over to the tree where there were still some bystanders, smiles on their faces, gazing up at the beautiful twinkling lights. Ryan caught one of the men erecting a barrier around the tree—heavy acrylic panels about four feet high—and asked if they could wait just a bit. He had one of the men go to his truck and retrieve one of the huge ladders and set it up next to the tree.

He held out his hand for the ornament and I gave it to him.

"Where did you want it?"

I pointed and he climbed. The city worker stood holding the ladder secure and smiled at me with a wink.

"Here?" Ryan said.

"A little higher."

"Here?"

"To the left a bit."

"Here?"

"A little lower."

"Geez lady," the city worker said. "It's no wonder you fell off the ladder."

"She didn't fall off it," Ryan said, placing the flamingo on a branch near where I wanted it. "How's that?" he asked me.

I nodded. I wasn't going to argue. It was high up. It was on the tree. And people could see it. Good enough.

He climbed down the ladder slowly, or was time dragging on? Was I really in shock? I couldn't be sure. We walked toward the railroad tracks to catch up with the Divas, but at the street, before crossing, Ryan stopped and turned me around. We stood there for a moment or two looking at the tree like all the others.

"Strawbridge may be small," he said. "But we do the holidays right."

We started to turn back to the street but hesitated, facing each other, smiling. I thought he was going to kiss me, and then chastised myself. I'd been there before, so many times. The guy was not going to kiss me. When would I learn?

"There's so much going on in your head," he said.

"How can you tell?"

"It's in your eyes. You've always been like that. I used to spend a lot of time watching you when you didn't know it. I'd try to imagine what you were thinking, what you'd be saying if all of your thoughts were spoken."

I chuckled. "That's not weird at all."

And before I knew what was happening, he put a hand to my face, leaned over, and kissed me. Slow, deep, and hungry, pulling my body to his. If it hadn't been for the kid screaming about losing his hula hoop, we might have stood there kissing for hours. I pulled away from him and took a moment to remember where I was—standing in the middle of Strawbridge Square with plenty of people who could be watching.

"Why did you do that?" I said and moved away from him. Seriously. It made no sense.

He raised his shoulders and said, "I don't know."

I nodded. Just one of those things, I guess. "Well, we *have* just been through a traumatic experience."

"You have."

"I'm the damsel in distress."

"I shouldn't have taken advantage."

And just like that, we were back to being...people who used to be friends. It was as if time rushed back to me in a dizzying blur. We met up with everybody else at the food trucks and, it seemed to me, didn't act as if something grand and important had happened between us. As we got in line for cinnamon sticks, I looked at Ryan and he looked back at me, and I smiled inwardly.

The festival ended at ten, when the food trucks closed up and the stage was being dismantled. We all headed over to Tracks for some dancing. The ten of us—Pari and Sam; Sophie and Reese; Vanessa and Sheldon; Karen, Kaya, me, and Ryan—found a couple of tables to push together in the room next to the big dance area and ordered a bunch of appetizers and drinks.

"There's Pat Willard," Sophie said.

Pat was dancing with some guy in a cowboy hat.

"And Buddy's nowhere to be seen," Pari said.

"He probably won't dance at Tracks anymore, because he knows Pat will be here," Kaya said.

"That's just sad," I said.

"Well, I have good news," Karen said. "We're all set with the big fix-up. They don't know who they're being set up with, but Pat's going to be with Mr. Cornell and Buddy's going to be with Trudy."

"Where are we taking them?" Pari said.

"Who's going with them?" I said.

"We're going to the Strawbridge Theater," Sophie said. "On the twelfth, to see *Guys and Dolls*, and then to the after party. I'm getting the tickets on Monday, so let me know if you can't go."

We all agreed we wanted to be there. This would be our first group fix-up and we were hoping it would be a disaster and drive each couple back to the ones they were meant to be with. Sure Pat Willard and Buddy Palmer seemed like opposites. She, a slim no-nonsense business woman and he, a food and fun loving downtown cop. But they got along so well this summer. There had to be a way for them to get over the age difference, if that was what was really keeping Pat from committing. Trudy Spencer and Billy Cornell were both in the antiques business, but instead of letting that blossom into the relationship they so obviously wanted with each other, they kept letting it get in the way. They were too competitive—we needed to get them to compete for each other.

By midnight, I'd watched Ryan dance, very badly, with about five different women. He spent little time at the table with the Divas. When we were ready to go, Vanessa left Sheldon to wait for him and Reese and Sam walked the Divas over to Creek Overlook Apartments where Sophie drove me and Vanessa home, dropping me off first.

My little house seemed so quiet when I got there. Dusty came to the edge of my bed when I went to change into my pajamas and meowed for a few minutes.

"I know, I know. I was gone a long time."

Meow.

"Yeah, I am a little perturbed. And confused. I guess I shouldn't have kissed him."

Meow.

"You're exactly right. He kissed me first. I just went with it."

Meow.

"Yes. It was nice. But it didn't mean anything, obviously. He's made it perfectly clear our entire lives that we're just friends. I don't know why I even wanted it to mean anything."

Meow.

I grabbed a yogurt from the fridge, practically inhaled it, brushed my teeth, turned out the lights, and nestled under my covers. Dusty curled up at my feet. The next morning my phone played Vanessa's theme from where it lay on the nightstand and I grabbed it, realizing I'd slept a bit into daylight.

"Don't read the paper," she said before I could mumble a hello.

"Huh?"

"I mean it. Not yet."

I sat up and flung my legs over the side of the bed. "What is it, Van? What's happened?"

"Lionel Beardsley happened."

Still holding the phone, and crying "no no no no no," I ran to my front door, pulled it open and dashed out into my front yard—still in my pajamas, neighbors be damned —and grabbed the paper off the lawn. I had it out of its little plastic bag before I got inside and threw it onto the coffee table.

"Don't read it yet," Van was yelling into the phone. "You need your Diet Coke, and maybe something chocolate. Can you make chocolate pancakes?"

"How bad is it?" I asked her.

"Don't read it until I get there. I'm bringing chocolate croissants."

She was crazy if she thought I was going to wait. I pulled the sections of the paper apart and found the weekly entertainment insert. Flipping through the pages, I stopped and gasped when I found the headline: Café

Flamingo? More like Mel's Diner.

"Wait," I said to Dusty who stared at me from the bedroom. "What?"

Chapter Twenty-eight

I'd read Beardsley's review three times by the time Vanessa arrived with the croissants. After each time, I had to go outside and walk around the house to let off steam. It's not that the review was awful. He did say that the food was good. But he spent so little time on the food that it hardly mattered. The review was more about me and my staff than what we served. And my customers.

"Loyal, repeat customers apparently enjoy the barbs and scowls of the owner and her staff. So, while the atmosphere of green palms and pink flamingos, leaf-shaped ceiling-fan blades twirling just for show—Florida charm overdone—might be appealing to some, and the food quite good, the experience of Café Flamingo is more like that of Mel's Diner. In the manager, we have Alice herself—stressed and trying to be helpful though her defeat echoes in every word. In the owner, we have Flo—wise-cracking, flippant, and careless. One expects to hear "Kiss my grits!" instead of "What am I supposed to do about it?," which was heard at least twice during my visits. And let's not forget Mel's addlebrained Vera, who can be found in more than one of the hapless waitstaff who populate the Café Flamingo team. And we even had the opportunity to glimpse Mel himself, in the person of a kitchen worker who strolled out into the restaurant to gripe at the manager over an issue with his schedule. The dirty ill-fitting t-shirt, the balding head. It was as if I'd been transported back to the Seventies, sitting on my sofa watching *Alice*. Just because television shows are funny to watch, doesn't mean we want to live them."

As soon as Vanessa walked in, she knew I'd read the article. Digging into the white bakery bag she carried, she forced a chocolate croissant on me.

"Three times," I mumbled. "It was worse each time."

"Honestly, it reads like a hit piece. I'm surprised the paper let him get away with it. I mean, that's a personal attack."

"It sure feels like it. What is this *Alice* show, anyway?"

She took a bite of croissant. "No idea."

I took my iPad off the coffee table and searched IMDb. "Here it is." We scrolled down to the cast and then I clicked over to YouTube so we could find some clips. We ate, drank Diet Coke, and watched as much as we could.

"Well," I said, dropping the iPad back onto the table. "Kiss my grits."

"Don't do anything drastic."

"Like what? Like, write a rebuttal? Call him a bloviating, frustrated old man?"

"You have to be the bigger person."

"Do I?"

"Yes. And you can't blame Ryan."

"Oh, yes I can. I told him to talk to his grandfather. It's a conflict of interest."

"Yeah, but this review hurts him just as much as it hurts you."

"No, it doesn't. If I go out of business, he can just find someone else to rent that space. I'm the one who'll be broke. I can't believe I kissed him!"

"Hold on. You what?"

"Oh, it was nothing. Believe *me*."

"You kissed him? When?"

"After I fell off the ladder."

"Were you in shock or something?"

"Whatever. He took me off to the side where things

were quiet."

"And he kissed you," she cooed.

"Stop saying it. You were there with us at the food trucks and at Tracks. You saw that it meant nothing."

"Maybe he was just playing it cool, you know? Maybe he didn't know how you felt about it."

"Don't defend him, Vanessa."

"This isn't his fault."

"I know, okay. I know."

And I did know. But I wanted it to be his fault. I wanted to be able to gripe about it without having to bring Beardsley into it. Mine wasn't the only restaurant to feel the sting of that man's pen. And none of the owners of those restaurants took any steps toward revenge, that I knew of. They just kept doing what they were doing, unless Beardsley was right, like about Brats' buns. They *were* flimsy and the guy who owned Brats switched to a different bakery and nobody made a big deal about it. But Beardsley didn't attack the food at Café Flamingo. He went after me and my staff—insulted us, turned us into sitcom jokes. Bad form.

"I'm going to work," I told her. "I need to talk to my team."

Susanne, my manager, was at the door with the paper when I entered the café before we opened to the public.

"Did you see it?" I asked her.

"I did, but—"

"I don't think there's anything we can do about it, but I'm so angry. Have you heard from anybody? Are they okay?"

"Nobody's called."

"Was he talking about Doug? The guy who came out onto the floor to talk about his hours?"

"I think so."

"But he didn't really look like that, did he?"

She went on to explain as best she could, but I wasn't going to get on Doug's case about it, anyway.

"Melissa, we have more important things to discuss."

"What?" That's when I noticed it wasn't the newspaper she was holding. "What's that?"

209

"The new lease." There was a tone of anger in her voice.

"What is it?"

"He's going to raise the rent."

"He can't."

"Our lease is up early next year," she said.

"So? Mr. Jenkins said…" But of course, anything Mr. Jenkins said meant nothing, apparently. He'd promised that if I took Mabel's storefront for my catering business, he'd make me a great deal on the two spaces together. So I waited to renew my lease. "Oh, no."

"Oh, yes."

"How much?"

"Another six-hundred a month."

"What? He can't do that."

She sighed. "Of course he can. I'm as mad as you are, but we can't do anything about it. The real problem is the food truck."

I shook my head. "It'll be fine. I can't rent Mabel's space, so I'll just put the extra money toward the truck."

"I'll get into the books and figure everything out," she said. "Really. You don't have to do anything. I just…well, of course you have to know about it."

"It's my name on the lease, after all."

He could have warned me. He should have let me know. Isn't there a rule or something about that?

"Sixty days," Ryan said when I let him have it over the phone a few minutes later. "I've given you three months' notice, that's more than required."

"But another six-hundred?"

"Look, I'm just bringing your rent closer to the market price. I could charge you more, but I'm giving you a break here."

"You call another six-hundred a month a break?"

"Compared to what I could get for that space, yes."

"You're unbelievable. And did you happen to read your grandfather's hit piece this morning?"

"I didn't have anything to do with that."

"Not as far as I'm concerned."

"Well, you're not exactly particular about who you

blame for all of your problems are you?"

"What's that supposed to mean?"

"I think it was pretty clear. Look, this is my day off. If you have more to complain about, call me during regular business hours."

And with that, he broke off the call. I was livid. So much so that Susanne insisted I leave the café to cool down.

"We've had enough bad press without you fuming and grousing around here."

"How do you stay so calm?"

She looked at me and smiled. "Sweetie," she said, putting a hand on my shoulder, "I'm not as emotionally invested in all of this as you are."

I was confused by her statement while I drove back home. Hurt, a little, because I thought she meant she didn't care about the café as much as I did. Not that she should. She's the manager, yes. But I'm the owner, so I would naturally have more to lose. But once I got home and plopped myself onto the sofa next to Dusty, it occurred to me that she might have meant I was emotionally invested because of Ryan. But why would she think that? Where would she have gotten such an idea? She didn't know my history with the guy, did she? No. Not possible. I decided she couldn't have meant Ryan. I was imagining things.

"Honestly, Dusty," I said as she purred and snuggled up against me. "The holidays make me nuts normally, so this is all just extra helpings of stuffing to deal with." And I was determined to deal with it as a mature, successful business woman.

So…how would a mature, successful business woman smack down an insufferable, conniving landlord? I had no idea.

Chapter Twenty-nine

How to Ruin a Scrumptious Recipe

Attempt Four: Add too much water

The summer after I opened Café Flamingo in Downtown Strawbridge, for some odd reason, my high
school class threw a five-year reunion. I first heard
about it from Kaya, but then received an invitation in the
mail. Kaya was right—it was a casual get together. A
picnic, actually, at Riverfront Park. I told her it made no
sense.

"Why would they have a five-year reunion? We just
saw those people."

And she said, "Girl, I'm there!"

"Not me." But let's face it, I was already thinking
about what I might wear.

"Isn't there someone you'd like to reconnect with?
You hung out with those smart kids. Jessica was one of
them, right?"

"And Josh and Karl and Kevin. Lots of J and K names."

"I would have fit right in." She laughed. "Come on.
Let's go."

"I'll think about it."

The truth was, I wanted to see Ryan again. We'd been such good friends in school. The least we could do was try to stay in touch. Vomit and cacti shouldn't dominate our memories of one another. The last time I'd seen him, after he broke my windshield, was so awkward. I figured we could use a reset. But, then, it seemed as if every time I saw him outside of high school something crazy happened. It was as if the universe was telling me to forget him. "Not the guy for you, Melissa!"

But, determined, I bought a new sun dress and a big floppy straw hat with a band to match. I kept telling myself that this was only a chance to talk to him again. My feelings for him were juvenile. High school nonsense. If he'd liked me back in school and we'd dated, I'd be completely over him by now. This wasn't about crushes, or love, or anything like that—although, I told myself, if he did try to kiss me, I wouldn't stand in his way. Nope. It was just about one of my best friends—actually my *best* friend—in high school. We both lived and worked in the same town. It was simply wrong for us to not still be friends. I hoped I could remedy that.

Riverfront park is tucked in a little hideaway spot off US1 south of downtown. The park was a roundish, jutting piece of land with a parking lot in the center surrounded by pavilions and picnic tables, and the outermost edges were dotted with Florida scrub, oaks, and palms against the boulder-lined water of the lagoon. My senior class had rented the largest pavilion and decorated it with our school colors of red and white. I purposely arrived late and sat in my car for a while trying to see if anyone I knew was there yet. I saw Kaya, but she was with some of her friends—people I didn't really know. When I saw Jessica, I was relieved and, leaving my purse locked up in my car, donned my floppy hat and finally joined the party.

I found her with several of our set at a picnic table a short distance from the main pavilion. Everyone acted like we hadn't seen each other in fifty years, but I had to admit, once I was there and chatting with the old gang, I realized that a lot had happened in the five years since we'd been in school together. Some of my friends were married and had children already. Karl lived in California and Jessica was in New York.

"And you traveled all the way back here for this?" I said.

She smiled and lifted a shoulder. "Who knows where we'll be in another five years, right? We should take every chance we can to get together."

"Ryan," Josh said, raising his beer bottle as if in salute.

I turned to find Ryan approaching. My heart raced as I managed a smile. He looked better than ever—his face a bit fuller, his eyes darker somehow. It had only been about a year since I'd seen him, but he'd changed. He wasn't a kid anymore, I realized. I suppose neither was I. For a while, we all talked and joked and it was as if no time had passed. The group shifted and morphed as familiar faces left and joined in, until suddenly Ryan and I were left standing alone.

"How've you been?" he asked.

I tried not to look directly at him, fearing I might stammer over my words. "Good. You?"

He said nothing so that I finally had to look up, expecting him to be watching the rest of our high school alumni having a good time. But he was looking at me, smiling.

"I've been by the café a few times," he said.

"Have you?"

"You're never there."

"I'm always there."

"I did see you run through once or twice. Once you came through the front door and made a dash for the back room. And once, you went the opposite way. You might have shouted stuff at people as you ran."

"Sounds like me. I'm sorry I didn't see you. Stop me next time."

"Maybe I'll call ahead. Catch you at a good time."

Something inside me fell. This was dull chitchat. The kind of civil talk people who hardly knew each other engaged in.

"You want to take a walk?" he said. "We should catch

215

up."

"I don't know what there is to catch up on. Unless you've got some news."

He started walking and nodded at me to join him. We made our way through the palms to the lagoon, where it lapped gently against the rocks, and strolled along the outer edges of the park. Occasionally, the boulders gave way to tiny sandy beaches where bugs and crabs scrambled away from us. Swarms of tiny gnats hung in the air like clouds that we worked hard to avoid and never managed to.

"Ew," I said. "I think I ate some."

"Close your mouth. Ew. Now I ate some."

"There's a dead fish somewhere," I whined.

"Could be that raccoon carcass." He pointed to something puffed and bloated, covered with flies, floating just off shore.

"I'm going to barf."

"Let's move along."

The smell was taken with the wind as we climbed onto the rocks and carefully avoided patches of slimy seaweed, balancing, our arms flying about, as we ducked under oak limbs.

"So," I said, not sure I wanted to know. "Do you have any news?"

"Not really. Do you?"

"Just the café. I might be starting a catering business, too."

"You really like to work, don't you?"

"This reminds me of Jetty Park. When I was little, you could climb on the rocks. I slipped once and my foot got sliced open by some kind of shell."

"Probably why they put up the walkway."

"You still live at home, or…?"

"I bought a condo a while back. You?"

"Still at home."

I was in the middle of a big step from one rock to another when he said, "Seeing anyone?"

Looking up too quickly, I stumbled. "Whoa," I said, my arms swinging wildly. I must have stepped onto a

216

slippery bit of seaweed and started to slide. He reached for my arm, I suppose to help me to solid ground, and I tried to take his hand, but instead, still not quite solid on my feet, managed to push him off balance. He was kind enough not to pull me down onto the rocks as he fell, but instead let me go, letting me splash backward into the lagoon. The water was only a couple of feet deep, but my back hit the soft sands before I flailed about and finally sat up, spitting out brackish raccoon-corpse-infested water.

I sat there like I'd been plopped down into a tub of runny pudding, my arms up out of the water as if I didn't want to be touched. I saw him where he'd landed, half on the rocks, half on the grassy dirt. He was laughing.

"At least I didn't vomit on you first," he said.

"Are you okay?" I called to him, wiping seaweed off my head. "My hat!"

I caught sight of it, floating away, and half crawled, half swam to get it.

"You could stand up," he called.

He was waiting for me, on the rocks, offering a hand to help me out of the water when I finally made it to shore.

"You're bleeding," I said.

"Your dress is see-through."

I looked down at my chest to confirm that, yes, my lovely white sundress was now drenched and stuck to my body, exposing every line and curve.

"Well, don't stare," I told him, covering myself with my soaked floppy hat.

He was still looking down at me, smiling. "Let's go see if somebody has a towel. I'm sure there's a first aid kit around somewhere, too." He turned to look at the back of his right calf where the edge of a sharp rock had cut into him.

"You go on," I said. "I have a towel in my car."

"You're not mad, are you?"

I tried to smile. "Just embarrassed."

He looked concerned. "Still friends?" he said.

"Always," I said. "Go on and get yourself bandaged up." I walked past him, heading straight to the parking lot and my car.

I dug through my emergency box in the trunk, found a dirty towel and spread it out on the front seat before getting in behind the wheel. The engine started up with a purr and I blasted the air conditioning onto my face. As I left the park, I mumbled to myself, "Okay, universe. I got the message."

Chapter Thirty

The holidays were in full swing the first week of December. I did my best to spend lots of time at home with Dusty and I was starting to get used to the idea of not having to be at the café, or oversee everything Lucy was doing with catering. Both my managers seemed to be capable enough. So that week, I met with Quinn at Café Flamingo so we could go over the specs for the food truck and I showed him some designs for the outside artwork.

"Love the huge flamingo idea," he said.

"How much is all this going to cost?"

"No worries; the grant will fund it."

"Are you sure?" It seemed too good to be true.

"Fully equipped truck, ready to serve the public, delivered to you. Whatever you want to do with it after that is on you."

"This is so great. I'm getting excited." I let my gaze wander out the window and across the street to Mabel's Pottery & Glass.

"She's doing well with her going out of business sale," Quinn said.

"Yeah. Not that it does me any good."

"You going to start looking for another storefront for the catering?"

"I don't know if I'll be able to afford it. He raised my rent here."

Quinn peered at me. "He's not trying to get you to move out, is he?"

For a brief second or two I considered it. "No. He didn't raise it that much. I did get a pretty good deal from Mr. Jenkins."

"With a bigger space for the catering business, you'll be able to bring in more money. It'll all work out in the end."

"Sure, but I really wanted a space really close to the café."

"Consider using the food truck to help with catering, then."

"It's a possibility."

He gathered up his notebook and the papers I'd given him. "Well," he said as he scooched out of the booth we were in. "I guess I'll see you on Saturday."

"What's on Saturday?"

"Our date."

"Our what?"

He smiled, teasing me. "Didn't Karen tell you?"

"She did not. Where are you taking me?"

"Meeting you there, actually. I don't think I'm allowed to say."

"But, I'm supposed to go to the theater Saturday night for the big fix-up conspiracy."

"I don't know anything about Saturday night or conspiracies. I'm meeting you somewhere in the morning. Don't worry." He tapped the table with his notebook. "It's going to be wild."

The zoo, I thought. I could handle the zoo. Unless it included zip-lining or the kayak tours. Maybe it would be a hike out in the wilderness. That wouldn't be so bad. Terrible idea for a date, but a lot less risky than skydiving. Other than those two ideas, there was nothing else in the area that would be considered a wildlife encounter. Maybe Quinn just meant crazy wild. But how wild can people be in the morning? Just to be safe, I was definitely going to plan for snakes and bears.

"Susanne," I called as I entered the kitchen. "Where can I get bear repellent?"

No luck on the bear repellent, but I did have some mosquito spray. It was December, though. The mosquito problem would be very low as long as the weather stayed cool.

Karen showed up at my door at eight o'clock on Saturday morning, smiling as if she'd been awake for hours, which I suspected she had. As for me, I was a tad hungover from a night out with Vanessa. We went to The Fort, as usual, and while she danced with Sheldon all night, I avoided Ryan like he was spoiled lunch meat.

"Well," I grumbled. "Am I dressed appropriately?"

She looked me up and down. Jeans. Ironic tee covered in colorful hearts. Tennis shoes. And a blue visor. "You'll do."

I was pleased, at first, when Karen didn't take me north. Instead, she turned west out of my neighborhood on the main road that cuts Strawbridge in half—Old Harbor Blvd, which turns into an Interstate.

"We're not going to Kissimmee, are we?"

"Not that far."

There was certainly a lot of area for wildlife on the way to Kissimmee. Riding that road always made me imagine being on a safari…if you were driving at seventy miles per hour and not being chased by rhinoceroses. (Rhinoceri?) Long before we got to Kissimmee, Karen turned off the road at Swampy's.

"Oh, no," I said.

The rough road tossed us a bit as she smiled. "Oh, yes."

Swampy's wasn't just a restaurant, with an outdoor bar and dance floor overlooking its little part of the St. John's River. And it wasn't just a picnic area, or a hot spot for birding on the Great Florida Birding and Wildlife Trail—I read about that on the sign. Most important to Karen, and Pari and Sam, and Vanessa and Sheldon, and Sophie and Reese, and Kaya and Ryan—of course Ryan had to be there—and Quinn, whose idea this whole thing probably was…Swampy's was home to air boat rides.

That's right. You get on something that looks like an extra wide, flat fishing boat, equipped with a ridiculously large fan on the back, and you let the gratingly loud fan propel you across the water. Why? Who invented this? Sure, I was given earphones that were so big I looked like an alien, to help mute the noise a bit. And I was slathered with sunscreen and fumigated with mosquito repellent, just in case.

I was warned not to put my hands or feet into the water because—hello!—alligators. Shoved onto the contraption's front row with Quinn, who seemed to be an avid fan of the experience, Kaya, and Ryan, I was given the choice between sitting on the outside, with the risk of being grabbed out of the boat and dragged under the water by a gator, or sitting in the middle next to Ryan, because Kaya definitely wanted to sit on the perilous, alligator nabbing side. I chose possible death-spiraling gators over sitting next to Ryan, which, I'm afraid, gave Quinn the idea that I was ready for a great adventure. The rest of our crew piled into rows behind us. The 'captain' sat at the back, on a platform just in front of the enormous fan.

Very loudly, the boat whizzed across the river at such high speeds my eyelashes felt it. But several times, it slowed or stopped, and we could remove our earphones. We saw alligators, lounging in the sun. Great blue herons, cattle egrets, wild turkey, bald eagles, and lots of osprey. Sam was happy to tell us all about the birds. Quinn and I dared to ride for a bit without our headphones on, leaving me with airboat hair—what you'd expect from a joyride in a convertible. All in all, it wasn't nearly as bad as I thought it would be. But I was still glad to be back at the dock.

We had lunch at Swampy's at a long table for the whole gang, Quinn and I at one end next to Sophie, Reese, Pari, and Sam, like we were just another couple. Quinn regaled me with stories of fishing exploits, alligator sightings—he saw one take down a small deer once—and the time he had to rescue a group of tourists trapped on a disabled fishing boat.

"You never struck me as the outdoorsy type," I told him.

"Why is that? I mean, sure, I spend most of my time in a dark restaurant and party place feeding people and forcing them to dance salsa. But that's exactly why I like to get outside on my off hours. What do you do when you're not at the café?"

"My café is light, so when I'm off, I go to dark places, like The Fort or your place."

"I guess that makes sense. So, did you have a good time today?"

"I did, actually."

"I heard about your other dates."

"The first two had me pretty scared. But these last two have been relatively calm and enjoyable. I didn't get dragged out of the boat by an alligator, so I think I foiled Kaya's revenge plan quite nicely today."

"Yeah, I heard all about the ghost challenges, too."

"Everybody knows all of my business these days."

"That's very true. And that's why I can tell you that, while I think you're prime dating material, I'm not the one Isabella told you about. Not that I haven't thought about asking you out. It's just…"

"You don't have to explain it to me. I'm clearly not your type."

"Oh, really?" He laughed. "What is my type?"

"Well, at first I'd have said your type was models and beauty queens. I mean, come on, I've seen you at Tracks with women."

"I have dated a Miss Strawbridge."

"But now, I can see that your type is not only taller than me—nothing wrong with that," I said as he began to protest. "But the outdoorsy sort. You're going to want a girl who loves being on the water."

"And you don't."

"Let's just say, it doesn't call to me. I like the beach, though. The shore part, not the water. I'll never understand why people want to swim in the ocean."

"We agree there. I do like to wade out into it with a big fishing rod, though."

"Could you see petite me trying to fish off shore? One bite and I'd be dragged under the waves."

"What are you two laughing about?" Karen called from the other end of table.

"We're finding common ground," Quinn said.

"Ooh," Vanessa said. "A budding relationship? Does Karen win?"

I caught Ryan's eye and tried to glare at him. I was still mad about his grandfather's attack, and the rent, even though I had to admit I didn't have much of a case. But then I turned to Vanessa. "What do you mean, Karen wins?"

"Never mind," Pari said. "You just concentrate on finding your mystery stalker."

I turned back to Quinn. "It's not like they're really trying to find that guy. None of my dates so far could possibly be him."

"But you do believe what Isabella said?"

"I believe she has a gift. But psychic readings aren't like science. She couldn't be completely sure what it was she was seeing."

"But you think there is a guy out there who likes you?"

"Of course. Look at me." I smiled and he laughed.

"So she didn't have to try very hard to come up with that story," Reese said.

"Maybe not. But that doesn't mean it's not true."

I peered down at the rest of my friends at the table, all of whom seemed to be listening in on our conversation. I thought I caught Ryan rolling his eyes, but I didn't care. He wouldn't be the only one who doubted Isabella's abilities.

Shortly after two, I said goodbye to Quinn and everybody left. Karen drove me back to my house, quizzing me about the date the whole time.

"You had a crush on Quinn a year or so ago, didn't you? I thought you did. Sure, he's a bit tall for you, but really, who isn't? He's definitely gorgeous. And you both own restaurants, so there's that. I think he likes you. Did you enjoy the air boat ride? I'm still sticky all over from the mosquito repellent. How about you? Anyway, I guess you'll see Quinn around. You two are friends, after all. A lot of romances start as friendships. But what do you think?"

It took several seconds of silence for me to realize she wanted a response. "I don't think we're going to find out who Isabella was talking about this way."

"It's worth a try, though. And it's kind of fun."

"Do I even want to find him?" I was musing out loud.

"Don't you?"

"I'm not sure. If he likes me, why doesn't he just say so?"

"Isabella said he was shy, didn't she?"

"If he's too shy to let me know he likes me, or to ask me out, then do I want to know him?"

"Are you mad at him?"

I suppose I did sound angry. "Maybe. I honestly don't know how I feel. So much is going on."

"Maybe he really is the guy for you. And seeing you going out on all these dates will push him to make his move."

"You believe in Isabella, too?"

"I believe in true love. And true love doesn't just happen when life is quiet and you're ready for it. It happens when it happens."

"Or not. Sometimes, I think love is like a window. The universe gives you a chance with somebody, and if you don't take it, the chance is gone. The window closes. And then you have to wait for someone else."

"That's an awful way to look at it."

"You don't think there's only one person for each of us, do you?"

"I don't know. I haven't really thought about it like that. But I guess I imagined that when you meet the right person, you just know. And everything falls into place and you live, hopefully, happily ever after."

"What if you screw it up?"

"You won't. Not with the right guy."

I could only hope that was true.

Chapter Thirty-one

After a long rest inside my very cold, air-conditioned house, a shower, a light dinner, and some quality cat time with Dusty, I headed over to the Strawbridge Theater for the Double Setup Conspiracy. It had all been arranged. Sophie invited Pat Willard, owner of the crystal and incense and all-things gypsy shop Namaste on a blind date with a surprise guy who she promised wouldn't be Buddy Palmer, the local traffic cop and parking meter checker. And Reese invited Billy Cornell, the long-haired, bearded owner of Old Geezer's Antiques who oddly seemed like a good fit for Pat, under the same guise.

Meanwhile, Pari invited Trudy Spencer, the plump, frazzled antique shop owner on a secret fix-up while Sam invited Buddy Palmer to be her date. Trudy was wildly too old for Buddy, but stranger partnerships have been made. What would happen if their fix-ups actually worked and Pat fell for Mr. Cornell, while Buddy and Trudy found love? I guess we could call that a win. But we were hoping that Buddy and Pat would both be so jealous of the other being out with someone else, they'd see the light and get back together. And Trudy and Mr. Cornell would realize they belonged together all along. Why couldn't these four people realize what they had?

We probably shouldn't have meddled, but I was just

glad to have all the attention off me and my love life for a change.

The Strawbridge Theater was on Manatee Road, in the area behind Burgers, which sat on the opposite corner of Woodplum and Strawbridge from my café. I could walk there from work. But as I was in heels and a little black dress, and coming from home, I drove. I'm not a theater buff, really. Not at all, actually. Never been. But I've heard the name *Guys and Dolls*. It sounded cute.

The fix-up ruse was put into play in the theater lobby where Karen handed out all the tickets after carefully manipulating the seating to our advantage. Sophie and Reese and Pari and Sam would unfortunately not be seated with their guests, "But we'll see you for the after party!" Putting the mixed-up fix-up foursome next to each other in the middle of the theater. And as we Divas stood at the big double doors on one side of the theater, we watched them find their seats, just as we hoped: Mr. Cornell and Pat in row eight, and in front of them, Buddy and Trudy. They all looked at one another, confused it seemed for a moment, then took their seats as we Divas did the same as the lights went down and the curtain rose.

The theater was pretty big and fancy for Strawbridge. Made it seem like our little city had some culture. The aisle was still partially lit as I headed downward on the slope to my seat on stage left, fourth row from the front. There, in the semi-darkness, I found Ryan Duval sitting in the seat next to the empty one that I guessed was mine. I turned to say something to Vanessa, but she wasn't behind me. I looked this way and that, until someone whispered, "Down in the front." So, I maneuvered in front of the people sitting in the first four seats, and sat.

"Where's Vanessa? Why are you in her seat?"

He showed me his ticket. The actors were already on stage singing the opening bit and in the dim light I could read his face. He wasn't any happier about the situation than I was. "Seems we've been set up. Vanessa's probably sitting with Sheldon."

"Well, that's just great."

I was hushed by the lady on my left.

I don't know what I was expecting, but it wasn't Madaline Richards, the real estate lady and president of the Historic Downtown Strawbridge Business Owners Management Board as General Cartwright of the mission ladies. And UPS Pete was Sky Masterson. I did my best to concentrate on the singing and dancing on stage, but I was constantly aware of Ryan Duval sitting next to me in the dark.

Finally, during the last song of the play, I leaned over and whispered, "Why are you even here?"

"Sheldon invited me."

"Why were you at Karen's for Thanksgiving?"

"What difference does it make?"

"Why are you everywhere that I am?"

"I get invited places. Do I have to check with you every time I go somewhere?"

The lights went up and I squinted a bit. "Are you following me around?"

He had the audacity to laugh. "Why would I be following you? Maybe you're following me."

"I'm being set up on dates. I don't have control over where I'm going and you're always there."

"And you just can't stand seeing me, is that it?"

I stopped short, surprised. "It's not that. I just... Never mind."

Our row had cleared by then so I got up and stalked up toward the door. Someone was setting us up; I was sure of it. And I didn't know if they were doing it because they, for some bizarre reason, wanted Ryan and me to be together, or if they were being mean, because they knew we could *never* be together. Either way, I was tired of it.

The after-party was held in a large room next to the lobby. I made my way, determinedly, through the crowd to find Karen and pulled her aside.

"Did you invite Ryan Duval to your Thanksgiving lunch?"

She'd been smiling and laughing and now looked at me as if I were drunk. "What?"

"Who invited him?"

"I don't know. I think he came with Vanessa and

Sheldon. Is it important? I didn't mind him being there."

"Thanks. Sorry to bother you."

Weaving around all the theater goers, with their tiny plastic plates piled with appetizers, drinks in clear plastic cups, I found Vanessa in a corner with Ryan and Sheldon. They each had drinks in hand and were whispering conspiratorially. As I approached, I heard Ryan say, "Incoming."

"Can I talk to you?" I said to her.

I pretty much dragged her out into the lobby and out the front doors of the theater. "Did you invite Ryan here tonight?"

"Not exactly."

"What does that mean?"

"Sheldon asked if he could come."

"And Thanksgiving?"

"Same. You said it would be okay. You said you could handle him being around."

"But I didn't realize he would be everywhere I am. What about paintball? Did you tell him about that?"

"I wasn't at the paintball thing."

"But Ryan Duval was."

"So you think I told him to go?"

"Did you?"

"Stop yelling at me. I don't control Ryan Duval."

"You told him about the paintball thing though, didn't you?"

"No, I didn't. What's the big deal, Mel? Get over yourself."

She turned and left me standing outside alone. I thought about leaving, but I remembered why I was there. We were all supposed to try to keep Pat and Mr. Cornell, and Buddy and Trudy in the same vicinity, in hopes they'd get jealous. By the time I got back to the party, I decided the whole fix-up thing wasn't right. I didn't like the idea that somebody out there was throwing Ryan at me every chance they could. I'd be a hypocrite if I involved myself in Pat and Trudy's business.

I got a plate of *hors d'oeuvres* and stood against a wall watching the party. I suppose I was pouting. I was angry with myself for letting Ryan get to me. And I shouldn't have been. It's not like he knew why I didn't want to be around him. He was clueless. A big, doofus of cluelessness. And of course, the doofus sidled up next to me.

He shoved his hands into his pants pockets. He'd loosened his tie and undid the top few buttons on his shirt. "Look, I'm sorry."

I rolled my eyes. "About what?"

"Everything."

"You may as well be sorry about nothing, then."

"I'm sorry that everything I do makes you angry."

I took a bite of a mushroom cap.

"I'm sorry I can't rent that space to you. I'm sorry I raised the café's rent."

"But you're not going to do anything about it."

"No. But I'm still sorry. And I'm sorry I kissed you."

I turned to glare at him so fast my head nearly hit the wall. "I'll bet you are."

I shoved my little paper plate at him and left.

Later, I heard that the Divas kept dragging the fix-ups together, only to see them meander apart again and again. But I got to see what happened when they left, because I was sitting in my little red Jetta in the parking lot fuming, mostly at my own ridiculous behavior.

"You're still so high school, Mel," I was telling myself. "Get over it already." And just as I was feeling confident about moving on and being civil to Ryan, I saw the whole thing.

First, Mr. Cornell and Pat Willard left the theater and I thought he was going to take her home, but he walked her to her car. They said a few words, shook hands, and parted. Pat stood at her car, as if thinking, while Mr. Cornell walked farther out toward his car, I assumed. But then Buddy Palmer was suddenly at Pat's car. She'd been watching him approach. And he was still with Trudy Spencer. Pat pointed the way Mr. Cornell had gone and Trudy left. As Pat and Buddy talked, I watched as Trudy caught up to Mr. Cornell. But, instead of leaving with him, she took his hand and brought him back to Pat's car. The four of them talked for a while and then they all started walking together toward Palmetto Road and The Fort.

I dug my phone out of my purse and called Vanessa.

"Are you going to yell at me some more, because, girl, I don't—"

"No, listen. I think it worked."

"What worked?"

"The Double Fix-up. I'm in the parking lot."

"We'll be right out."

Within a few minutes, all the Divas, their dates, and Ryan, were at my car and I told them what I'd seen.

"So…The Fort?" Kaya said.

"Let's go," Sophie said.

The couples headed out together, leaving Kaya, Karen, Ryan and me to stand around looking awkwardly at each other, as if we each expected something different to happen. Ryan threw up his hands when he caught me looking at him, as if I'd accused him of putting bacon on a pizza.

"Kaya," he said. "Walk with me."

"I'd be happy to," she said, taking his arm.

"I guess you're my date for the rest of the evening," Karen said to me with a smile.

We linked arms and skipped past the others, ready to watch our matchmaking miracle unfold.

Chapter Thirty-two

The Fort has a large open-air front porch with lots of seating and we caught sight of our two couples right away at a table to the left of the entrance. So we pushed a couple of tables together on the opposite side so they wouldn't think we were spying on them, which we definitely were.

We ordered drinks all around and then sent Sophie and Pari over to talk to them because they were the ones who set up the dates. The rest of us watched as the two Divas stood at the table and chatted for a few minutes. At one point, Pat Willard peered over Trudy's shoulder and waved at us. We all suddenly tried to look at other things, but I think we were caught.

"It's hard to say," Pari said when she and Sophie returned to our table. "But I think it might have worked."

Sophie said, "Pat and Buddy are sitting together on one side and Trudy and Mr. Cornell on the other."

"They could be sitting across from the person they're with," Kaya said.

"Nah," I said. "The table is round. You're going to sit closer to the person you're with."

"Did they suspect anything?" Karen asked.

Sophie shook her head. "I don't think so."

"Well, look at us," Kaya said. "Matchmakers."

I hmphed. "That setup was easy. They had history with each other."

"So you don't think we can match you any better?"

"You haven't done a great job so far."

"Come on," Vanessa said. "We've picked out great guys for you."

Sam, Reese, Sheldon, and Ryan all looked a tad uncomfortable, but interested just the same.

"I don't think you're taking the challenge seriously, that's all," I said.

"We are," Kaya protested.

"You really thought these guys might be the one Isabella was talking about?"

"We tried," Pari said.

"Tildon Frakes?" I said.

"What's wrong with him?"

"Nothing. But I just can't picture him being interested in me at all."

"But he eats at the café, like, three times a week. And he adores Reese Witherspoon."

"What does that have to do with it?"

"She's blonde and I think she's petite. So…you do the math. I'm sorry if you two didn't get along."

"We actually got along great. But I don't think Tildon wants to date. I think he wants to fall in love at first sight and move right on to marriage and kids."

"Nothing wrong with that," Vanessa said and Sheldon shot a wide-eyed glance her way. "And you can't say my choice wasn't a possibility."

I thought of Diego West, owner of Burgers. He was at the café a lot too, and he did flirt with me all the time. "I suppose."

"We're taking it seriously," Kaya said. "And at the same time trying to torture you a little bit."

"I'm glad it's almost over."

"Only one mystery date left," Kaya said and we all turned to Sophie. Except the guys. They were bewildered.

"How bad is it going to be?" I asked her.

She smiled. "You'll see."

"Let me put it another way. How high off the ground

will I be and how fast will I be going?"

"You'll be glad to know that both of those things will be entirely up to you."

"So when is it?"

"I'm not sure yet."

"You just want to spring it on me so I'll be unprepared."

With that, the couples left for dancing inside, and Ryan invited Kaya to join them. I was left with Karen. We sipped our drinks for a few minutes, sitting with our own thoughts.

"You're uncomfortable when Ryan Duval is around."

I started to deny it, but it was true. "Yes."

"I don't think we all realized just how much you didn't like him."

"I'm glad no one's set me up with him. I really thought Vanessa was going to."

"There must be something there, though, right? I mean, for you to be that unnerved by him."

"I'm not unnerved. I just don't…" I was going to say I didn't like him, but that wasn't really true, either. "I just don't like being around him."

"Well—" she pulled her purse off the back of her chair, "—I'm heading home. Go find someone to dance with. I don't want to leave you sitting here by yourself."

"I'm watching the purses," I said.

She sank back into her chair.

"Go on," I said. "I've been purse watcher before. Why don't you go dance?"

"It's not really my thing. I'd rather go home and curl up with a book or a movie. It's getting late."

I talked her into leaving and did purse duty for a while. The couples made their way back and forth from dancing to the table and at some point, well after midnight, I turned the purses over to Sam and Pari and went home.

The next morning at nine-thirty, Vanessa was at my door, as she often is on Sundays. She brought sausage biscuits from Brunch and we had to lock Dusty up in my bedroom to keep him from bothering us as we put our

235

feet up on the coffee table and ate on the sofa.

"Next Sunday, I'm making you breakfast," I told her.

"You're going to cook?"

I shrugged and took a bite of biscuit. "I'm not sure it'll be real cooking. I ordered a waffle maker online."

"Waffles?"

"Yeah, I like Belgian waffles. We could put strawberries and whipped topping on them."

"Or syrup."

"Syrup's good."

After we ate and let Dusty out, Vanessa pulled her feet under her and turned toward me on the couch.

"You need to explain yourself."

I knew exactly what she was talking about. "I'm sorry."

"You really went a little nuts last night. What was that all about?"

"He's just everywhere all of the sudden. It's like he came out of nowhere, well, okay, he came out of my past. And now he's my landlord and he's involved in all the things I'm involved in. And for some reason every place I go, he's there."

"And you thought I was making that happen?"

"I did. I'm sorry, but I thought you were trying to get around not making him your choice for the whole Pink Diva Man Hunter Plan by just having him coincidentally show up at all of my dates."

"That would be a great idea and it does sound like me. But I didn't do it."

"So you think it really is just coincidence?"

"Probably. But why do you care? I get that you guys had some lousy encounters, but...what really happened? Why do you dislike him so much."

"I don't dislike him. I mean, I do. Oh, all right." I sighed. "I had a huge crush on him in high school. I mean huge."

"Mm hm. I thought so."

"It's not that obvious is it? I don't want him to know. You wouldn't tell Shel would you?"

"Never. I promise. And about that."

"No, I really meant it when I said I could handle it. I don't want to come between you and Shel."

She grimaced. "It's okay. I like him and all. But he's not *the one*."

"Are you looking for *the one*?"

"Sure. I think it's time. I want a family. And kids."

"Ugh."

"Seriously? You don't?"

"I don't know. And if you ask me, not knowing means *no*."

"I don't think that's what it means. I think you're holding back for some reason. You're not letting yourself get too close to anyone. When you find the right guy, it'll happen. You'll see."

"You think?"

"I know. That's how love works."

I didn't like to think of myself like that—as someone who isn't willing to be open to life. Dusty hopped onto my lap and curled into a warm furry ball. But I did sense that I was waiting. For something. And I had a nagging feeling that Ryan Duval had something to do with it.

"I need to just forget it," I mumbled.

"Huh?"

"Getting another cat," I said. "I think Dusty would like a cat companion. But it's just too much."

"You never know. You might fall madly in love with Sophie's pick and he could come with a cat of his own. Or a dog."

"Ew. Face licks. No thanks."

Chapter Thirty-three

On Monday morning I went in to work at the café to help out with the holiday uptick and got word that Kaya had ordered lunch.

When we were in school together, Kaya was a cheerleader, not that there's anything wrong with that. It's just that in high school, in Strawbridge at least, cheerleaders were a different species. It's funny to us now, looking back on it. Why do we act that way when we're teenagers? I thought cheerleaders were destined to be models or celebrities and Kaya thought debate and chess club students would become scientists and CEOs and here we were, both of us shop owners in beautiful Downtown Strawbridge.

Kaya ran her shop mostly on her own and often ordered lunch from Café Flamingo. I loved it when I got to be the one to deliver it to her. It gave us a chance to chat. When you first think of Kaya's vintage clothing, you might imagine clothes from the 1800s. But it turns out that the Seventies and Eighties are vintage. She has a lot of clothes from the Sixties, a few pieces from the Fifties, and every once in a while, something from even earlier shows up. When you walk into her store off Strawbridge Avenue, you're surrounded by clothing—racks along the walls and in the center—and it acts as a buffer to the noisy activity outside.

"I love your store so much," I told her when I approached her sales counter along the left wall.

She invited me to take a stool with her behind the register.

"Compared to the café," I said. "This place is calming." I closed my eyes and smiled. "You hear that? Nothing."

"Nothing can drive you nuts after a while," she said, digging into the paper bag I'd brought to get at her ham-and-Swiss sandwich and chips. "I'll have to put on music later to keep myself sane."

"We should do some kind of job switch. You run the restaurant and I'll come here. We could do it with all the Divas."

"That would be a disaster."

"A lot of disasters." I laughed.

"So," she said, sticking a sour cream and onion chip into her mouth. "What was the deal with Karen Saturday night? It looked like you were yelling at her about something."

"It was dumb."

"I'm sure it was. Tell me all about it." She was smiling devilishly.

"You know I ended up sitting next to Ryan Duval, right? I told you guys I didn't want to be fixed up with him."

"And you haven't been."

"But he's everywhere. Ever since I dumped that tray onto him, he's suddenly everywhere I am. All the time. I guess I got it into my head that somebody was making that happen."

"And you thought Karen did it? She doesn't strike me as the conniving type."

"Are you kidding? She's writing a romance novel. You've got to connive all sorts of ways to throw the lovers together. She could have been doing it as research, you know. With me and Ryan Duval has her guinea pigs."

"You don't really think that, do you?"

"Not now. I was asking her how he got invited to her

Thanksgiving party. I was out of sorts. He's just always around lately. Reminding me…"

"Of what?"

"Nothing."

"Oh, no. You don't say something like that and then deflect."

I rolled my eyes and stole one of her chips. "Okay. So I liked him back in high school."

"Ooh, girl. You had a crush on Ryan? Please. Everybody knew that."

"They did not."

She gave me a patronizing smirk. "Well, I did. You were always googly-eyed when he was around."

I laughed and playfully smacked at her. "I was never googly-eyed in my life."

"I guess nothing ever came of it, huh?"

"We hung out a few times—"

"The infamous pool party vomit."

"You were there, weren't you?"

"Me and most of the senior class."

"So embarrassing."

"For him or you?"

"You know, every time we—I don't know what to call it. We didn't go out, or meet up. We…had encounters. And every time something awful like that happened. If that wasn't enough to put me off, he always made it clear that we were just friends."

"Until he kissed you."

"You saw that? Did anybody else?"

"Not any of the Divas that I know of, if that's what you're worried about. But, you don't think he likes you now?"

"You saw him at Tracks. I was 'friend-zoned' again. I guess he just kissed me for the heck of it."

"Sure," she said, sounding skeptical. "Maybe he was caught up in the moment." She took a big bite of her sandwich and chewed for a bit. "So, is that why you don't want to go out with him? Because crazy stuff always happens when you get together and he says he just wants to be friends?"

"Seems like enough to me."

"But he kissed you. So there's a nugget of something there that you could pursue."

I thought for a moment. "I suppose there is more to it."

"What is it? Come on, get honest with yourself."

I shrugged.

"It's the cat," she said.

"The cat?"

"Remember what Ryan said at Triple F that time? Something like, why would you think you wouldn't have a cat if you got married. Like, you couldn't have both."

"What's that got to do with anything?"

She rolled her eyes. "I've known you for a long time. And I know that since high school, or maybe earlier, you looked at some of your friends and thought, 'I don't want to be like that. I don't want to lose myself in a guy, in a relationship. I want a career—a life I can call my own.' And you've been laser focused ever since."

"That's true."

"So every time you get close to Ryan—or maybe any guy, I don't know—you remember that promise to yourself and you back off. Or you find some excuse not to lean in."

"Okay, but I've never been close to Ryan. So let's leave him out of it. There's nothing wrong with wanting to be independent and having a career."

"Of course there isn't. But look at the cat."

"Why do you keep bringing the cat into it?"

"Mel, you've made it. You have the career. And you have plenty of leisure time, you just don't take advantage of it. You got a cat; you've proven that you can have creatures in your life, responsibilities, interests, besides work. Maybe now is the time for a real relationship."

"Maybe. But Ryan's not the one."

"Are you sure?"

"Pretty sure."

"Then someone else is. Start opening yourself up to the next chapter."

"If I were ready to do that, I wouldn't be so afraid of

it." I looked at her, my eyes wide. "I'm *afraid* of it. I guess I never realized that before. Why would I be afraid?"

"Change is scary. I mean, come on, your first test was a cat. That's not really much to go on if you're looking to calm fears."

"There you go with the cat again."

"The cat's the canary."

"Huh?"

"The canary in the Melissa Romance coal mine."

I got up from my stool and walked to the other side of the counter. "Sometimes I think you're too smart for your own good, Kaya. But thanks. As usual, you help me make sense of myself. You're a rock."

"No, please. I don't want to be the rock of the Divas."

"Okay, okay. You're a flake. But thank you." As I left, I turned back to her. "That'd make a great Broadway musical. *Rock of the Divas*."

On my way back to the café, I had a sudden thought. Of course Kaya was right. Maybe I'd been holding on to this Ryan thing—being friend-zoned—because I was too afraid to have a serious relationship. It was like this subconscious excuse. *My high school crush didn't like me, so why bother?* How stupid was that? I realized it wasn't the Divas who weren't taking the Pink Diva Man Hunter Plan seriously. It was me. I thought back over the dates I'd had so far. Ignoring Isabella's prediction, were any of them promising? My paintball experience with Steve was a lot of fun, but neither of us felt a spark. It wasn't impossible, but I didn't feel like I wanted to date him. Rock climbing with Diego was more frightening than fun, but Diego was really nice about it. He was definitely a flirt, but again, I wasn't feeling it. Tildon Frakes was a no. For him more so than for me. He was looking for lightning and marriage right away. And I was looking for…what was I looking for? And Quinn, my HDS BOMB pal, my jokester friend. As much as I liked him, he wasn't the one for me.

There was one more fix-up left. Sophie's pick. He could be the one, if there really was such a thing. I could feel my hopes rising but I calmed myself. If this last one wasn't Mr. Right, it would be okay. I felt ready, anyway.

Ready to settle down, take some time for myself and whatever might be next for me.

I could hear my dad in my head as I entered Café Flamingo, "So, you're finally ready to grow up?" I laughed. And there was a tingle of excitement rising up within me. I tried not to get my hopes up, but it felt as if everything was starting to fall into place.

Business Success Mel was ready to give way to Life Success Melissa!

Chapter Thirty-four

How to Ruin a Scrumptious Recipe

Attempt Five: Add Some Sting to the Mix

After a couple of years running Café Flamingo, I was ready to buy a house. It's not like my debt to my family had been paid, but they encouraged me to forge onward into independence. I had my eye on this really cute little place not far from Downtown Strawbridge. I could walk to work, if I had to. It had an added-on garage, which was a big plus, and lots of personality. The lot was fairly small, but I wasn't that thrilled with the thought of lawn work in Florida, anyway. I was sure I could find a neighborhood kid to mow it for me. I called the number on the sign and made an appointment to meet a realtor there on a hot, summery, Tuesday afternoon.

When I pulled up to the curb, there was Ryan Duval standing on the little front porch waiting for me. It had been a while since I'd seen him and even when I did, we never moved beyond a brief hello.

"Nice to see you again," he said as he unlocked the house. "How's business going? Must be good."

"It is, actually."

"The place is always hopping when I go in for lunch."

He pushed the door open and I followed him into the house. It was empty, which made it look more spacious than it was. I worked hard to imagine furniture in each room. The limited front area would have to do for the living room, but I could see a sofa and coffee table there easily enough. Beyond that, a small space for a dining table across from the kitchen on the right. Between the living and dining rooms, on the left, the wall opened into a short hallway with a tiny bedroom on the front of the house, a bathroom in the middle, and the master bedroom and bath on the right. Though the master bedroom was at the back of the house, there was only the little bathroom window above the toilet through which to see the back yard.

"Small lot," Ryan was saying as I leaned over the toilet, opened the window, and peered out.

"It's too bad you can't see it from the bedroom."

There were two small windows on either side of the far wall which looked out over the side yard and the neighbor's house. "I'd have to put the bed between those," I said, pointing at the space as I walked back toward the living room.

"Big front and back windows, here, though," he said.

True enough. I could sit on my sofa and see anyone approaching my front door. And the dining room area had a sliding glass door. I went to it and pulled it open. "That'll have to be replaced."

"French doors would be nice."

I looked at him, surprised. "They would." He was a realtor, after all. I don't know why I didn't think he'd know about French doors and house-y stuff. I pointed toward the kitchen where there was a door on the far wall. "Does that go out to the garage?"

"It does, but there's a laundry room first."

Through the door, there was a cozy room with shelves on the walls and hook-ups for a washer and dryer. And through yet another door we walked along a covered walkway to the garage where he unlocked the side door.

"It's a one-car garage," he said, leading me inside. But there's plenty of room here for storage. The previous owners installed those cabinets. And there's a shed in the back yard as well, for a lawn mower or whatever."

The owners had also left some junk behind. A few cardboard boxes. A stack of plastic bags labeled 'potting soil' and 'fertilizer' and a few flower pots. I saw a button on the side wall that looked like it was for an automatic garage door opener and pushed it. The old door creaked its way slowly up, filling the space with light.

"Not too bad," I said. We stood there for a moment, looking around and I think he was waiting for me to move back toward the house. "What's that noise?"

"What noise?" He tilted his head.

"Listen." I was sure there was something humming nearby.

"Somebody using a drill?"

"That's not a drill." I moved closer to the cabinets in the far corner of the garage. "It's coming from in there." I pointed upward, to the top. I'd never be able to use those cabinets. I'd forever be up and down a step stool. Even then it'd be pretty high.

"What is it?" he said.

"Open it up. Let's see."

He dragged a few bags of fertilizer over to the cabinet and stood on them to pull open the door. With a yelp, he staggered backward, falling off the bags, as bees flew out into the garage and buzzed all around us. As he clamored to his feet, I ran outside to the front lawn. I turned to see him swatting his arms like a madman.

"I'm hit," he said. "Ouch."

"Don't bring them over here," I screamed as the bees followed him toward me. I ran again, this time into the house, slamming the door behind me.

He followed and when he opened the door to run in, I yelled at him.

"You're letting bees in the house."

"What am I supposed to do?" He swatted himself all over—legs, head, stomach—and twisted around trying to get to his back. "Are they still on me? Mel, where are you?"

"I'm in here," I called after I made it to the master bedroom. "Don't follow me."

I waited until the sound of him slapping himself stopped and left the master bedroom, peering into the living room from the hallway. He was standing there in his underwear.

"Did you get them all?"

"I don't know."

"Why did you take your clothes off?"

"I don't know," he said sarcastically. "It just seemed like the thing to do at the time."

"You've been stung."

"You don't have to tell *me*."

"A lot."

He turned around. "How many on my back?"

I counted. "Five. You'd better get to a doctor. Just in case."

"You go on." He stepped into his jeans. "I'll have to lock up. You can call the office if you want to make an offer."

"Want any help?"

"No, thanks."

I could hear a silent 'you've done enough' on the other side of that. "Sorry I made you look in the cabinet."

"My fault. I should have checked the place out before you got here."

"So, you'll go to a doctor? What if you go into ana-phylactic shock?"

"I'll let you know."

He was already making his way around the house, checking that the windows were secure, locking the slid-ing glass door.

"Okay, then," I hesitated. "I'll see you around."

"Call the office soon. Once we get the bees taken care of, I think the place will go fast."

After talking to my dad about how much I should offer, I called the realtor's office and a lady named Bernice said she'd be handling the sale.

"Is Ryan okay?" I asked her.

"Oh, I'm sure he's fine. He told me to take over for him, that's all. He's very busy."

I could have sworn I heard her mumble after that, "He says he'd still like to be friends." But I suppose it was my imagination.

After that, whenever I saw Ryan Duval, I hid. I didn't want to see that look again. As he stood in the living room of my soon-to-be house in his underwear, blaming me. So I avoided him. Until I dumped a tray of dirty dishes all over him in Café Flamingo.

Chapter Thirty-five

The Saturday before Christmas had finally arrived. The weather had chilled considerably with highs in the Seventies. Woohoo! Break out your sweaters, Divas. Downtown Strawbridge was buzzing with excitement. All the stores were packed, the restaurants at capacity, with just a few shopping days left before the big day, after which everyone could relax and wonder where they would store that huge gift they didn't know they wanted, or declare a week of fasting once the leftovers were depleted.

After taking an early afternoon break to lunch with Dusty, I changed into my fancy duds because later that evening I'd be judging the Holiday Baking Contest. I got back to the store by four, just in time to watch the parade. The stream of floats, musicians, dancers, and more started just west of the café where they gathered on sides streets north and south of Strawbridge Avenue waiting their turn to join the spectacle. They'd march all the way to the east side of downtown, make that sharp right turn onto Mangrove, and disband, packing up instruments, driving floats back home, or handing off batons to their mothers before heading over to the food trucks across the railroad tracks for another fabulous evening of festivities.

The only customers in the café at four o'clock were a couple feeding potato chips to each other in a booth along Woodplum, and old Mr. Pritchard sitting by the front window reading last Sunday's newspaper. Susanne volunteered to keep an eye on them as the entire staff joined me outside to watch the parade pass by. The calls to clear the street of cars had started at noon leaving just a few stubborn people unable to leave until the parade was done. Worse, they ran the risk of having spectators climb on their cars for a better view. Officer Palmer could only do so much with such a crowd, after all. The parade route was understood to be between the marked parking spaces, but any store owners handing out candy were allowed beyond those lines. A few of my employees— Doug, Dean, and Petra—were the official candy tossers, wearing pink flamingo hats. They'd go up and down the street, though not too far from the café, throwing treats to kids and grown-ups alike.

Right on schedule, we heard the whistle, and the drums began their rattling opener before the Strawbridge High School band began to play Christmas carols. The sounds echoed through the corridor, rendering them almost unrecognizable.

"Is that…Here Comes Peter Cottontail?" Lucy asked from behind me.

I laughed. "I'm pretty sure it's Jingle Bells."

Behind the band came the baton twirlers, cheerleaders, the Chamber of Commerce float with the board members dressed as elves. The Shriners, Strawbridge RC Club and behind them, their offshoot Strawbridge Drones. The Strawbridge Theater cast were all decked out as characters from *Scrooge*, which they'd started running after *Guys and Dolls*. Strawbridge Middle School band and associated were next, playing "Up On the Housetop." Strawbridge Clown Club—I'm not a fan, and it turns out, not alone in that, as two little kids ran screaming from the front of the crowd with their parents chasing after them. On and on, the parade went. Choirs, triangle players, Hula Hoopers, MacAuley Awley's staff dressed all in Kelly Green. And then, the Strawbridge Gazette float, shaped like an opened newspaper, with none other than Lionel Beardsley sitting at a desk in the middle.

Boos rang out in the crowd and I cringed. I turned to catch sight of my staff and was pleased it wasn't them. But if not them, who? I stood on my tiptoes, but, trust me, that didn't help. As soon as Beardsley drifted out of sight, the boos ceased and along came the Strawbridge Brass Band playing "Here Comes Santa Claus." Next up trotted the Strawbridge Riding Club on their horses. Every year they begged to be last in line, but were over-ridden by traditionalists who insisted that Santa Claus must always bring up the rear. Behind them, the men with shovels. And through anything that might get left behind, came Santa's float with the red-clad jolly elf himself sitting in a rocking chair atop a snowy mountain covered with gaudy plastic pinwheels and lollipops.

The crowd joined in the parade and followed it all the way down Strawbridge Avenue.

"You going?" Lucy asked me when we were the only ones left standing in front of the café, our staff already having retreated back to the air conditioning.

"In these heels?"

"You've got to get down there eventually for the contest. You'll never get a parking spot if you drive."

"I'm going to wait until the crowd clears out and use the sidewalk. I'm not taking a chance with horse poop."

She chuckled.

I checked on the store, made sure everything was well, and headed toward the festival, meeting up with Kaya, Karen, and Vanessa on the way. At the east end of Strawbridge, there was a big stage set up, with a curtain from which performers emerged. There was a magic show, a barber shop quartet, plenty of speeches by the local bigwigs, and lots of food to be eaten.

"Not me," I told Pari when we met up with her and Sam and she offered me a Christmas cookie. "I've got a contest to judge."

By the time the Holiday Baking Contest was an-nounced, I was starving. Madaline grabbed me away from the Divas with Quinn already in tow. "You're late," she said. "Get a move on."

We were crowded into the dim, warm space backstage

with the other judges and the contestants who would come out as each of their entries was judged.

"You look nice," Quinn said.

And I had to say, I did. Cute little green dress with a full, twirl-worthy skirt. I quickly pulled my little elf hat, the brim lined in white fur, out of my purse and slapped it on my head. "You don't look so bad yourself. I see you wore a suit for the occasion."

"Well, I am an official judge."

I heard Ryan announce Melanie, from Brunch, and caught sight of her in the darkness backstage, as the curtain was pulled back to let her out.

"So Ryan Duval is definitely the emcee," Quinn said.

"What? Oh, yeah."

"And our next judge," Ryan's voice echoed beyond the curtain, "the renowned critic, and your worst nightmare, Mr. Lionel Beardsley."

I gasped, surprised Ryan would say such a thing. Mr. Beardsley passed Quinn and I without a word and was met with a smattering of applause.

"This feels like a scene from some kind of psychological thriller," I said.

"What's behind the curtain?" Quinn teased. "Will we survive?"

Next, I heard my name and was shoved in front of the curtain to mild applause from the crowd. They'd set up the judges tables to the left and I took my seat, which was, unfortunately, next to Lionel Beardsley. Across the stage were tables displaying the contest entries in the categories of holiday breads, holiday cookies, holiday desserts, and holiday pies. The pies, we'd been assured, would not be the same ones used in the pie eating contest that would occur shortly after our winners were announced.

"Mr. Beardsley," I said, as I sat down next to him.

He harrumphed.

"I'm sorry you were booed in the parade."

"Beg pardon?"

"I heard boos. I just wanted to assure you it wasn't me or my staff doing it."

"I've no idea—"

"Not that it wouldn't surprise me if they did. What you wrote was pretty insulting. But I guess you were just doing your job. And I suppose your job is getting people to read your column and I imagine a lot of people like that kind of mean-spirited stuff. Look at reality TV today, right?"

"Who are you?"

My mouth fell open and my eyes widened to the point of discomfort. I was just about to let him have it when I saw a half-smile light up his face.

"Well," I said, confused and not a little bit relieved. "Kiss my grits."

He laughed loud, beginning with a huge "Hah!" and tamped his hand on the table. I realized everyone was watching us and it was perfectly understandable. Had anyone ever seen Lionel Beardsley laugh?

Once all the judges were seated, Quinn, to my right, leaned in and whispered, "Consorting with the enemy. I see you've chosen your survival strategy."

"What's yours?"

"I think there's a clue hidden in one of the desserts, so I'm going to eat my way out of this."

Ryan was in his element as emcee. Charming, witty, and rarely had to read a joke off of his lined index cards. We tasted all the sweet stuff and filled out score cards for each round. Then we were allowed to discuss amongst ourselves while the crowd were handed out samples of all the entries.

"Okay, folks, we'll take a short break and be back in a few with the results of the Strawbridge Holiday Baking Contest. Good luck too all of our participants."

The stage was to be cleared and reset for the handing out of prizes and while everyone else stepped outside for some fresh air—and probably in search of some protein to counteract all the sugar we'd just consumed—I hung around backstage, not wanting to be late again.

After a few minutes, Ryan joined me.

Chapter Thirty-six

We both stood there in the dim light of the small space behind the curtain, awkwardly, for a few moments. Finally, he said, "Mel, about last Saturday—"

"Don't bother. I already know what you're going to say."

"You do?"

"The answer is yes. We're still friends. I guess. As much as we have been in the last few years. We're not friends like we were in high school, but yes. You don't have to worry about it. Still friends."

"What are you talking about?"

"That's what you're always worried about, isn't it? Making sure we're still friends. After the pool party senior year—"

"I vomited all over you!"

"Yes you did. And you called me the next day to make sure we were still friends."

"I was embarrassed," he mumbled.

"And then at the beach when I pushed you into the cactus plant."

"What does that have to—wait, you pushed me?"

"I thought you were going to kiss me, okay? Dumb me. I was so surprised, I lost my balance and grabbed hold of you, which made you fall."

"So you didn't technically push me."

"Is that what's important right now? And then when I heard you in the bathroom with your real friends, as they were pulling cactus spikes out of your back, they asked you who I was and you said I was just some friend from school."

"I'm sure I didn't say it like that."

"Well, that's how I remember it. And then at the reunion, after I fell in the lagoon?"

"At least I didn't vomit on you."

"That's what you said then. And again, you had to make sure we were still friends."

"I don't get what's wrong with that."

"And you cracked my car windshield with your fly ball that summer."

"I paid for it."

"And as you left after that...well, I don't think you said anything, but you gave me an I'm-glad-we're-still-friends look."

"I did?"

"You did. And then when I made you open up that cabinet in my garage and you got stung by bees—"

"You didn't make me do that."

"—and what did you do?"

"Asked you if we were still friends?"

"No. You gave me to another realtor. You just pushed me off onto someone else without so much as a let's-stay-friends."

"She was supposed to tell you. I was out of work for days. Covered with bee stings."

"Well, if we were really friends, you'd have called me yourself."

"I didn't think you wanted to talk to me."

"Why would you think that?"

"You didn't call to find out if I was okay."

"Well, I didn't think you wanted me to."

"I didn't want you to."

"Then why is it my fault?"

"I didn't say it was."

Stunned, I took a step back. It felt as if we were going around in circles. But wasn't that our relationship since that first ridiculously embarrassing encounter, anyway? "Maybe we aren't friends, anymore."

"No," he said. "That's not—"

"Melissa!" Vanessa ripped open the curtain, filling the hot space with fresh air. "Everybody is listening to you two."

She was panting, as if she'd just run the entire length of Strawbridge Avenue. Behind her, the microphone sat on its stand and beyond the stage, the crowd waiting for the announcement of the winners smiled sheepishly at us. And it was then that I remembered I was dressed in a green dress, wearing a green elf hat. My face burned hot and I could think of nothing else to do but run. So, I ran. Down the backstage steps, across the crowded street to the shops nearby. I made it all the way to Pub's Sports Bar before I was surrounded by the Divas.

"We're so sorry," Vanessa said.

"We were over at the food trucks," Sophie said.

"We didn't know anything was going on until we got back," Pari said.

"I'm so embarrassed," I said.

"It wasn't that bad," Kaya said. "Not the bits we heard."

"Not really," Vanessa said.

"Who put the microphone there?" I said.

"They probably moved it out of the way so they could take down the tables," Karen said.

"But all those people! Why didn't they stop us?"

"Maybe they thought it was part of the show," she said.

We all looked at her and she smiled and shrugged.

After a bit of coaxing, they convinced me to go back for the awards ceremony. It would look bad if I weren't there. The Divas stood around me, as if protecting me from any points and stares, as we watched the presentation. I was still embarrassed, but I didn't really care that much about it by that time. I stood there, not really paying attention, trying to remember what Ryan and I had said to each other. It was just a blur of senseless words without meaning. All there was left was what I felt—sorrow. Thinking back, I realized that since that first crazy incident—the pool party—nothing had been the same between us. Our friendship died away. But wasn't that going to happen after high school anyway? How many friends, crushes, even supposedly true loves actually lasted beyond graduation? Every time I saw Ryan after school, the universe had tried to tell me, "This is the past. This isn't where you should be looking." But every time I caught sight of Ryan's face, I forgot. Instead, all I could think about were those days in school when all I cared about was seeing him, talking to him, listening to him, and laughing with him.

I felt stupid. I was too old to be having such realizations, wasn't I? I'd held onto this for too long. Well, no more. I was ready to grow up.

Loud laughter and applause brought me back to the world around me as I found myself watching the beginning of the Downtown Strawbridge Holiday Pie Eating Contest, emceed by our honorable Mayor Hawn. They'd just announced Lionel Beardsley as one of the contestants.

"What the…?" I heard Kaya say.

Next up was Buddy Palmer and Sam Preston.

"Sam!" Pari said. "What does he think he's doing?"

"Eating pie," I said.

Then Kaya was introduced. All the Divas twisted and turned, looking at each other.

"How did she get away from us?"

The final two contestants were Carolina Davies of the Christian gift store, Begotten, and my own manager, Susanne. That little sneak!

"This is going to be epic," Karen said.

We all had our phones out, cameras ready. The contestants were covered in plastic capes, their hair put in netting—Sam looked ridiculous, his full, round cheeks pulled into a huge grin. A two-crust pie was put in front of each of them as Mayor Hawn announced the flavor.

"Cranberry pear," he said with great fanfare. "You may use your hands. Your pie tin must be emptied and nothing spilled can remain on the table. Your hands must be licked clean and held up before you are declared 'finished.' First one to finish is the winner. Oh, wait…"

The contestants turned to him in wonder as the audience laughed.

"There are two pies."

We all cheered and the chant "two pies" rang out.

"Well, this is a first," Karen said.

"Everybody finished too fast last year," Pari said.

"Can they even eat two pies?" Sophie said. "Look at Kaya, she's scared to death."

"Not Carolina. That girl's pumped."

"Chocolate bourbon pecan," Mayor Hawn announced as a second pie was put before the not-at-all-professional competitive eaters.

"Ooh," we all said.

"I could go for that," I added.

Without further delay, the whistle was blown and our friends dove into their pies, shoving handfuls of sweet gooey mess into their mouths. Mr. Beardsley was a clear frontrunner, having swallowed half a pie before Kaya could finish her second portion. And he was the only contestant who managed not to laugh at some point.

"Stop looking at everybody else," Karen called out to Kaya. "It's just making her giggle. You can't shovel pie in when you're giggling."

Sam made good progress as well, but the surprise was Carolina Davies. She meant business. Still, Beardsley took on the chocolate bourbon before anyone else. They all shoveled and chewed—though not nearly enough—and swallowed. Pans were lifted in front of faces so they could be licked clean. Bits of crust were slurped off the tablecloth and plucked off cheeks. And we watched, laughing and applauding, as Sam—our Pari's Sam—be-gan licking his fingers.

"Hurry!" Pari screamed. "Hurry!"

Up went his hands and we all roared. Beardsley was second. And Kaya third. Carolina fourth and Officer Palmer fifth with my dear Susanne still eating her chocolate bourbon pie when it was all over. When one of the crew attempted to take the remains from her, she pulled the tin closer. She was going to finish that pie if it killed her.

I forgot completely about the open-mic incident and strolled around the festival with the Divas, except for Pari who was helping Sam carry his award, which included six pies, to his car.

"Can you believe Lionel Beardsley?" Kaya said. "He was even nice backstage when we were waiting to be announced."

"He was nice to me, too," I said.

"You think he's drunk or something?" Sophie said.

"Maybe we just don't know him," Karen said.

"I guess not," I said.

"Well," Karen said. "Christmas is next week."

"Is everybody coming to my place Christmas eve?" I said.

"We wouldn't miss it."

"What about Mel's last date?" Vanessa said.

They all turned to Sophie, who smiled. "Tomorrow."

"Don't tell me. Eight o'clock?"

"Nope. Nine-thirty."

"So I get to sleep in," I said sarcastically. "Stretchy clothes? Shirt I don't mind getting covered in mud? What's the deal?"

"You can wear whatever you want. But pants would probably be better than a dress."

"Wait. You mean, I'm not going to be doing some kind of extreme sport or wrestling an alligator?"

Sophie just smiled. "Jeans would be best."

Chapter Thirty-seven

Sophie was at my place by nine-thirty the next morning, but she spent a good ten minutes petting Dusty before we could leave. As I climbed into the passenger seat of her dark gray Elantra, I said, "Don't tell me. You're taking me north."

"How did you guess?"

"All the horrible stuff is north of Strawbridge."

"This isn't horrible; it's fun. You shouldn't have believed Kaya. We're not monsters, you know."

"Sure," I mumbled. "Paintball attacks, Ninja Warrior goo, enormous-fan-propelled boats on the St. John's, having to be helped down from a fifty-foot high fake wall. I had no idea Strawbridge was so dangerous."

She drove us up to the same area where the paintball place was and I looked longingly at it as we passed it by. It was at least something familiar. Several blocks later, past flower shops, pool halls, a dance studio, and a pizza joint, she pulled her car into the parking lot of the roller rink.

"This place is still open?"

"Obviously. Did you used to come here?"

"I don't know how to skate."

"That's okay. You can learn."

"Sophie," I said after getting out of the car and standing in the parking lot, staring up at the building. "It's called Disco Boogie."

"So?"

"We're seriously going to go inside a place called Disco Boogie?"

"It's always been Disco Boogie."

"Which is probably why I've never gone inside."

We went from the sunny, but cold Saturday morning, through the front door into a dark chilly room. Disco music filled the space and the smell of popcorn hung in the air, so buttery I was sure I'd leave with a layer of grease on my face. On the left was the snack bar with a bunch of metal benches for seating. To the right, the shoe rental. And in front of us, with benches all around facing it, was the rink, surrounded by a low cement wall, the shiny mirror-faceted ball spinning slowly near the ceiling in the middle. I'd lied of course. I'd been to Disco Boogie a few times as a little kid, for birthday parties—there were huge booths all along the right-side wall where kids could be penned-in around one large table for cake and ice cream. I'd had skates on a few times. But I never learned to do much more than walk around the rink hanging on to the wall.

"Well, I'm going to leave you here."

"Wait. You're leaving?"

"Get some roller skates on and get out there."

"But, who's my date?"

"You'll figure it out."

"You can't just leave me here by myself."

She put her hands on my shoulders and said, "You'll be fine."

I watched her walk out the door feeling like an abandoned puppy. I turned around, looking for anyone I knew, anyone who might be my date. The rink was filled with teenagers and children, mostly. Their parents were sitting at the snack bar eating nachos and checking emails on their phones. I took a seat on one cold bench next to them and waited. After about ten minutes, I decided he was late. The least Sophie could have done was to make sure he was here. I figured I might as well get some skates on. I put my purse and shoes in a locker and got my wheels. Taking a seat on one of the benches in front of the rink, I pulled them on and began lacing them up. When somebody sat down next to me, I looked up with a smile.

"Ryan!"

"Hi." He was already wearing skates so he must have been there, in the crowd.

"Of course you're here," I groaned.

"I am."

"Look, I don't know what kind of crazy game the universe is playing with us, but I have a date right now." Standing up, I walked and slid gingerly toward the opening in the wall to get to the rink with him following me.

"I know," he said.

I turned to him and nearly lost my balance. "Good. So…do you mind?"

"Mind what?"

"Leaving me alone so my date can find me."

He smiled, nearly laughing, his brows punching up his forehead.

"Wait," I said. "No."

"Yep."

"You're my date?"

He just stood there, smiling that nerdy smile.

"After everything Sophie heard last night—the insane stuff that happens whenever we get within a hundred-eighty yards of each other—she fixed us up?"

"Yep. A hundred-eighty yards is awfully specific. Have you been around town measuring?"

"Us! On a date?"

"Yes. Are you ready to skate?"

"Are you nuts? I'm not going out there on wheels with you." I turned and baby-stepped back to the bench. He sat down too, much more comfortable on skates than me.

"It was Sophie, wasn't it?" I said. "She told you to go to the paintball game. And rock climbing."

He just kept smiling.

"Why?"

"I asked her to keep me in the loop," he said.

"Why would you do that? How do you even know her?"

"Our families go way back."

"But I told them not to—"

"I know what you told them. But I'm your date." He stood up and offered me his hands. "Come on. Let's skate."

I sighed. "Oh, all right." I let him help me up and guide me to the rink. "But if I fall and break my neck, it's on you."

I clung to the wall for a while with him patiently rolling beside me. Finally, determined, I let go and we moved away from it, but just a bit. I didn't want to disturb the actual skaters. After one full go around, I started to feel more confident, like I was really skating. We moved a bit faster and glided over into the throng. The others didn't seem to mind that we weren't going as fast as they were. They whizzed past us, turning to skate backwards, spinning, doing little jumps.

"When did you learn to skate?" I asked Ryan.

"*I* don't know how to skate," he said.

Instinctively, I panicked. I'd been led around the skating rink by someone just as incapable as myself. Like a weirdo, I grabbed at him, as if he could help me. He lost his balance, his skates running without moving him anywhere, his arms flailing about as if he were being attacked by bees. And I just continued to paw at him as if he could save me *and* himself. I fell to the floor on top of him and we lay there for a few seconds, stunned. Then I looked at him and he looked back at me and we burst out laughing.

"I warned you," I said.

"You're the one who got a soft landing. I could have cracked my skull."

I grabbed his cheeks. "Turn your head, let's have a look. No blood. I think you'll live. But—" I managed to climb off him and sit on the dirty rink floor. "I warned you. The universe doesn't want us together."

"I'll have to start listening to you, now that I know how wise you are. You could see Isabella about an apprenticeship."

We tried to stand, still clinging to one another, but it was useless. In the end, we crawled, laughing, to the wall where we turned and sat, leaning against it. After we caught our breaths, he pulled himself up and helped me to my feet. We were on the right side of the rink along the party booths. Making our way to an opening in the wall, we inched across the carpet to the nearest one and scooched along the semi-circle of padded seating to the center, our backs against the wall. The skaters went around and around, ignoring us, probably glad the obstacle had crept off the floor. "You Spin Me Round" was playing and the disco ball was flooding the darkness with shards of color.

"I don't think the universe is trying to keep us apart," he said after a while.

"I disagree."

"I think we're just nervous around each other."

I thought about that for a few seconds, remembering how easy it was to be around him back in school. "When did that start?"

"At the pool party. Why do you think I got drunk?"

"I never really thought about that. But you're right. It wasn't like you."

"I was nervous."

"Why?"

"I'm sorry I wasn't honest with you from the beginning. I was going to tell you. But it was scary. So I drank a little."

"A little?" I couldn't process all of what he'd said quickly enough for it to make sense, so the only thing to hit my brain was the last part. "Wait, were you going to tell me you liked me?"

"I wanted to kiss you. But I vomited all over you, instead."

"You *were* going to kiss me. I thought I imagined it. And again at the beach house. Were you going to kiss me then? Before the cactus thing?"

"I was definitely thinking about it."

Again, we sat and watched the skaters rolling around

the rink, now to Donna Summer's "MacAurthur Park."

"I just feel like," he said. "You've been mad at me. Since I vomited on you. I mean, I get it. And at the same time, I don't."

"Because friends don't let a little vomit come between them."

He nodded.

"I thought you were mad at me," I said.

"Why would *I* be mad? I'm not the one who got vomited on."

I lifted my shoulders and put my palms up. "I don't know. You seemed mad."

"I was embarrassed. And there's something else I should apologize for."

"The windshield?"

"I already said I was sorry about that."

"The bees?"

"That wasn't my fault."

"What else was there?"

"When I called you after the pool party."

"And you wanted to make sure we were still friends."

"Yeah. And you said, 'what, no more loving me from afar?'"

"You remembered that?" I turned in the booth so that I could face him. "Why did you act like you didn't?"

"I was just so embarrassed. The whole date was a disaster."

"You mean...we were on a date?"

"I know you didn't think we were, but I did."

"You should have told me."

"I was a coward."

"Anyway, you were drunk when you said that. "

"But I meant it."

I sighed and watched the skaters for a bit. "We're so stupid."

"And clumsy."

"But why did you apologize for kissing me at the tree lighting ceremony?"

"You obviously didn't want me to."

"How do *you* know?"

"You asked me why I did it."

"Oh. Yeah, I guess I did. It was unexpected, that's all. I'd decided that it was all just my imagination…you *ever* wanting to kiss me."

His lips curled into a silly grin. "So, you wanted me to?"

"Since high school. I had the biggest crush on you. You have no idea."

"Me, too. Wait. I didn't have a crush on myself—"

"I know what you mean." I laughed and poked him in the ribs.

"But how do you feel now?" he said.

"I feel like if you don't kiss me right now, it'll never happen again."

And there we were, like two teenagers on a Sunday morning at the skating rink, making out in a party booth. I was doing it! I was kissing Ryan Duval. And neither of us were surprised by it. After a moment, he looked at me, his hands on my face, and said, "There's something I've been wanting to ask you…"

It sounded unsettling. "Okay?"

"A while back, at Triple F, your friend Kaya said something about the Pink Diva Man Hunter Plan."

"Please don't talk about that now." I made a move to start the kissing again, but he put a finger to my lips.

"Hold on. It's not that. It's the Pink Diva thing. Sophie said you all have names."

Pouting, I turned away from him a bit and watched the skaters. "Yeah. I suppose it is sort of childish."

He shook his head. "I just want to know why you're the Pink Diva. I mean, Flamingo Diva, Sassy Diva, Diva in an Elf Hat."

Laughing, I begged him to stop. "Everybody thinks it's my favorite color."

"Your favorite color is green."

"You remember." I felt as if my heart were melting like ice cream under hot fudge sauce.

"Dark green, right? No, wait. It starts with an H and has something to do with deer."

I chuckled, watching him puzzle it out.

"Hunter green," he said.

"You have no idea how much I want to kiss you right now." And the making out began again.

At some point, the rustling of tissue paper and giggling brought us back to the real world and we both looked up to find about a dozen kids in party hats, and a few parents, brows raised, staring at us.

"We reserved this booth," one lady said, pointing upward to where I supposed there must be a sticker of ownership tacked overhead.

I'd like to say we skated gracefully away, but...well, you know us by now.

"Come on," Ryan said, once we had our street shoes back on. "I've got something to show you."

We talked nonstop all the way from Disco Boogie to Downtown Strawbridge, filling in all the blanks of our lives and going over old memories. Everything was suddenly easy again. As if there'd been some kind of fence dividing us that we'd taken down—or more likely, crashed through. When Ryan pulled his car into a parking spot in front of Café Flamingo, before I could register where we were, I had the sudden thought that I had to do something to hang on to this moment. It was too unreal. It couldn't last on its own. I was going to have to do something to make it stick. But what?

I looked up to see my restaurant in front of me. "You wanted to bring me here?" And then I saw the big ribbon attached to the front door. "Oh, the Best Holiday Decor results are in. What did we get?" Before I could get out of the car and make my way to the door, however, I saw that our ribbon was for second place.

"That's not too bad," Ryan said. "Who won, though?"

Susanne pushed the door open to greet us with the answer to that question. Pointing across the street, she said, "Old Geezer's Antiques won. But second isn't so bad."

The three of us moved to the sidewalk and gazed at Old Geezer's prize-winning display. Santa clinging to the rooftop, his pants pulled down by rascally reindeer. On the roof, a tree lay on its side, decorations scattered about.

Hapless reindeer, lacking opposable thumbs, not being able to stop the annihilation of Christmas. And peeping out of a fake chimney, the Grinch, smiling with glee.

"Okay, so he deserved it," I said. "But," I turned to Ryan, "how did you know before I did?"

"Know what?"

"That we got second place."

"I didn't."

"Then why did you bring me here?"

"Not for this." He took my hand. "Come on."

I waved at Susanne as Ryan took me around the corner to the back of the café where there was a small parking lot that we shared with the accountant's building behind us. We walked along the sidewalk until we were at the corner of Woodplum and the main highway through town where he turned and held out his hand to Wilbur and Sons, C.P.As.

"Okay," I said, slowly.

"What do you think?"

"It's Wilbur and Sons. I've driven past it on my way to and from work a million times."

"Did you know it used to be a little café? Mostly outside dining."

"I did not know that."

"That was pretty long ago, though. So, you'll probably have a lot of updating to do…on the kitchen."

I turned to look up at him, but he was still beaming at Wilbur and Sons. "What are you talking about?"

"Your catering storefront." He held out his hand again, like Vanna White.

"Are they moving out? Who owns the building?"

"I do. Well, my corporation does. And yeah, Wilbur and Sons are moving out in a few months."

"Seriously? It's perfect."

"I know. And I can give you a good deal, what with you leasing two spots. There might be a little bit of extra preferential treatment, what with you being my girlfriend and all."

I blushed and turned to him again. "Am I your girlfriend?"

He put his hands on my shoulders and gazed intently at me. "Melissa, I think I've been in love with you since tenth grade when you spilled chocolate milk all over my new Nikes."

"I forgot all about that!" I laughed.

"And every time we get together and something ridiculously awful happens, it just makes me want you more. How does that sound?"

"What are you saying, exactly?"

"I'm saying that if you will be my girlfriend, I have no doubt that if we haven't managed to mortally wound each other within six months, we'll be together for the rest of our lives. Are you willing to brave that danger with me?"

I put my arms around his neck and kissed him. "Yes," I said. "Let's do it."

Epilogue

The Divas and I sat around my coffee table after lunch on Christmas Eve. We, along with several other guests, had just finished watching *It's a Wonderful Life* while munching on turkey-dressing-and-cranberry-sauce sandwiches and chips. Most of the others were already out in my back yard playing croquet while some of the guys—Sam, Reese, Ryan, and Shel were gathered in my little dining room still sampling desserts and talking about who-knows-what.

Kaya, Sophie, and Vanessa were perched on the sofa, drinks in hand. Karen practically lay on the easy chair, bemoaning repeatedly how stuffed she was. Pari and me were cross-legged on large floor cushions with Dusty curled up between us enjoying having two people petting her. I'd decorated the house a bit, nothing like Karen could have done. But Ryan put twinkle lights along the front eaves outside. A wreath hung on the door. And I had a little tree next to the television set across from the sofa, displaying the few ornaments I'd asked everyone to bring.

"So," Vanessa said. "It's been a busy few days for you and Ryan."

I smiled, blushing as they all stared at me.

"It looks serious," Kaya said.

"It is. We're going to my parents' for dinner tonight and to his tomorrow morning where I'll meet the entire family." I turned to watch Ryan, leaning on the kitchen counter, a napkin in one hand and a piece of pie—no plate or fork—in the other.

"Why do we do this?" Karen said. "It's sexist or something, isn't it? The way we split up into gendered groups?"

"That's psychology," Pari said.

"Does biology have anything to do with it?" Kaya asked.

"Is there a branch of science called psychobiology?" I said.

"I believe there is," Pari said. "Sophie, look it up."

"My purse is across the room," she said, lazily. "Either way, we should do something about it."

"Let's solve gender mixing in social situations later," I said. "Right now, I have news."

"So soon?" Vanessa said.

"Wedding bells already?" Karen said.

"So, Isabella was right."

"That's true, enough," I said. "Does that mean you all believe in ghosts now?"

"How do you get from Isabella being right to ghosts?" Kaya said.

"It's evidence of the spiritual realm, right?"

"Or," Sophie said, "evidence that Isabella has known Ryan's mom for, like, fifty years."

"Is that true?" I said. Then I yelled, "Ryan, is that true?"

"Is what true?"

"Does your mother know Isabella?"

"You mean Aunt Izzy?"

I turned back to the Divas. "Never mind. And how is it that you know Ryan so well, Sophie?"

"Gramps is pretty chummy with Mr. Beardsley."

We all gasped.

I said, "Did you know he wasn't as mean as he seems?"

"Gramps tried to tell me. But any time I've been around him, he's been really grumpy."

"He was probably being nice to you because he realized Ryan liked you," Pari said.

"Or that he's in love with you," Karen cooed.

They all laughed and I rolled my eyes. "Sometimes we all act like we're twelve. But that's not my news. We're not getting married; not yet, anyway. But Ryan is moving in with me."

"That was fast," Kaya said.

"A second ago you thought we were getting married."

"Totally different," Vanessa said. "It takes months to plan a wedding."

"Not always," Sophie said and we all turned to her, suspicious.

"Oh, my god," she said with a laugh. "I'm just saying. What is *with* us? The Divas have gone wedding crazy, lately."

"We don't all have to get married," Kaya said. So we all then turned to her, shocked. "What? I'm just stating a fact of life. And you guys moving in together is happening pretty quick."

"Well," I said. "As a wise romance writer once told me—" I winked at Karen. "When true love hits, you know it's right." They looked skeptical, but hopeful.

"Gosh," Karen said. "Did I say that?"

"Something along those lines. Anyway, that's still not the news."

"What could be more—" Karen said. "Wait! Are you pregnant?" She shrieked and all the guys stopped talking and looked over at us.

"No!" Panicked, I glanced at Ryan. He pulled the guys' attention back to whatever they were arguing over. "We had our first date four days ago. Before this gets way too out of hand, come on. I'll show you."

I jumped off the floor and told them to follow me into the little hallway between bedrooms to the closed guest-room door.

I whispered, "Ryan got a cat."

"You're kidding," Sophie said.

"She's done it," Vanessa said. "She's become a cat

person."

"Tell me about it. I used to prize my simple lifestyle and independence. Now I've got two cats, a fridge filled with food, and a fully furnished guest bedroom."

"The horror," Karen said.

"Which one of you is next?" I peered at Karen, Vanessa, and Kaya.

"Oh, no," Kaya said.

"Not me," Vanessa chimed in.

"No way." Karen raised her hands in defense.

Diva laughter echoed in the small space we'd crowded into.

"Quiet down," I said. "She and Dusty have gotten to know each other, but we thought a party might be too much for her so soon. Do you want to meet her?"

They all nodded. Even the cat-less Divas were eager. I quietly pushed open the door and we entered the room where a concert of "Aw" rang out. Atop the twin bed by the window, curled into a tiny ball, was Tux.

"You called it Tux?" Kaya said, after I introduced them to our new black-and-white kitten.

"We're not good at naming cats," I said. "Nothing we can do about it."

Our little Tux lifted her head to see what the commotion was about and meowed at me.

"Tux is a fine name," Sophie said. "It looks like she's got a shadow of a bow tie to go with her suit."

Everyone took their turn petting her until she stretched and curled into another ball.

"All right, Divas," Kaya said, trying to usher us out of the room. "I'm calling it. The Pink Diva Man Hunter Plan was a huge success."

"Which reminds me," I said. "I got the distinct feeling that each of you was pushing for me to end up with the guy you picked. Was there some kind of bet going on?"

"What?" Vanessa said with mock horror. "We would never do such a thing."

"Especially after we found out Sophie had set you up with Ryan," Pari said. "It all fell apart after that."

"You were all *that* sure that he would be the one?"

Every Diva's head was bobbing.

"What was the wager?" I asked.

"Just bragging rights," Kaya said. "So, what's next for the Divas?"

"Don't you mean, who's next," Sophie said.

"I don't want to go on a bunch of blind dates," Karen said. "So not me." She plopped herself onto a floor cushion, offering Pari the easy chair.

Vanessa and Kaya agreed.

"After all, Sophie and Pari didn't need our help," Kaya said.

"Hey," I said. "I didn't *ask* to be set up."

"But if I hadn't made you go skating with Ryan, you two would still be avoiding each other."

"I suppose that's true. But they're right. They don't need blind dates."

Karen said, "We don't need any help at all. Love will happen naturally."

"What's natural about falling off a ladder on top of a guy in the bookstore?" Sophie said.

"Or catching you soul mate on his hands and knees at your office door?" Pari said.

We all giggled like school girls.

I said, "Well, I happen to know that one of our Divas thinks all great romances start with a cute meet."

"Meet cute," Vanessa said. "It's meet cute!"

"Now that," Pari said, "is a fabulous idea."

"What?" Vanessa said. "What idea? I didn't come up with an idea."

We realized the guys were quiet and turned in unison to look at them standing at the table like lost ducklings.

"Croquet?" Ryan said.

"You guys go on out; we'll be there in a second."

Their conversation started up again as if in mid-argument and they left the kitchen through the laundry room door. I heard Ryan saying, "Be on the lookout for bees."

Turning back to the Divas, I said, "I'll set up the first meeting of the Dating Divas so we can choose the first victim." I knew who I wanted to set up. But the Divas were, if nothing else, democratic.

"Victim of what, exactly?" Kaya said.

"I'm thinking...a series of perfectly timed, disastrously and hilariously executed cute meets."

Vanessa rolled her eyes.

"Okay, okay. Meet cutes."

"Damn to the depths—" Karen started, and we all joined in yelling. "—whatever muttonhead thought up meet cutes!"

Books by Dianna Dann Narciso

Fiction by Dianna Dann
Camelia
Always Magnolia
Bury Me

Romantic Comedy by Dianna Dann
Bookish Meets Boy
Pari and the Ghost Whisperer
Matching Melissa

Fantasy by Dana Trantham
Children of Path: The Kell Stone Prophecy Book One
The Wretched: The Kell Stone Prophecy Book Two
Mark of the Faire: The Kell Stone Prophecy Book Three
The Kell Stone Prophecy: Complete Trilogy

Paranormal Humor by D.D. Charles
Zombie Revolution

Children's Fiction by Dana Trantham
Wayward Cat Finds a Home
Wayward Cat Saves the Day
Zombie Cats
Franken Lizard

For more, visit
waywardcatpublishing.com

www.ingramcontent.com/pod-product-compliance
Lightning Source LLC
Chambersburg PA
CBHW021951170626
46808CB00001B/105